M000159300

THE
BRIDE

BOOKS BY WENDY CLARKE

What She Saw
We Were Sisters

THE BRIDE

WENDY CLARKE

bookouture

Published by Bookouture in 2020

An imprint of Storyfire Ltd.
Carmelite House
50 Victoria Embankment
London EC4Y 0DZ

www.bookouture.com

Copyright © Wendy Clarke, 2020

Wendy Clarke has asserted her right to be identified
as the author of this work.

All rights reserved. No part of this publication may be reproduced,
stored in any retrieval system, or transmitted, in any form or by
any means, electronic, mechanical, photocopying, recording or
otherwise, without the prior written permission of the publishers.

ISBN: 978-1-83888-246-4
eBook ISBN: 978-1-83888-245-7

This book is a work of fiction. Names, characters, businesses,
organizations, places and events other than those clearly in the
public domain, are either the product of the author's imagination
or are used fictitiously. Any resemblance to actual persons, living or
dead, events or locales is entirely coincidental.

For my two girls

PROLOGUE
The day it happened

Fingers are on my eyelids, first one then the other, prising them gently open. A circle of light. Too bright and then merciful darkness again. When my hand is lifted, it's like it's made of lead. There's a pressure on my finger as something is clipped to it. The rasp of Velcro, then tightness around my arm.

I try to remember what happened. Why I'm here. But there's nothing.

Through the fogginess of my brain and the pain in my head, I hear voices. A man. A woman. Words moving in and around one another, some coming to the fore before drifting away again: *concussion, vital signs, lucky.*

Who's lucky?

The covers of my bed are too heavy, and I try to push them down, but the sharp pain in the back of my hand stops me. When I force my swollen eyes to open a slit, I see that taped to the skin is a thin tube attached to a metal stand.

Where am I? Why am I here?

Then more sounds. The clink of the side rails being raised on my bed. The metallic slide of a curtain. A small jolt as my bed begins to move.

Sliding doors. More voices. A cool hand on my forehead.

It's a hospital, but why am I here? I'm looking down on my pale face as though from a great height desperately searching for answers, but all my fuzzy brain can conjure is a memory from the distant past – a time when I felt just as alone. Just as scared.

Instead of a hospital ward, I'm standing in the doorway of a classroom, two other new girls beside me. A sea of faces I don't recognise staring up at us from their desks.

'Who would like to look after these new girls today?' The head teacher places a hand on my shoulder and prompts me to step forward. 'Shall we start with Alice?'

One girl's hand shoots up before the others, the smile she gives full of reassurance. She looks older than the others. A head taller than the girl who sits next to her and whose expression is registering hurt. 'I'd like to look after her, Mrs Talbot.'

Pushing her chair back, she stands and walks between the desks, her hand outstretched. Tall. Confident. Everything I am not.

I force my way through the fog that's enveloping the memory and realise that the little lost girl, with her pale face and ginger ponytail, is me.

'You're awake at last. Thank God.'

I'm brought back to the present. There's a dark shape beside my bed. Someone sitting there. How did I not notice? As they speak again, the warmth of their voice enfolds me, and tears of relief start in my eyes.

'Is it really you?'

Despite the incessant pain in my head and the memories that hover, refusing to be captured, I know I'll be all right now.

'Hush. Don't talk.'

Her hand slips into mine; the gentle squeeze of my best friend's fingers is reassuring.

Through chapped lips, I force the words out.

'What happened?'

'You've been in an accident, but you're going to be all right.'

'But I don't remember.' I thump my forehead with my fist, sending a jolt of pain through my skull. 'Why can't I remember?'

Reaching out, she takes my hand and lowers it to the bed. The pressure of her fingers warm and reassuring. 'Hush now and rest,' she says. 'There's nothing to be afraid of. I'm here now.'

Why don't I believe her?

CHAPTER ONE

Three weeks earlier

The feeling that I'm going to die isn't new to me, but it never gets any easier.

The first jolt shakes me into wakefulness, bumping the side of my head against the plastic edge of the window. Once. Twice. Three times. The noise of the engine is louder than I remember it being before I'd closed my eyes. Before I'd let sleep mercifully enfold me and blank out the awful week I've just had.

Trying to ignore the fearful twist of my stomach, I cup my hand to the cabin window in an attempt to centre myself, but, outside, the sky is no longer blue. Where earlier I'd been able to see the land spread out like a huge map below me: green fields and clusters of towns bisected with threadlike roads, there is now nothing but blackness.

Suffocating blackness.

It's why I never take flights overnight, but the plane had been delayed, and there was nothing I could do about it.

The plane shakes again, and I grip the armrests, glad that the middle-aged woman who's sitting beside me is too engrossed in her *Hello!* magazine to notice me. Next to her, the man she's travelling with, *Keep Calm and Drink Beer* emblazoned across the front of his sleeveless vest, sleeps on, unaware of the turbulence.

I'm wrong, though; the woman's seen my white knuckles. She stares at them, and then at me, and I want to scream at her. *Stop looking at me. You're making it worse.*

She'd tried to engage me in conversation when we'd first embarked, asking me where I'd been staying. Was it Corfu Town? Had I enjoyed my holiday? Why was I travelling on my own? I could have told her how my visit to my father in Benitses had been a disaster. How instead of bringing us closer, staying with my father, his partner who's barely older than me, and their baby, had only served to confirm what I already knew – that even if I'd wanted it, there's no place for me in their lives. How my fiancé Drew's idea had backfired.

Drew. In the week we've been apart, I've done a lot of thinking. I hope he has too.

I'd said nothing about my troubles to the woman, though. Why would I? Instead, I'd given innocuous answers, which she'd seemed satisfied with, and when I'd given a yawn and closed my eyes, the questions had stopped. I guess she must have got the message.

It's the Easter holidays, and the flight is full, but despite this, and my neighbour's unwanted attention, my growing discomfort is isolating. There's no one to hold my hand, no one to help quell the growing fear before it overwhelms me. I force myself to look around me. The people who fill the cabin are mainly families returning from their Easter break and groups of teenagers. They look unconcerned. Surely, I can't be the only one feeling trapped on this shaking plane, the darkness outside pressing in. The only one bothered by the rhythmic bumpiness that pushes my seat belt into the flesh of my stomach. The only one scared the lights might go out, and we'll be plunged into darkness.

Our row is near the back of the plane, and the queue for the toilets spreads past our seats. A teenage girl, with pink hair extensions, waits with her friend and, despite my distress, I still notice the band of red sunburnt flesh above the waistband of her denim shorts. Corfu had been unseasonably hot.

Another jolt and I gasp. The girl lurches sideways, grabbing at the seat of the man on the end of my row. When her shiny pink nails make contact with the skin of his shoulder instead of the chair back, he wakes and glares at her.

'For fuck's sake.'

The girl wipes her hand down her shorts as though contaminated. 'All right. Keep your hair on.'

Sweat beads at my hairline, and I wipe it with the back of my hand. My fingers are trembling, and I link them before the woman next to me can see. Am I imagining it, or is the plane getting hotter? The night outside blacker?

There's a sharp ping above my head. The yellow seat belt sign has come on. Instinctively, I feel for the metal buckle around my waist and tighten it, my heart rate rising.

Why is it so hot? Reaching up a hand, I twist the air vent one way then another, but it's not making any difference. In front of me, there's nothing but heads. All the way to the front of the plane. Row upon row.

Somewhere near the middle of the plane, a baby cries. Then another, nearer. The woman beside me tuts and shifts in her seat, taking a sip of her wine just as the plane gives another lurch.

'Damn,' she says, mopping at her top with a serviette.

Her tray is down, strewn with the detritus of her in-flight meal: the remains of an egg sandwich, its sulphur smell making me feel sick. A small pot, with the foil lid peeled back, offering up a view of the vivid orange jelly that's stuck to the bottom. Next to her, her husband's head lolls against the red nylon cover of his fat horseshoe-shaped neck rest, his fingers linked across his large belly. Even if the seat belt sign hadn't been on, it would be a struggle for me to get out.

Fighting my instincts, I press my forehead against the Plexiglas, forcing myself to breathe slowly and deeply. The reason I always choose the window seat is so I can pretend I'm a bird, free to fly where I like in the huge expanse of sky – not stuck in a metal tube along with hundreds of people. But there's nothing to see except the blackness. It's as if we're no longer moving.

Desperately, I search for the red blink of a light somewhere on the wing, but I'm too far back in the plane to see it. My anxiety rises a notch.

'Hot, isn't it?' The woman next to me is reaching up, twiddling the nozzle of the air vent as I had a few moments ago. 'Is this thing even working?'

She's dressed in an orange, sleeveless T-shirt, the half-moon of sweat on the stretchy material under her arm disappearing again as she lowers her hand. I don't want her to talk to me.

The plane shudders, making the table that's secured to the seat in front of me rattle, and I wish that Drew was next to me instead of the woman whose bag is wedged on the floor between her legs and mine. He'd know the right thing to say to calm me. Explain how there's nothing to worry about. That thousands of planes fly through turbulence every year and nothing happens. Only he'd be wrong about the reason for my shortness of breath and dry mouth. It's the fear of being trapped in the dark with no way out that's sending my pulse racing.

If I could just get to the toilet, splash cold water on my face, I might feel better, but there's nothing I can do as we're no longer allowed to leave our seats. Besides, it looks like it would take more than a bit of turbulence to wake up the man on the end. A child behind is pushing the back of my seat with his feet and the teenage boy in front has reclined his slightly so that the space I have is reduced. I think of the oxygen mask tucked behind its panel and long to breathe in the sweet air.

The woman next to me is talking again, wondering how many people it would take to use up all the air in the cabin. I want to scream at her to shut up because the whine of the engines, the shuddering of the plane and the press of the bodies is becoming unbearable.

The cabin crew are no longer in the aisle with their drinks trolley. It's been stowed away in the galley. They must be in their jump seats by the emergency exits, their seat belts pulled tight. It does nothing to quell my rising panic.

There's a humming in my ears that's competing with the vibration of the engines, and my fingers are starting to tingle. 'Please,' I whisper to myself. 'Not now.'

Because I know what's happening. Recognise it from before.

As I think of the pressure of air outside the window, I start to imagine the walls of the fuselage crumpling and crushing. The space inside shrinking. I want to get out, but there's nowhere to go.

Without knowing it, I've unbuckled my seat belt and pushed myself up, one hand on the back of the seat in front of me, the other to my throat, pulling at the neck of my T-shirt.

I stare desperately at the woman in the seat next to me, nearly falling into her as the plane drops then settles again.

'Please. I've got to…'

She's staring at me wide-eyed. 'What are you doing?'

In front of me, a few heads have turned. They're wondering what's happening. Why this red-haired woman is standing up, her eyes wild. Pupils dilated.

'I… I can't breathe.'

I feel a tug on my arm. 'Sit down. The seat belt sign's on.'

When I don't move, the woman stretches, her damp T-shirt brushing my arm, and presses the call button; the *ding* as the light comes on, causing a physical pain through my skull.

I don't remember anything else.

When I come around, I'm in the aisle seat and a flight attendant is holding out a glass of water to me.

'Here, drink this.' She wraps my fingers around the plastic cup. 'You fainted. How do you feel now?'

'I don't know.'

'You had a small panic attack, but it's nothing to worry about, Alice.'

I don't remember having given her my name, but I must have done. She's crouching in the aisle and, although she's not old, her face is so close to me I can see where her make-up has settled into the creases around her eyes. Her dark hair is scraped back from her face into a rolled bun at the top of her head, tightening the skin at her temples, but her eyes are kind. The light from the reading lamp catches her name badge, and I fix my eyes on it, repeating the mantra. *You're safe. You're safe.*

'We'll be landing soon. Is anyone meeting you at Gatwick? Can I call someone for you?'

The words are out before I can stop them. I could have said Drew, but for some reason his name isn't the one that comes into my head. Instead, another name is on my lips.

'Joanna.'

CHAPTER TWO

By the time I finally get home, after paying the cab driver the extortionate amount of money he's asked for the twenty-five-mile trip from the airport, I've calmed down considerably. My meltdown on the plane is no longer something life-changing, just an embarrassment I'll have to put behind me.

What I don't understand is how I let myself get into such a state. Over the years, I've learnt how to control my claustrophobia by practising the breathing techniques my doctor showed me and repeating to myself that my fear is irrational. The dark can't hurt me. But today, it hadn't worked. Something had gone wrong.

Of course, I hadn't let them ring Joanna. Why would I? It was just the stewardess's name badge that had put her name into my head. A name they both shared. No, it was Drew I'd needed. Drew who I'd really wanted to call, to hear his reassuring voice telling me it was all right to be scared. But I didn't make that call either. He'd still have been in the warehouse, driving his forklift between the tall metal shelves of cardboard boxes. Doing an extra shift. I couldn't expect him to drop everything for me.

And why would he after the things we both said.

While I was away, I could pretend that it had never happened. Pretend he hadn't said he wanted to leave. I'd pushed down the hurt and the pain – my anger at my father, and his new family, a good distraction. Now my misery has returned.

The taxi driver has dropped me on the opposite side of the street from my house. The street light picks out the number on the gatepost and, as I slam the door and watch him drive away, the tail lights disappearing around the corner, I wonder what made me give him the wrong number when he first asked me. 87, the flat I'd shared with Joanna in our university days. It was only when he'd stopped the taxi further along the street that I realised my mistake. *Strange.*

Compared to Corfu, the evening air feels chilly, and I'm glad I have my coat with me and didn't pack it in my case. The street looks drab: the sodium glare of the street lights picking out the petrol-black puddles on the pavements and the beige pebble-dash on the fronts of the semi-detached houses. More autumn than spring. There are no lights on in the house, but there wouldn't be. Drew won't be back for at least another hour. And when he comes home, we can talk properly about things. Sort everything out. I'll tell him that I didn't mean what I said… that we'll have a baby, if that's what he wants. Anything… as long as he doesn't leave.

Taking the handle of my case, I start to cross the road. What is it I'm scared of? Why have I been so reluctant to give him the child I know he wants? I wonder if it's the conscience on my shoulder that holds me back. The whisper in my ear telling me I don't deserve to bring a new life into the world. That I should be punished for what I did.

Deciding I should let Drew know I'm home and that I want to talk, I pull my phone from my pocket, typing as I cross. When I reach the kerb, I stop and, one-handed, try to bump the case onto the pavement. I don't see the car that rounds the corner until it's almost upon me, just hear the skid of its tyres as it brakes hard. The shock makes me stumble, and I lose my footing. As my foot twists and I make contact with the ground, my phone skitters into the middle of the road.

Through a fog of shock, I hear a car door slam and a woman's voice.

'Christ Almighty. Are you all right?'

She's standing in front of me, and I squint up at her, mortified, realising how much worse this could have been for both of us. The woman's older than me, about the age my mum would have been had she still been alive. She's visibly shaken, and my guilt grows. Sitting up slowly, I assess the damage, touching my fingers to my ankle, relieved that it's probably only twisted.

'I'm fine. Really.' Taking her offered hand, I try to stand and, as my damaged foot touches the ground, I find that, although it hurts, I can put my weight onto it. Taking my arm, the woman helps me onto the pavement.

She's near to tears. 'I didn't see you. I didn't expect anyone to be crossing so close to the corner and—'

'No, it's my fault. I was distracted. I should have been paying more attention.'

Seeing my phone, the woman goes over to it and picks it up. She hands it back to me without a word, but I can guess what she's thinking.

'Thank you. I'm sorry for giving you a scare.'

'Have you far to go? Can I give you a lift?'

I point to the house. 'No, I live just here.'

Taking the handle of the case from me, the woman helps me up the front path and waits while I find my keys. 'Are you sure you'll be all right? Is there anyone I can call?'

It's the second time someone has asked me this question today. The second time the name Joanna has been on the tip of my tongue.

'No, I'll be fine now, really. Thank you.'

'Well, if you're sure.'

She walks back down the path, and I let myself in, lifting my case into the hall and shutting the door behind me. Turning on the hall light, the first thing I see, half blocking the hallway, is a red plastic box. I take it to school with me every day, or rather I used to, and the sight of it causes a hollow pain in my chest. It's something else I've tried not to think about while I've been away.

The box is filled with folders of different colours. One for each subject I've taught this term at St Joseph's. English. Maths. Music. Their names clearly labelled on the spines. But I won't be using them again. Not since the devastating decision to close the school after pupil numbers fell. It was my unexpected redundancy that had instigated my spur of the moment decision to see my dad. That and the thing with Drew. A picture of my father stealing kisses with his young wife when he thought I wasn't looking, rubbing sun cream into the plump arms of their baby, comes into my head. I wish now I hadn't bothered.

Reaching my arms behind me, I press the heels of my hands into the small of my back and stretch. I'm too tired to sort the box out now. It will have to wait until tomorrow. Besides, I've too much on my mind to think about school.

I hang up my coat on the hook by the door. Without Drew here, the house feels empty. Lonely. Nothing like it was when we first moved in. In those days, it was full of noise and laughter. Drew was home more and on days he finished work after me, he'd call out, *Honey I'm home* in a terrible American accent as he let himself in. The bear hug he pulled me into would make me laugh and gasp for breath in equal measures.

I smile at the memory. We were idiots then.

I bend and unlace my trainer, wincing as I pull it from the foot I twisted. Using the wall for support, I take off the other one, then hobble into the kitchen and switch on the kettle. The room faces north and even on sunny days feels cool. Tonight, it's decidedly chilly. As the kettle boils, I look out at the dark little garden. There's nothing to see except my reflection, but I'm not missing anything – just a square of crazy paving, grass pushing through the gaps. There's a cluster of terracotta pots that I've never got around to filling and in the middle of the paving is a small green wrought-iron table and chairs. We'd bought them at a car boot sale, imagining sitting there on sunny evenings, me with a glass of wine and Drew with a beer. It hadn't happened, though. I'd been too busy with my lesson prep and, once it got warm enough to sit out there, it was rare that Drew was home before the sun left the garden.

I feel a stab of sorrow that now it's something we might never do.

My throat tightens, and I sit down at the little kitchen table, the reality of my life beginning to sink in. My relationship is in tatters, I have no job and, if the woman hadn't braked when she did, I could have been killed outside my own house. Turning my engagement ring around my finger, I start to shiver. My teeth chattering against each other.

I take out my phone, the message I was writing to Drew still there. Pressing send, I touch my finger to the screensaver before it disappears. The picture is of me and Mum taken on Brighton seafront. Walking along the promenade was something we used to do a lot back then when I was home from university. Ten years after her death, I'm still not over the loss of her. Still expect the phone to ring and to hear her voice. If she was still alive, I'd ask her what to do.

It's getting on for eight. Drew should be home soon, and I wonder if he'll be hungry. The kitchen is so small that I only need to reach behind me to open the fridge. There's not a lot in there, just a few bottles of lager, and I wonder what he's been eating while I've been away.

Deciding I'm not hungry, I close the fridge door again, a little kernel of worry lodging in my stomach. Why isn't he home? Pushing back my chair, I test my bad foot on the floor, then walk carefully into the living room. It's at the front of the house, and I part the net curtains, yellowed from the cigarette smoke of the previous owner, to look out onto the street.

The drive is empty. The street is empty. But there's also an empty feeling in my stomach that has nothing to do with the fact that I've eaten little since the very British-looking sandwich

I'd picked up at Corfu Airport. The truth is, I don't like my own company. Without Drew, I'm afraid I'll become what I used to be: afraid of my own shadow; my belief in myself faltering, then slowly ebbing away.

When my phone pings a message, I have my forehead pressed to the cold glass, my eyes straining to catch the first sight of the car's headlights when it turns the corner into our road. Snatching my mobile out of my pocket, I stare at the screen, presuming it's from Drew.

It isn't. The name that appears on my screen isn't my fiancé's. It's a name that's been in my head since the stewardess helped me down the aircraft steps and asked me if I was sure I was all right. The number, the one I gave her before changing my mind. It's as if what happened on the plane has conjured her out of nowhere. That by saying her name, I've cast some kind of magic spell.

Another message pings as I'm trying to get my head around it, and her name fills the screen.

Joanna.

CHAPTER THREE

As I stare at her name, a feeling of weightlessness comes over me, and I sink down onto the old settee. Once, the fact that its cover is faded from the sun would have bothered me, but not now. What's important is that Drew and I chose it together.

I trace my finger over her name thinking of all the other messages she's sent me in our years of friendship. The note she'd slipped under my pillow in the dorm when she knew I'd been homesick. The excited email she'd sent when she knew we'd both got into the same university.

My hand rises to my mouth to cover my smile. What can Joanna want? As always, when my friend has messaged me, it's as if all my senses are on high alert. I try to analyse my emotions and realise what I'm feeling is a combination of anticipation and excitement. Not for the first time, a sixth sense tells me that if I look at what she has to say, nothing will ever be the same again.

The part of me desperate to find out what Joanna wants vies with the one that tells me it's better not to know. My head wins over my heart. Throwing the phone onto the table, I sit on my hands and look at it, until eventually the screen goes black again. My foot has started to throb, and I'm overcome with a sudden tiredness. There's a throw on the back of the settee. Dragging it off, I wrap it around me, then squash one of the cushions under my head. It's then I hear the door.

'Drew?'

He comes into the room, and I notice how pale he looks. Dark circles under his eyes.

'I thought you'd be home earlier than this.'

'You know what it's like. We're up to our bloody necks.' He rubs his jaw with the flat of his hand. 'I could murder a beer.'

No kiss. No *how was your trip?*

He hesitates, then walks into the kitchen. Soon I hear the fridge opening and the sound of a bottle being placed on the worktop. 'Want one?'

'No.'

'Sure?'

'I said no, didn't I?' I don't mean to snap, but the sight of Joanna's name on my phone has unsettled me.

There's a clink as the bottle top flicks onto the laminate worktop, and then he comes back in. Rather than sit next to me, he sits opposite, his work boots leaving marks on the cream carpet we'd thought a good idea when we chose it. He raises the bottle to his lips, tipping his head back as he swallows down a few mouthfuls before catching sight of my puffy ankle.

'What have you done?'

'It's nothing. Just a twist.' I move it experimentally and am relieved when it does what I want it to do.

'How did you do it?'

I think about making something up, then decide it's pointless. 'I was crossing the road and almost got knocked down by a car. I'm fine, though. It was my fault. I should have been looking.'

'Shit.' His brows pull together, and he puts his beer bottle on the coffee table between us. 'That looks painful.'

'I'm okay.'

We sit in silence for a while, the air thickening with tension. We both know we need to clear the air, but it's as if neither of us wants to be the one to start the conversation.

Eventually, Drew speaks. 'I take it you didn't make it up with your dad then?'

I fold my arms around my body. 'The two of them made it clear I wasn't wanted. I was like a spare part.' I screw up my eyes, remembering how awful it was. How awkward. 'It was a terrible idea, Drew. I should never have let you persuade me to go.'

Once, he would have come over to me and wrapped me in his arms. Now, he stays where he is, picks up the TV controller and flicks through the channels.

'I've only got an hour, then I need to be at the club. There's a problem with the door staff or something. I told Sean I'd sort it out.'

Four nights a week Drew's out at his second job as a music promoter, checking the sound levels and visuals. Making sure everything's ready for the DJs and that the venue manager's happy. When we were first together, I used to go with him, but I soon got fed up with sitting at the bar while he chatted to the DJ or checked the speakers. They're four nights I spend on my own, but if Drew didn't do this second job, we wouldn't be able to afford this house.

A sick feeling worms its way into my stomach. I've no job now. No means of paying the mortgage if he leaves. Panic overcomes my reluctance to broach the subject. 'Tonight? Do you have to? We need to talk, Drew.'

There. I've said it.

His eyes slip away from me. 'There's nothing to talk about, Alice. We said it all before you went away.'

'But…'

On the coffee table my phone pings, lighting the screen with Joanna's name, and I stop what I was saying. She's sent another message. Drew points to it, looking relieved the conversation has been interrupted. 'Read it if you like?'

I shake my head, though I want to. 'I can read it later.'

'That's not like you. You're usually all over your phone.'

He gives a half smile, the tension in the room easing a little. I want to go over and kiss him, but of course I can't.

'It's not important,' I say, instead.

Reaching out a hand, Drew turns the phone towards him and looks at it. 'Joanna? Really?'

'Yes. Give it to me.' I snatch the phone back.

'Okay. Okay.' He frowns. 'What do you think she wants?'

'What do friends usually want when they message you? She probably just wants to see how I am.'

I've an overwhelming desire to know if I'm right, but I don't want to read what she's written while Drew is here. I put my phone back down.

Drew gives a shrug. 'Where's she living now?'

'I'll have it in my address book. Why are you so interested?'

'No reason.' Tipping the bottle to his lips, he takes another mouthful of beer, then wipes his mouth with the back of his hand. 'I'm going to shower and change. I'll finish this upstairs.' He sniffs at the armpit of his green sweatshirt. 'Christ, I stink.'

'But, Drew…' It's too late, he's already gone. I sigh heavily, realising we're no closer to sorting things out.

There's the slam of the bathroom door, and soon I hear the shower. Usually, Drew sings as he washes his hair, but tonight he doesn't. Leaning forward, I pick my phone up from the table and click onto my messages. The two from Joanna are at the top. Heart racing, I open the first one and start to read.

It's short. *Alice, are you there?*

But it's not this message that makes me sit up straighter, it's the next. It's not what I had been expecting at all.

Hi Alice. I just had to tell you! I've met the most amazing man and, guess what? Drum roll… We're getting married! Yes really. I know I've only known him a month, but you'd love him. I know you would. And you just have to come up and meet him. No one gets married without their best friend's approval. Please say you will. Please. Please.

CHAPTER FOUR

Even though it's only a message, I can hear Joanna's voice. The breathy excitement and the lack of pauses that, if we were face to face, would give little space for reply. Without realising it, I'm touching a finger to her words – feeling how they're drawing me in. Warmth spreads through my body and my skin begins to prickle. My fingers itch to reply straight away, but I supress the urge. With me and Drew so up in the air, I can't think straight.

Drew's out of the bathroom. I listen to him as he gets dressed in the bedroom, hear the wardrobe door slam shut and imagine him slipping his arms into one of the patterned shirts he likes to wear on club nights. It isn't long before his footsteps are on the stairs. I put my phone back in my pocket.

When he comes into the room, I see his hair is gelled, and he's wearing an aftershave that I don't recognise. It's spicy with a hint of sandalwood.

'You smell nice.'

'Do I?' He sounds pleased, his eyes slipping to the clock on the wall.

Soon he'll be gone and, before he goes, I need to tell him. Make him understand.

Grabbing his arm as he walks by to get his jacket, I pull Drew onto the settee next to me. 'There's something I need to say to you, Drew. Something important. I know things have been difficult between us these last couple of months, and I know what you said, but while I was in Corfu, I did a lot of thinking… about us.'

Drew sighs. 'There is no us, Alice. Not any more. I told you that before you went. I can't stay when we both want different things.'

I take his hand. 'No, you don't understand, Drew. I was wrong… I know that now. Maybe being made redundant was a blessing. Maybe it's what we need for a fresh start.'

He puffs out his cheeks, then exhales. 'How did you come to that conclusion?'

It's now or never.

'You said you wanted a baby. You said our relationship would never work if we weren't on the same page. But I've changed my mind. It was selfish of me to think we could carry on as we were when you were thinking this way.'

Drew's eyes won't meet mine. 'It wasn't your fault. It wasn't just you who was selfish, but it doesn't change anything.'

'It does, Drew. We could have a baby… just like you wanted. In fact, it's the perfect time. I could get a part-time job while I'm pregnant, and then, once the baby's born, I could stay at home and look after it. It would be a fresh start. Things happen for a reason, and I think this is it.'

I'm gabbling. Scared at the way he's looking at me, the colour drained from his face. I thought he would be pleased, that it was what he wanted to hear, but now I'm not sure what he's thinking. What he's feeling.

My smile slips a little. 'Say something, Drew. Anything.'

He shakes his head. 'You throw this at me now?'

'What do you mean? I'm not throwing it at you… it's what you said you wanted. We don't have to decide now. We can think about it.'

Drew looks away, scratching at his forearm. 'We can't have a baby. Not now.'

'But why not?'

His lips are pressed into a thin line. I know something's wrong.

'Tell me… please.'

He's looking at me now, and my gut twists when I see the guilt in his eyes.

'Look, Alice, there's no easy way of saying this.' The breath he draws in is loud in the otherwise silent room. 'I'm seeing someone else.'

For a minute, I think he's joking, but when I see the way his body angles away from me, desperate to get away, I know he's not.

I stare at him, the muscles of my face aching with the effort not to cry. I can't let this be the end. 'I forgive you.'

Drew drops his gaze to the floor. 'Don't say that, Ali. I don't deserve it.'

'But I mean it. I don't care. Whatever it is… this fling… we can put it behind us. I love you, Drew.'

I try to take his hand, but he pulls it from me. 'Please, Alice. You've got to stop this. You're only making things worse.'

'I'm not. Don't you see—'

'She's pregnant.'

The bottom drops out of my world.

'Are you okay?' he asks.

If it wasn't so tragic, I'd laugh. How can he ask this? How can I be okay when my life has fallen around me like a pack of cards? A wave of pain and nausea hits me, and I press my hand to my stomach, the shake of my head giving him my answer.

'I'm sorry. I don't know what else to say.'

I didn't want to know before, but now it's important to me that I do. I need to know what sort of woman has taken my place… who it is that's having his baby.

My whole body feels numb with shock, but I force the words out. 'Who is she?'

'Just someone at the club.'

Just someone at the club. It's said so casually. Can't he see what his words are doing to me?

'It wasn't planned… it just happened.'

I look at the man I've shared the last few years of my life with. It's as though he's a stranger. 'And that's supposed to make me feel better?'

'I still care for you, Ali.'

With difficulty, I stand, my ankle sending a shock of pain up my leg, and point at the door.

'I'd like you to leave now, Drew.'

'I don't want it to be like this.' His eyes are pleading. 'If you'd just let me explain.'

The hurt is a solid pain in my chest. But it's not just the hurt… it's the realisation of how naïve I've been. Remembering how I'd sat in the spare room of my dad's house struggling with my conscience before talking myself round to the idea of having Drew's baby.

Not knowing it was too late.

The hurt is turning to anger. 'There's nothing you can say that I want to hear. Just get out.'

'I didn't plan it this way. You have to believe me. It's just that you've held me at arm's length for so long, I decided you didn't care. Look, I'm not trying to make excuses or make out it's your fault, of course it isn't. I just wanted you to understand why I…' His voice falters. 'Why it happened.'

I can't look at him. Can't bear to see the way his eyes plead. How desperate he is for me to understand. To absolve him. 'Go on. Tell me, Drew. Tell me what it is I did that was so bad it made you run into the arms of the first girl who'd take you.'

His shoulders sag. 'That's just it, Alice. You didn't do anything. It was just a stupid mistake. The baby… it wasn't supposed to happen. We should have been more careful.'

I stare at him incredulously. The bitter taste of jealousy in the back of my throat. *A stupid mistake.* I want to cry at his words. How could a baby be a mistake?

'A mistake,' I say, my voice flat.

Drew crosses his arms defensively. 'I've never felt that I'm good enough for you – that I'm just filling a gap in your life. Some sort of emptiness that you won't talk about. Do you know how that feels? Do you? It feels like shit.'

Shock makes me take a step back. 'But that's not true. I've always been here for you.'

'Have you? Have you really? In body maybe... but not up here.' He taps his forehead with his index finger. 'Is that why you always changed the subject when I said I wanted children? I've always felt like you settled for me, like you were biding your time with me until someone better came along.'

'Of course not—'

'Because that's what it looked like to me.'

Part of me wants to tell him the truth. That I've been too scared. But what's the point? It's too late now. Drew's moved on. He's leaving me behind.

I turn away, swallowing down the hot lump that's formed in my throat. 'Just get your things and go, Drew. This is only making it worse.'

Drew stands. 'You probably won't believe me, but I wanted things to work out between us, Alice. So badly.'

'You have a funny way of showing it.' My voice is filled with bitterness.

Ignoring me, Drew carries on. 'For months and months I tried, but you need the other person to try too. It's not something you can do on your own. A relationship should be equal, but when I talk to you, I don't feel as if you're really listening.'

My head feels heavy, numbed by the unfairness of what he's saying. 'You've never said any of this before.'

Drew bats at his forehead with the heel of his hand. 'And why is that? Because every time I mention anything that might involve, God forbid,' he makes quote marks in the air, 'an *emotion*, you shut down. What is it you're scared of, Alice?'

I can't talk about it. Can't afford to have my words twisted and used against me. The silence lingers, and I know he's waiting for me to answer.

Eventually, he speaks, his voice raw with emotion. 'For Christ's sake, Alice, you're even doing it now. I'll get my things.'

With a loud sigh, he leaves the room. I have my back to him, but I hear him as he climbs the stairs. Hear the wardrobe doors opening and closing, the thump of a case as it's pulled from the top of the wardrobe. There's a silence, and then the soft scrape of the case against the wall as he carries it down the stairs.

I stand frozen in the middle of the living room, holding my breath, telling myself his leaving doesn't bother me. That he's a cheat and a liar and I'm better off without him. I wait for the sound of the front door to open and when I don't hear it, I turn. Drew is standing in the doorway looking at me, his fingers grasping the handle of the case.

'I'm sorry,' he says at last. 'I've made things worse waiting until you got back. I planned to pack up my things and leave while you were away, but then I found out about the baby, and it just didn't seem the right thing to do. It would have been easier for us both if I'd slipped out the back door, but you deserved to hear about the baby from my lips, not someone else's. Of course, I'll carry on paying my half of the mortgage, until we can sell the house. But we'll need to get someone in to value it sooner rather than later. There's no point in dragging this out.'

'No,' I say coldly. 'There isn't.'

As the front door finally opens and shuts, I refuse to let myself cry. Instead, I twist my engagement ring round on my finger, my bruised heart thudding in my chest, before slipping it off. It nestles in the palm of my hand, the diamond sparkling in the overhead light. Is Drew right? Did I really shut him out? I think back to the day he gave me the ring and try to remember what I felt as I opened the velvet box. With a shock, I realise that on what should have been the most wonderful day of my life, there was still a little piece of me that held back.

Not knowing what to do with it, I pull open a drawer in the hall table and place it in there. I'll make that decision later.

My phone pings. It's Joanna again. *You didn't reply!*

If she was here, I'd tell her everything that's happened these last few days: my dad, my job, the car that nearly ran me down… Drew leaving me. I wonder what she'd say in reply. I hear her voice in my head. Feel the touch of her slim hand with its narrow, manicured nails. *It's a blessing, Alice. He's not worth it, you know I'm right. I'm here for you, just as I've always been.*

Knowing she'd be right, I sink down onto the settee, the phone pressed to my heart, and let the tears come. Seeing Joanna is the one thing that can make everything better.

CHAPTER FIVE

I lie in bed watching the sun flicker behind my curtains. See how the hem is edged in gold. I've been awake for hours, but there's nothing to get up for. In the week since Drew's been gone, I've hardly been able to function. Everything I see, everything I touch, reminds me of him. The kitchen table we salvaged from a skip and repainted, the stain on the carpet where Drew knocked over his red wine, the TV controller only he really understands how to work.

It's hard now to remember what happened after I found out the man I thought I'd known was someone I didn't know at all. He had proved me right. Provided evidence that the barriers I'd put up had not been for nothing and that I'd done the right thing by not allowing him to know the true me. See my vulnerable side. He's called once, but I haven't answered, not wanting him to know how his actions have turned me inside out. Laid my nerve endings bare.

Since then I've shut down. Not left the house.

I barely eat.

Barely sleep.

And, on the days I bother to get up, when I drag myself to bed again later, I lie awake in sheets that still smell of Drew. Replaying my life with him and wondering what I did wrong before rewinding my memories to wander again. A continuous loop.

Today is the tenth day, and I'm feeling different – as though, little by little, my senses are returning. At first, it's just tiny things: the stale smell of the duvet and the sound of next door's recycling bin as the lid shuts. But then I become aware of my body. How my arm is cramping where I've lain on it, and the insistent growl of a stomach that's trying to remind me I haven't eaten properly in days. My ankle is better now, but there's a dull pain in the area of my heart as it thaws. It's mild enough to ignore, but I know from experience it will continue to grow until I'm longing for the earlier numbness to return.

The bedroom is stuffy, smelling of the clothes I haven't bothered to wash but have left on the floor beside my bed. My hair is greasy, and I really should shower, but it's too much of an effort.

I hear Joanna's voice telling me to pull myself together. *He's not worth it, Alice. You're better off on your own than with someone who doesn't love you.* If she was here, she'd make me get out of bed, steer me to the bathroom and search my drawers for fresh clothes to put on. Then, even if I hadn't wanted to, she'd drag me out to the cinema, or pub, or café – anything rather than have me wallow in my own self-pity.

Why haven't I rung her before? Pride, I suppose.

Hit by a sudden yearning to hear Joanna's voice, I grab my phone and punch in her number, not sure yet what I'm going to say. It rings and I wait, acknowledging the thud of my heart.

'Hi, it's Joanna.'

She sounds so happy, so full of life, that immediately I feel calmer. I'm about to speak when I realise it's just a voicemail message. She's unavailable right now. Can I leave a message? My mind goes blank. What can I say? Before I've decided, a beep signals the time is up. Annoyed with myself, I write a text instead.

Great news! Who is he? Where did you meet him?

The small act of messaging her has coaxed me out of my lethargy. Even though I want to, I know I can't stay in the house forever and, despite my lack of appetite, I'll eventually need to go to the shops, if only for some more loo roll. With no one to talk to, the small house is starting to feel even smaller. With super-human effort, I make myself get up and open the curtains, the sun blinding me.

Not bothering to get dressed, I go downstairs and make a mug of coffee, which I take into the garden, surprised to find that it's midday already. The small garden is hemmed in on all sides by a high grey fence. I used to like the privacy, but now it just feels oppressive. I look at the blank glass faces of the patio doors, the pebble-dashed walls, the heavy black guttering. Things I'd managed to overlook in my desire to make a home with Drew, but which now I know to be ugly. If I stay here, I will disappear and, if that happens, I'm scared I might never find myself again. As I sip my coffee, I listen out for the ping that tells me Joanna has replied.

There's nothing.

Instead, through the open door, I hear the sharp trill of the doorbell. At first, I decide not to answer it, but then the ring comes again. Whoever it is will have seen my car and guessed that I'm in. On the third ring, I give in. It's clear they're not going to leave until I answer. Forgetting I'm still in my night stuff, an old T-shirt of Drew's and a dressing gown that has seen better days, I force my legs to take me to the front door. Opening it, I see it's Sally, the classroom assistant with whom I used to share a lift. Her round face registers surprise as her eyes take in what I'm wearing.

'Oh,' she says, taking a slight step backwards. 'Sorry. I wasn't interrupting anything, was I? Drew got a day off work?'

I pull the belt of my dressing gown tighter, the mention of Drew tugging at my heart. 'No. I've been in bed. I've had a migraine.' Sally's face rearranges itself into one of concern and I quickly add, 'I'm fine now, though.'

Sympathy is not what I'm looking for. I know that if she's kind to me, then I'm in danger of telling her what's happened and I'm not ready to do that. Not yet.

'Well, I just popped by to tell you that, as it's such nice weather, a few of us from school have decided to have a barbeque tomorrow evening, round at mine. About five? You don't need to bring anything… just a jumper. It will be a chance to let it all out – say fuck to them all. It would be great if you could come. Oh, and bring Drew… it's not as if I can get rid of Alan for the evening.'

She laughs and, not knowing what else to do, I laugh with her. 'No, I suppose not.'

'So, you'll come then?'

I can see her looking past me into the hall. Can imagine her wondering why my big red box of school stuff is still there and why the curtains are closed in the living room. I don't want to go to her barbeque. Don't want to make up a reason why Drew isn't with me or, worse still, tell them the truth and have to endure their sympathetic smiles and words of advice.

'I'm sorry I can't.' I search for something I can say. Some reason to give that won't sound like an excuse. 'I'm going away.'

Sally raises her eyebrows. 'Didn't you just go to Corfu?'

I flounder, caught out in my lie. 'Yes, but—'

'Mind you,' she continues. 'I don't blame you after the bombshell they dropped. Anywhere nice?'

It comes to me like a lightning bolt. What an idiot I've been. I know exactly where I'm going. Her hand stretched out to me in her message, and it's a hand I'm struggling not to take as she's the only person I know who can make things better.

'I'm going to stay with my best friend, Joanna,' I say, the finality in my voice surprising me. 'She's getting married. Wants me to meet her fiancé…'

I tail off. That's all the information Joanna has given me.

Sally leans back against the little porch. 'Must have been a whirlwind romance if you haven't met him before. Lucky girl. Took Alan nine years to get his act together and propose.'

I can see she wants to know more. She's probably surprised that I haven't invited her in for a gossip. But although I like her well enough, ours has never been the sort of friendship where we've opened up to each other. Why would I start now?

'I'll tell you all about it when I get back,' I say, even though I have no intention of doing any such thing. Now I've made up my mind to go, the time I have with Joanna will be precious. Not something to share. 'Look, Sally, I really have to go. Tell the others I'm sorry I couldn't make it and that I'll catch up with them another time.'

I don't want to see these people who have only known me as Alice the teacher... Alice Drew's fiancée. I've started to lose touch with who I really am, and I want to find that person again. The person I can only be when I'm with Joanna... The person I was with Jez. I haven't thought of him in years, but now his face comes back to me as he was then. Laughing blue eyes. A flop of blond hair that he'd push back with his fingers. What's brought him to mind now?

Sally nods and straightens up. 'I'll tell them. They'll be sorry to have missed you. Maybe another time.'

'Maybe.'

I go back into the house, the silence when I close the door behind me deafening. Without Drew between its walls, the fabric that holds everything together – the carpets and the curtains, the furniture and pictures – has no meaning. It's just an empty vessel. My hand slides to my stomach, and I screw up my eyes in pain as I think of what I've lost, and all Drew's new girl has to look forward to. One thing I know for sure is that I can't stay in a house where there are memories of him in everything I touch. The promise of a future that is no longer mine.

Soon, our joint friends will hear of the new girl who's taken my place at Drew's side. Maybe, after a short interval for decency's sake, they'll even be introduced to her. Will they congratulate them both? Wish them all the best?

I can't help wondering if this girl will fit in better than I did.

The only person who can really understand how I feel is Joanna. Why shouldn't I go?

Snatching my phone from my pocket, I click on her name. I haven't heard back from her about my previous message, but it might be because she's been busy planning her wedding. I know how time-consuming it is to search for venues. For photographers. For dresses. With a pang, I look at the wedding magazines that are strewn across the coffee table. Inside are pictures circled in red pen. Notes scribbled in margins. Scooping them up, I dump them in the recycling bin in the kitchen, reminding myself that it's not the first relationship to have ended. The last time it happened, I lost so much more. I was strong then and I can be now. Picking up my phone, I tap out a reply.

I want to come. Tell me when.

CHAPTER SIX

I feel like an alcoholic who's had their first sip of wine in years. A warmth spreading through my veins. I smile at the thought of Joanna, and a memory comes back to me. We're sitting in a math's lesson, our heads bowed to our work, when she leans across the desk and scribbles something in the margin of my book. When I look at what she's written, I see it's the answer to the question I've been struggling with. I smile my thanks and she mouths, *you owe me*, though we both know I'll never pay her back. Unless you count playing the piano, Joanna is better than me at everything.

The ping of her reply comes so quickly it startles me. *Come on Saturday*. It's followed by her address.

I stare at the screen, my heart thudding. Saturday. That's only three days away. Already my mind is racing through the things I should take. The clothes I have that aren't jogging bottoms or the black trousers and blouses I used to wear for work. Maybe I should go out shopping; get myself something half-decent.

For the first time in ten days, my hurt and anger at Drew nudges aside a little, leaving room for a little frisson of excitement to edge in alongside it. A reminder of what I always feel when Joanna rings. Just thinking about her voice and the smile that never fails to lift my spirits, is helping me come alive again.

It's as if she knows something has happened. Has found out my world has fallen apart and is going to be there for me just like she's always been. Joanna's the only person in this world who knows me well enough to understand what I'm going through.

The only one I can bare my soul to. I have a sudden urge to look at the photos of us when we were teenagers. The ones taken on our backpacking trip around South East Asia in the month before we went to university.

The albums are kept in the cupboard under the TV, but it's only when I slide the first one out that I remember I no longer have the ones I'm looking for. Instead, I go to the computer and switch it on. I might as well see what Joanna's new place is like.

I don't know what I've been expecting when I type Joanna's address into the search engine, but it's not this. The images that jump out at me are like something from a film. Some are of stylish bedrooms with low-level futons and gauzy curtains. Others feature kitchens with shiny black units and integrated appliances – inserts showing close-ups of marble islands, the shiny surfaces of which hold strategically placed coffee makers and glass and steel juicers. But it's the pictures of the vast living areas that hold my attention. Neutral-coloured walls contrasting with the dark wood floors, the furniture all clean, minimal lines. Their pièce de résistance the floor to ceiling windows that look out over the Thames and the London skyline.

When I click on one of the images, it brings up the developer's brochure, and I read the brief introduction. New Tobacco Wharf is a renovation of an old tobacco warehouse by Maitland Belmont Developments. It's situated in one of the last London docks to be redeveloped. Black Water Dock. The name conjures images of pirates and smugglers, and I smile as I remember the Captain Jack Sparrow outfit Joanna had managed to carry off at one of the many parties we'd gone to back in our student days. The beard she'd painstakingly stuck to her chin and the beaded braid she'd fixed to her dark hair.

There's a small photograph of the developer, Mark Belmont, a serious-faced man who looks to be in his early forties and, beneath it, a picture of the red-bricked warehouse and its surroundings as it was in its heyday in the 1800s. I enlarge the black and white image and see that the area in front of the building is busy with dockers carrying barrels and hauling on ropes. Lining the quayside are ships with tall masts, clusters of wooden barges jostling for space nearby.

How different it is to the architect's design that's printed next to it. In it, the imposing warehouse containing the apartments looks much the same, but that's where the similarity ends. Here, the regimented lines of windows, instead of having a view of a bustling dock, now look down onto an elegant area of landscaped gardens and outdoor living spaces. It's modern. Cosmopolitan. And, when I read the developer's spiel, I find out that, as well as this lovely area, there's a gym and a large underground car park for residents.

Clicking through the pages, I come to the asking price. It takes my breath away for the sum is more than I'd guessed – around three million for a two-bedroom apartment. I try to remember the last job Joanna had. Something in telesales I think. Whatever it was, it's unlikely she'd be doing it now as she was never one to stick to anything for long. Could she really have found something that would enable her to live in such luxury?

It's only as I remember her breathless words that the answer comes to me. Of course, it must be something to do with her fiancé.

I look at Joanna's message again. *Come on Saturday.*

Finding her number, I phone her, but there's no answer. Like before, it goes straight to voicemail. It's frustrating as there are things I need to know, like the best way to get there and how long she's happy for me to stay, but it's typical Joanna. With no answer to my questions, I look up trains. There's no way I'm going to take the underground, but there's an overground train that runs from Clapham Junction to Wapping which I could take. As I check the times, a yellow exclamation mark comes up; I'd forgotten about the train strikes that are starting tomorrow. With fewer trains running, the carriages will be heaving, and there's no way I'd be able to cope with that. It's then I remember that the apartments have an underground car park. It would mean braving the Blackwall Tunnel, but I could drive there.

I type in a message.

Saturday's perfect. I'll be there. I can stay the weekend if you like.

CHAPTER SEVEN

It should only have taken me two hours to get to Joanna's apartment, but I'd underestimated the traffic: the continuous jams, the roadworks, the constant stopping and starting at lights that always seem to be red. A glance at my petrol gauge shows I've a quarter of a tank left. I just hope it's enough to get me to the end of my journey. Drew would tick me off for not stopping at a garage sooner.

Drew. Over the last few days, I haven't had time to think about him much. I've been too busy deciding what clothes to take, how to wear my hair. From the look of the apartment in the online brochure, Joanna has done all right for herself, and I don't want to show her up. I try to imagine Joanna in one of the trendy warehouse developments that make up New Tobacco Wharf and fail. This wasn't the kind of place either of us had imagined ending up in when we'd talked about our futures. During those long terms at St Joseph's, we'd pictured ourselves living side by side in semi-detached cottages in the country. One with roses around the door. Our husbands would be best friends, and our children would go to the same school.

I look at my bare ring finger. Now it seems it's only Joanna who will have a husband. A month though – that's all the time she's known him. Joanna has always been impetuous, buying clothes without a second thought, deciding within seconds if she likes someone, but marriage is a different thing entirely. Choosing someone to spend the rest of your life with isn't something to be rushed into. But that's not the only thing that bothers me. I'd always thought that when she met that special person, she'd want me to meet him straight away. That she'd care what I thought before saying yes.

With fingers gripped tightly on the wheel, the points of my knuckles whitening my skin, I slavishly follow my satnav as it takes me round roundabouts and across intersections, hoping upon hope that it really does know the way. Because if it doesn't, I've no idea what I'll do as I haven't brought a map.

Still, the Blackwall Tunnel is behind me now. I'd survived it by turning my music up loud and singing even louder, telling myself over and over that it wouldn't be long before I saw the circle of light that would signify its end. I hadn't let myself picture the thick walls of concrete and the press of water above me.

But, now I'm across the river, my troubles are far from over. I must have taken a wrong turning somewhere, and the next thing I know there are signs for Canary Wharf. It's not where I want to be. There are cars everywhere, and I'm starting to feel overwhelmed. The pavements are crowded with people, men in slim blue suits and women with shiny hair and expensive-looking shoes and bags. When the lights are red, I watch them hurry on their way: successful people who know what they're doing. Know where they're heading… or so I believe as I wait with sweating palms praying that the satnav will find me, and guide me on to the correct route, before the lights go green again.

It doesn't, so I've no alternative but to follow the stream of traffic because, even if I'd wanted to, there's nowhere I could stop. In a desperate bid to keep my panic in check, I turn the air conditioning up to maximum and take long slow breaths.

I'm just thinking that it's worked when a car sounds its horn, making me jump. I've drifted into the lane next to me, only luck making me avoid a collision. Mouthing an apology to the driver, I move back into my lane and force myself to calm down. Soon, my drive will be over, and I'll be sitting on Joanna's balcony looking out at the boats on the Thames, a glass of chilled wine in my hand. My nightmare journey reduced to nothing more than an anecdote to be laughed at – as we used to laugh back then about everything and nothing.

The blue arrow reappears on the screen and, reassured that I'm back on track, I continue to snake my way between the concrete and steel office blocks and residential developments either side of me. Dropping down my sun visor to block the occasional flash of sunlight that dazzles from their glass windows.

I pass between colonnaded shopping malls, crawl round huge roundabouts and through grey underpasses that spew me back out onto bollard-lined shopping streets. The only thing to add contrast to this futuristic landscape of glass and steel and concrete are the red buses that follow each other, nose to tail.

At the next roundabout take the first exit.

Thank God.

Relief flooding through me to be leaving this busy thoroughfare, I do as the woman's voice says, taking the exit that leads me away from the endless shining windows, the colonnaded walkways and the wide road hemmed in by glittering skyscrapers. But, as I drive on, I tell myself that what I've just experienced is something I'll have to get used to over the next few days. From what I saw of the architect's drawing of the area, Black Water Dock will be as much of a gleaming example of modern living and retail spaces as its sister. Joanna really must have landed on her feet.

The digits at the bottom of the satnav tell me that I'll be arriving at my destination in twenty minutes, and I start to relax. But, as the minutes count down, I notice a gradual change in my surroundings. The roads are smaller now and not nearly as congested, the pavements edged, not with cafés and bars, but with kebab shops, hairdressers and dry-cleaners. A pub on the corner advertises a steak night on Friday, and instead of the smooth road surface I left behind at the last roundabout, the road is made up of flat cobbles. It's like I've entered a different world, one far removed from the one I've just been through.

Passing under an iron railway bridge, just as a train rattles by, I see my first sign to Black Water Dock. Taking a left, I drive through an area of social housing, narrow verandas running along each length of their flat brown fronts. Past a Tesco Metro. A dilapidated bus stop. An electricity substation, its grey fencing barbed with vicious-looking spikes.

There follows a stretch of wasteland where houses have been demolished and, with nothing to now block the view, I get my first proper sight of the river, a brown stripe, the buildings of South London rising behind it. I pass a disused pumping station, and then my satnav tells me I've reached my destination.

Slowing the car to a stop and turning off the engine, I look around me. Surely, it's a mistake. How can Joanna live here? It's a far cry from the images I saw on the internet: the continental-looking bars, their green umbrellas shading metal tables overlooking the water. The landscaped gardens and courtyards that filled the spaces between the converted warehouses and shiny sharp-edged new builds. I must be in the wrong place. But the sign to my right is telling me otherwise.

WELCOME TO BLACK WATER DOCK

The sign is large. Impressive. But the solid black lettering is half-obscured by the remnants of the blue paint that, at some time in the past, has been thrown at it. As I stare at the words, I wonder, not for the first time today, why I've come... what made me so impetuous. I could simply have waited until I spoke to Joanna. Made sure I knew where I was going. Why was coming here so important to me anyway?

Taking out my phone, I ring Joanna's number. The call tone carries on until her voice tells me to leave a message.

'Joanna, it's Alice. I'm at the entrance to Black Water Dock. Where should I go? How do I find you?'

I wait a few minutes then, when nothing happens, I realise that unless I'm going to turn around and drive back home again, I have no option but to set out in search of New Tobacco Wharf myself. Turning the engine back on, I follow the new-looking road ahead of me. It's covered with chippings, and I have to go slowly to avoid flicking them. It seems to be the only way into the area. My tyres crunch on the stones and, through the open window, I can smell the river. Briny. Seaweedy.

It's not long before the road I've come in on fans out into a labyrinth of smaller ones. They wind between the huge brick warehouses and storage units that line the quayside. The buildings look sad. Neglected. Some of their windows whitewashed. Others broken. Many of the walls are embedded with solid ironwork, evidence of their functional heritage, and a few have rusting scaffolding attached to their faces.

Remembering the black and white photograph on the website, the tobacco warehouse's blank windows looking down on the tall ships waiting to be loaded, I don't turn off but follow the road I'm on as it heads down to the river. If only the place wasn't so deserted. If only there was someone to ask.

When I reach the waterfront, I park alongside a sprawling low-rise building covered in graffiti and get out, shading my eyes. The waterfront is a mishmash of dockside buildings, warehouses of differing sizes and cargo vaults, standing cheek by jowl with each other. But whereas these buildings are in keeping with the area's maritime heritage, when I look further along the abandoned quayside, I see, in front of a desolate wasteland of rubble, four new-looking developments in all their shining glory. They're angled in such a way as to represent the prow of a ship, and the deck-like wooden balconies that jut from their sliding patio doors, continue the nautical theme. Leaving the car, I go to look at them – hoping for signs of life – but when I tip my head to see above the sturdy hoarding that encloses them, their windows look back at me. Empty. Silent but for the scream of a seagull that struts the boards of one of the balconies.

An interpretation board attached to the hoarding boasts that Calypso Wharf, the name of the development, and Black Water Dock are the Covent Garden of Dockland. But as I walk back the way I've just come, it feels just the opposite. It's nothing like Covent Garden… it's more like a ghost town.

When I reach my car, I don't get back in but walk in the other direction, being careful not to catch my feet in the grass and weeds that push up from the cracks in the paving. New Tobacco Wharf must be here somewhere. I walk past a warehouse with bricked up doorways and another whose empty shell harbours piles of car tyres and other abandoned car parts. I've just passed a building with Units to Let printed on a board outside when I see it. Unmistakeable because of the name and date printed across the top line of brickwork. *New Tobacco Wharf 1812.*

Compared to the buildings either side of it, this one is vast. Its tall, regimented windows staring down at me from a flat red-bricked frontage. It's imposing. Austere. And, although the building is clearly old, there's something about it, apart from its size, that sets it apart from the others. It's a while before I realise what it is. New Tobacco Wharf is the only building in the area that doesn't look either derelict or unfinished. In fact, it's magnificent – the brickwork repointed, the wooden window frames newly painted, the paved space in front, with its miniature box hedges in their square planters, freshly swept.

In the middle of the building is a large archway, edged in darker brick, which houses two glass doors that I presume is the front entrance. Going up to them, I cup my hand to the glass and peer inside, gasping at what I see. There's a huge marble atrium, in the centre of which is an ornate fountain. Even with no water cascading from the mouths of the dolphins that raise themselves up from the base, it's impressive. At the back of the hall is a shiny lift and, to the left, an unmanned reception desk.

Alongside the door is a brass panel with buzzers. For some reason, I'd been expecting name cards, but there are only numbers next to them. I can't see the apartment number Joanna gave me. I'm certain it was number thirty. Getting my phone out, I check Joanna's message to make sure I've remembered correctly. Yes, it definitely says thirty. I'm just wondering what to do when I notice, on the other side of the door, another panel mirroring the first. Number thirty is near the bottom, and before I can chicken out, I press the button next to it.

There's no welcoming voice, just silence. Maybe no one's in.

I'm just wondering whether to press the buzzer again when the intercom crackles into life.

'Yes?'

It's a man's voice. Fairly deep. Not particularly young. Could this be Joanna's mysterious fiancé?

'I've come to see Joanna.' I pause awkwardly, wondering how much she's told him about me. 'I… we… arranged it on the phone.'

Even to my ears, I sound ridiculous, and it's no surprise when there's no reply.

'Is she in?' I hurry on. 'I came by car and I don't know where I should—'

'Joanna? No, I'm sorry, but she's not here.' There's a finality to his words that takes me by surprise.

My finger rubs at the brass button. 'But she must be. She asked me to come.'

'I rather think I'd remember if Joanna had told me she'd asked someone to stay. Who did you say you were?'

'Alice. Alice Solomon. We were at school together. Uni too. She's my oldest friend.'

'That's funny. She's never mentioned you.'

I swallow, frustration growing. 'Please… um…' I stop, realising I don't even know his name.

He sounds amused. 'Mark.'

'Sorry. Yes… Mark.' I'm consumed with embarrassment. Why didn't Joanna tell me his name? 'Anyway, I've driven all this way, and it's been a really awful journey. Could I at least come in and have a glass of water? You don't know how difficult it is trying to explain myself to a metal grill.'

I think I hear him laugh, then there's a buzz. 'I'm sorry. You must think me terribly rude. Please… come up. It's the sixth floor. Number thirty halfway along.'

In one smooth silent movement, the doors in front of me slide open. I step inside, and it's only as they start to close behind me that I wonder how I'm going to get out again. Beside the door is a large silver square marked *press*. Leaning across, I thump it with my fist, closing my eyes in relief as the doors slide open again. I'm being stupid. A huge building such as this would be full of emergency exits and fire escapes.

Bypassing the lift with its shiny steel doors, I climb the stairs to its left. It's only six flights, I tell myself, and then I'll be able to find out what's going on. The stairs are wide, uncarpeted, their walls painted the colour of hessian. Mindful of my recent injury, I take it slow, but by the time I reach the sixth floor, I'm out of breath and my ankle is aching. Leaning against the wall, I put a tentative finger to the flesh around the ankle bone. Thankfully, it doesn't appear to be swollen.

A door brings me onto a wide corridor, its walls lined with black and white prints of the wharf when it was still in use. I recognise one as being the photograph used in the developer's brochure. I'd expected the landing to be carpeted, but it isn't. Instead, long boards of dark wood run down its length, presumably to stay in keeping with its industrial roots. On either side of the corridor are heavy wooden doors and, as I walk by, I find myself straining for a sound: a television, music, voices… anything. But there's nothing but the echo of my footsteps.

The corridor seems endless, and it's only as I reach number thirty that I realise how nervous I am. I'm about to meet the man Joanna's going to marry, and she's not even here to greet me. It doesn't seem right somehow.

Seeing a spyhole in the door, I compose myself and smooth my hair before pressing the buzzer, half-expecting it to be ignored. It isn't. Before my hand can return to my side, the door opens to reveal a dark-haired man with a neatly trimmed beard. Heavy-framed glasses draw my attention to his serious blue eyes. He's very tall, and as he leans against the door, he appraises me, his gaze prickling my skin.

'Hello, Alice. I'm very pleased to meet you. In fact, I'm intrigued.'

Mark holds out his hand and I shake it, feeling awkward at the formality. He says nothing more but continues to look at me, a quizzical expression on his face. Even though it's Saturday, he looks as though he's just come back from work as he's wearing grey suit trousers, the jacket of which is hanging from a stainless-steel hook beside the door.

'I guess you must be Mark,' I say, to break the silence.

'Yes.' He loosens his blue silk tie and steps aside, gesturing me through. The door closes behind us with a soft click. 'I'm Mark. Who else would I be?'

CHAPTER EIGHT

It wasn't how I imagined our first meeting to be. In fact, I hadn't imagined Mark being here at all. Did he live here at New Tobacco Wharf with Joanna? Yes, of course he would. They were getting married; why would I think they lived apart?

Suddenly, I feel nervous. What if Mark doesn't like me? What if he's wondering what on earth his fiancée is doing with a friend who can't even be bothered to check the details of her visit before turning up unannounced?

I'd pictured Joanna at the door, greeting me with her infectious laugh. Maybe a bottle of Prosecco chilling in the fridge to toast her engagement. But she isn't here, and in her place is this man with his serious expression and impeccable manners. He's older than I thought, in his forties and not a bit how I imagined a future husband of Joanna's to be. When we were younger, she'd favoured guys with a past, an edge to them that would sometimes concern me. But this man, in his fitted shirt and cufflinks, couldn't look more conventional. How on earth did she meet him?

Since I saw her last, her taste in men has certainly changed. Maybe *she's* changed too.

Mark turns and gives an ironic smile. 'Welcome to our humble abode.'

I drag my eyes from his intense gaze, and it's only now that I look properly at the room we're standing in. And when I take it all in, I have to stop myself from gasping out loud. For the area is huge: a combined sitting, dining and kitchen area, one flowing into the next, that takes up the whole of the front of the apartment. Sunlight streams in through the small panes of the four tall, arched windows that stretch from floor to ceiling, through which I can see the river. Between these are industrial-looking black wooden doors that I presume lead out onto a balcony. Beneath the Farrow and Ball paint, the tasteful furnishings, I can almost smell the old warehouse. A faint musty smell that's slightly unpleasant.

The impression the living space gives is one of openness, the polished wooden floorboards taking the eye from one area to the next. The windows, the exposed brickwork of the walls and the glossy black iron columns that support the ceilings make me feel as though I've gone back in time. Yet, despite the authenticity, the apartment has a foot firmly in the present. As I follow Mark through the dining space towards the kitchen area, I take in the slim metal up lights either side of the settees, the tiny recessed lights that twinkle in the bright white ceiling, despite it still being daylight outside. Did Joanna choose these things or did Mark?

Feeling like a prospective buyer being shown around by an estate agent, I compose my face so as not to look too in awe. Not that Mark looks like an estate agent. Or a man who's just got engaged, come to that. From his slightly stooped posture and the lines between his eyebrows, despite the effort he's making, he looks more like a man with the troubles of the world on his shoulders.

'Won't you sit down?'

Four high chrome stools, with white plastic seats, are neatly arranged under the white wooden kitchen island. I pull one from under the overhanging stainless-steel worktop, but as I do, something catches my attention. On the sleek door of the fridge is a photograph fixed with a magnet in the shape of a champagne bottle. I can't tear my eyes from it.

'That's not me, is it?'

'I don't know. You tell *me*.' Walking over to the photograph, Mark lifts the magnet and slips it out. 'I hadn't noticed it before.

I'm not sure when Joanna put it there. I'm not very observant at the best of times, but I've got a lot on at the moment.' He hands it to me. 'Now you mention it, I can see the likeness. I'm guessing it's the two of you when you were kids.'

In the picture Joanna and I are sitting on the wall outside the art room, laughing at something I can't remember, Joanna's arm around my shoulders. We look happy.

I put the photograph down on the worktop. 'You never said where she was.'

'Who?'

I frown. 'Joanna.'

'No, sorry, I didn't. Tea? Coffee?'

Mark turns his back on me and fills a shiny silver kettle from one of the slim taps above the butler's sink, then stands looking at it as though forgetting what it is he's supposed to be doing. Eventually, he puts the kettle down and opens the stainless-steel fridge instead, pulling a bottle of white wine from its depths. 'Or maybe something stronger after your drive.'

I nod.

'Joanna,' I say encouragingly. 'Where is she?'

Mark studies the label on the bottle, then, frowning slightly, returns it to the fridge and brings out another one. 'She's on a course.'

'A day course?'

'No, it's a weekend one.'

I watch him, my mind in a whirl trying to work out why Joanna has gone away on the day she knew I was coming to stay. When she'd invited me.

'And you're sure she didn't say anything about me? That I was coming?'

'Didn't say a word, no, but we don't tell each other everything. In fact, we try not to live in each other's pockets. I think it's healthier that way, don't you?'

Live in each other's pockets. It's an expression people used to use to describe Joanna and me. I didn't mind it. In fact, I liked it. Why would I have minded if people thought I was close to my best friend?

'I suppose so.'

Mark takes two glasses from a glass-fronted cabinet and places them on the island. 'You don't have a bag with you. I thought you said Joanna had asked you to stay.'

'She did. I left my things in the boot of my car.' I think of my Mini, abandoned by the graffitied building. 'Joanna didn't get back to me with details of where to park or anything, so I left the car further along the quayside. Thought I'd better check what was going on first. Only, of course, she's not here, is she? When did you say she'd be back?'

I'm not sure what to do now. I hadn't exactly planned somewhere else to stay if Joanna wasn't here. Where is she?

'I didn't say. I'm not sure myself. Look, she must have just forgotten she'd invited you. I apologise on her behalf.'

'You don't need to apologise, it's not your fault.'

I watch as Mark twists the corkscrew with long slim fingers. As he puts the bottle between his knees and pulls out the cork, I try to remember when I last had wine from a bottle that hadn't had a screw top.

'So,' Mark says, pouring the wine into the glasses and handing one to me. 'Have you come far?'

'Not really. I live in Brighton, but I timed it badly... hit the worst of the traffic. It's taken forever.'

'I can believe it. Traffic's a bugger... gets worse every day, I swear.' He leans forward, his elbows on the counter. 'Sometimes, I think it would be nice to live in the country. Fresh air. Open spaces. Can't see it happening, though – not until I retire at any rate. Have you always lived by the sea?'

'Yes, though I didn't appreciate it as much as I should have when I was a child.'

'I'm not sure any child does.' He looks wistful. 'And adults can be as bad. Sometimes, we don't appreciate what we have until it's too late.'

I stare into my wine glass, the truth of his words hitting home. 'No.'

Mark lifts his glass and holds it up to the light, swirling the wine a little before putting it back down on the counter. 'Have you decided what you're going to do?'

'Do?'

He smiles. 'Yes, now that you're here and Joanna clearly isn't.'

'I'm not sure.' I take out my phone. "I'll give her another call."

The number rings and then, just as before, it goes on to voice-mail. Deciding I'll try again later, I sip my wine, and as the chilled liquid slides down my throat, I look around the kitchen, taking in the smooth black circles of the induction hob and the stainless steel American fridge freezer that sits flush with the brick wall. Above the hob is an industrial-looking extractor fan that could grace any celebrity kitchen, the white squares of the windows opposite reflected in its shiny surface.

I imagine myself driving back through the heavy traffic. The red lights. The roadworks. The tunnel. The motorway. The thought makes me want to cry. Did Joanna really forget, or did she just change her mind? But if she'd had a change of heart, wouldn't she have let me know? I think of the times in the past that she's let me down when a better offer has come her way. No, maybe she wouldn't.

Straightening up, Mark puts his hands in his pockets. Despite the suit, the striped work shirt and the loosened silk tie, he looks strangely out of place in this cavernous room. I try to picture him and Joanna snuggling up on the purple crushed velvet settee that faces the windows on the other side of the living area, or on the button-backed leather chesterfield that's placed opposite, and fail. Mark doesn't look the type of man to snuggle up with anyone.

'Then I think you should stay,' he says.

'Stay?' I put down my wine, my cheeks reddening. 'I couldn't.'

'But of course you can, Alice?' His tone is formal. Polite. 'I couldn't possibly expect you to drive back tonight.'

I'm unsure. It hadn't occurred to me that I might stay without Joanna being here. Seeing my discomfort, Mark points to a door on the other side of the living space.

'We have a rather nice spare room with an en suite. Joanna would never forgive me if she knew I'd sent you back home after you've made the effort to come all this way.'

Any awkwardness I felt is pushed aside by my relief at not having to join the traffic again. 'Thank you, but don't feel you have to entertain me. I've got a book with me and am more than happy to just sit and read.'

Mark nods, although I can't imagine him reading books. 'That's settled then.'

My glass is half-empty, the wine helping me to relax. The whole reason I came here was to get to know Mark, and it seems like I'm going to get the chance. When Joanna comes back tomorrow, I'll be able to tell her what I think. I look at Mark, taking in his thick-rimmed glasses, the well-cut suit, the neat beard. Despite his kind offer of a bed for the night, he seems a little on edge.

'Thank you.'

'You'll be wanting to park your car.' Going over to one of the kitchen drawers, Mark rummages inside and pulls out a key fob. He tosses it to me. 'It's a spare remote for the underground car park. The entrance is round the back of the building. You can't miss it. Park anywhere. It's not as though you'll be fighting for a space. You'll find the lift on your left near the back, so it might make sense to park near it. It's what I do. The lighting's on a motion sensor, so don't be alarmed if it seems dark when you first drive in.'

My heart gives a double thud at the mention of the lift. 'I presume there are stairs too?'

He raises his eyebrows. 'There are, but it's a bit of a climb. I wouldn't bother if I were you.'

'I don't mind,' I say quickly. 'I've been sitting a long time. I could do with the exercise.'

'Please yourself. I'd do that now if I were you. You don't want to leave your car outside for any longer than you need to.'

I want to ask why, but Mark is pulling at his tie again. Sighing as he undoes the top button of his shirt. 'God, I hate these things. I'm going to get changed. I'll leave the door on the latch for you.'

Downing the last of his wine, he hangs his tie over his shoulder and makes for a door on the far side of the living area. It must be their bedroom. I watch him as he pushes open the door, catching a glimpse of more wooden flooring and a king-sized bed with a large ceiling fan suspended above it. On the wall behind the bed is a painting of a reclining nude. It takes a moment to realise it's Joanna and, when I do, I dip my head to my glass, my cheeks burning. Hoping Mark won't turn and see.

Letting myself out, I take the stairs as quickly as I can without turning my weakened ankle and come out into the sunlight. As I make my way back to the car, I'm hit once more by the strangeness of the place – the contrast of old and new. Ahead of me, the glass and steel walls of the Calypso Wharf apartments tower above their blue hoarding, but when I turn and look behind me, all I see are dismembered buildings, rusting cranes with nothing to lift, rubble and broken asphalt. And, beyond it, New Tobacco Wharf rises from this apocalyptic wasteland like a phoenix from the ashes. The place where Joanna lives. The place where Mark is waiting.

As I walk along the quay, I consider my first impression of him. He's been warm and friendly, there's no denying that, and when he smiles, his serious face is transformed, but there's something else about him… something that contradicts what I see. Maybe it's that he's tired or simply that he's put out having a strange woman arrive at his flat out of the blue.

Reaching my car, I'm glad to find it's just as I left it. I get in and start the engine, then turn the car round and follow the narrow road past the front of Joanna's building and around to the back. Here the arched ground floor windows have been bricked in – all except for the furthest one where a sloping driveway leads to a shiny metal door.

Stopping in front of it, I press the button on the key fob Mark gave me and wait as the door rises to reveal a cavernous darkness. I don't drive straight in but wait, breathing deeply while I tell myself there's nothing to be afraid of. Mark said that the lights were on sensors and there's no reason not to believe him. Screwing up my courage, I drive in, relieved when the overhead lights immediately come on to reveal a vast, empty space – the vaulted brick ceiling, and the warehouse above it, supported by wide brick pillars. Apart from my own Mini, there are only a handful of other cars. Expensive-looking ones. A silver Mercedes. A red Mazda convertible, its black roof up.

As the door rolls down again, sealing me in, my panic returns. There are no windows in this place. No natural light. Just this huge great underground space. Wanting to get out as soon as I can, I drive down the empty lanes to the back of the car park where a panel of doors break up the brickwork. A navy Lexus, which I presume is Mark's, takes up one of the spaces in front of them. Parking next to it, I see one door is for the lift and the other leads to the emergency staircase. On the wall to the side is a security camera and when I look around, I see another trained on the exit.

Getting out of my car, I take my bag from the boot, lock it, then head for the stairs. As I press against the door, it doesn't give and I freeze, the part of my brain I find hard to control at times like this expecting it to be locked.

When I try again, my anxiety making me push harder, it swings open. Of course it wasn't locked. Why would it be?

CHAPTER NINE

'Find it all right?' Mark holds out his hand for the key fob and puts it back in the drawer.

I nod. 'Yes. It's the white Mini. I parked it next to the Lexus.'

'That's mine.' Mark has changed out of his work clothes and is wearing jeans and a light-blue short-sleeved shirt. He looks younger now. Less serious. Maybe he and Joanna are suited after all. It's something I plan on finding out.

He's refilled my glass of wine and holds it out to me, and I'm surprised to see that outside the windows, the sky has turned navy. The lights in the buildings across the water starting to come on.

Picking up a remote, Mark points it at the windows and presses a button. With a soft whir, heavy metal blinds start to lower from some hidden recess, and the tops of the buildings begin to disappear.

'No, don't!'

The blinds stop moving, and Mark looks at me, puzzled. 'Why? What's the matter?'

I wrap my arms around my body. 'Nothing. I just like to see what's outside, that's all.'

'It's just London.' Mark walks to the window. With a press of the button, he raises the blinds again. 'Just buildings and cars and people. Just the same old.'

'Not to me it isn't.' I think of my small house, the uninteresting street in an area not far enough out of town to have its own name, but not close enough to be part of the community. Black

Water Dock is strange, not like any place I've come across before. 'It couldn't be more different.'

'Each to their own.' He smothers a yawn, and I see how tired he looks. I'm desperate to find out more about him, but I don't want to inconvenience him further.

I take a sip of wine. 'Please… Whatever it is you do in the evenings, don't mind me. As I said, I'm happy just to read. If you could just show me where I'll be sleeping.'

I've seen the huge flat-screen TV on the wall and wonder which of them watches it. What they watch. When Joanna and I were teenagers, we used to binge on episodes of *Friends*, huddled up under a tartan throw, pulled from the back of her parents' overstuffed settee. There's nothing like that here. Nothing to soften the sleek lines of the furniture unless you count the neat cushions covered in the same velvet fabric as the settee.

Mark turns. 'Of course. Yes, I'm sorry. I'm not much of a host. We don't have many visitors. Joanna…' He stops and sighs. 'Let me take your bag, and I'll show you your room.'

Despite the fashionable clothes, the expensive haircut, there's something old-fashioned about Mark. Letting him take my bag, I follow him through the living area to a door at the end. He opens it and gestures for me to go in.

'This is our second bedroom.' He goes over to the bed and lifts a pillow to his nose. 'We're not accustomed to having guests, so I'm not sure when the sheets were last changed.'

'Please, It's fine.'

Finding it strange that Joanna hasn't put fresh sheets on the bed for me, I put my bag on the chair and take another sip of wine, surveying my surroundings. The floor is the same dark wood as the living area as are the two large, small-paned windows that reach almost to the floor. But, in here, there are no rugs to soften the effect. No billowing curtains. Just the double bed at one end, its plain iron frame contrasting with the crisp white duvet, and a solid-looking wardrobe at the other. Above the bed, three twisted iron arms hold candle-shaped bulbs.

The effect is stark – reminding me of a cell in a monastery.

'Will this be okay?' Mark has seen my expression. 'It used to be the one Joanna used when she first lived here as she said she liked to see the river. But, after I moved in, it made more sense to move to the other room as it's quite a bit bigger.' He points to a door on the right. 'There's an en suite, though.'

'It's very nice.' I search for the right word. 'Minimalist. Like something from a magazine.'

I hope he won't be offended by this, but he just shrugs. 'Tell me about it. Joanna sees these ideas and likes to take them to extremes, but I let her do her own thing. It keeps her happy.'

There was a time when just being with me made her happy. Making up silly rhymes about the teachers. Mucking out her horses when I stayed with her family in the holidays. Sending valentine cards to each other because, going to an all-girls school, we knew they'd be the only ones we'd get. And later, when we were older and discovered school wasn't the only place to meet boys, getting drunk on alcopops when we'd been stood up at the cinema or had our hearts broken.

Desperate to find something to remind me of her presence, my eyes scan the room, but find nothing. No evidence that my best friend has ever been here. No alarm clock on the bedside table. No bedside light even.

I want to ask about Joanna, but I hold back. The way he talks about her makes her seem different.

Mark sees me looking. 'I'll bring in one of the lamps from our room… in case you need to get up in the night. If there's nothing more you need, I'll leave you to settle in and make a start on the supper.'

It's the first time he's mentioned food, and I'm grateful. My stomach is rumbling, and I've nothing in my bag except for a packet of mints. I don't want to be a burden, but the way he's said it is so casual I'm put at ease.

'Thank you. I hadn't expected you to cook for me as well. Is there anything I can do?'

Mark's eyes flick from the expensive-looking watch on his wrist to the living room. He seems ill at ease, his brows pulled together, and I wonder what it is he's waiting for.

'It's kind of you to ask, but you're my guest. I wouldn't dream of it. Do you like pasta? I don't have a lot in.'

'I like anything. Please don't go to any trouble.'

'It's no trouble. Really. Come and join me when you're ready.'

He leaves me and, through the open door, I see the fridge opening. Watch how he bends his tall frame to it before straightening again and opening cupboards. Taking out packets and jars and reading them.

Not sure what to do, I take out my phone, wondering if Joanna has left a message. She hasn't. Instead, there's one from Drew. *Hope you're okay*. I stare at it, wondering how it is that since I've been here, I haven't thought of him at all. Now he's in my mind, I wait for the pain of the last week or so to return and am surprised when it doesn't. Being somewhere new is already making it easier to bear.

The bedroom is cold, and I rub my arms. Its starkness reminds me of the room in my university halls of residence before I filled it with my junk. Covering the walls with posters and my bed with cushions bought in a flea market. I remember Joanna reaching over and picking up the photograph of the two of us in its charity shop frame, the one I kept on the desk beside my laptop. She'd joked that I was turning into a regular Del Boy.

A wave of disappointment washes over me that Joanna's not here. Seeing her would have made everything that's happened recently so much better. Her invitation had been the perfect distraction. She always had this way of making everything seem less serious, and I know she'd say all the right things.

Knowing I can't sit in the bedroom forever, I take my book out of my bag and carry it, with my wine, to the living room. Mark is still in the kitchen area, so I take myself over to the purple velvet settee and try to make myself comfortable.

Mark looks up from the island. 'You were limping a bit as you came out of the bedroom. Are you all right?'

I touch my ankle. I'd almost forgotten. 'I turned my ankle the other week, and it's still a bit tender. It must have been all the stairs that did it, but I'm fine. Really.' I change the subject. 'Is there anything I can do?'

'No, you're my guest. I wouldn't expect you to do anything.'

'Well, if you're sure.'

I try to concentrate on what I'm reading, so Mark doesn't feel pressured to entertain me. But I feel out of place. If only Joanna were here, it would be different. We'd giggle together just as we used to, and she'd call Mark a goofball as the pasta water boiled over, forming hissing bubbles on the induction hob, or when his glasses steamed up, and he had to take them off and wipe them.

It's the way she'd always been whenever I'd met one of her boyfriends, and I'd found it funny then… but perhaps I wouldn't now. I've grown up and Joanna has too. Would she really make fun of the man she's going to marry?

Giving up, I put my book down. I need to find out more. 'How long have you lived here?'

Mark takes a handful of spaghetti from a stainless steel cylinder and adds it to the pan in front of him. Pressing it down with the flat of his hand until it disappears.

'Not long.'

I wait for him to say something else, but he doesn't.

I try again.

'How did you meet Joanna?'

'Through her parents.' He says matter of fact. 'I work with her father. In fact, it was he who introduced us. I suppose her parents thought we'd be a good match.' He smiles to himself. 'Turns out they were right.'

I look at him, trying to decide whether I agree. It's hard when I know nothing about him. Thinking back to the holidays I spent at Joanna's house, and the way Joanna and her parents, Gary and Denise, were with each other, I'm finding it hard to believe she would be interested in anyone they suggested for her. Quite the opposite in fact. Her choices of unemployed musicians and perpetual students weren't solely for her own benefit – they'd been a way of thumbing her nose at her parents, knowing how it would irritate them. She'd never succumbed to the pressure to reach the high standards they'd expected her to achieve. Had never wanted their lifestyle.

'That sounds like something from Jane Austen. It's not often your parents choose your fiancé for you.'

It's meant as a joke, but Mark doesn't laugh.

'And you think that's odd?'

Wishing I could take back my words, I feel my cheeks redden. 'Not odd, just unusual. I'm sorry, I didn't mean to be rude.'

He looks at me, then shakes his head. 'No, *I'm* sorry. It was unforgivable of me to snap at you like that. I'm just tired. Work's difficult at the moment. Bloody difficult.'

'What do you do?'

Mark frowns. 'What do I do? Hasn't Joanna told you?'

'Well, no. Not exactly.'

Mark opens his arms wide to encompass the room. 'I do all this.'

I look around to find a clue as to what he's talking about. 'All this?'

'New Tobacco Wharf. I'm the developer.'

I stare at him in surprise, and then gradually a picture comes into my mind. Of course. He's the man in the photograph from the company brochure. Only in that picture he hadn't had a beard, nor was he wearing glasses. No wonder I hadn't recognised him.

'You're Mark Belmont?'

'I am.' He picks up his glass and swallows a mouthful. 'But the question is, who are *you*?'

'You know who I am.'

'But do I?' He stares at me intently, a deep crease forming between his brows, then looks at the photo of me on the fridge. He looks back at me. 'I've answered the questions you've clearly been dying to ask me all evening and now I have a few of my own for you.'

CHAPTER TEN

'You still haven't really told me why you're visiting, Alice. Though, of course, you're very welcome.'

I clear my throat. 'Joanna wanted me to meet you before you got married.'

'I see.' Mark puts the lid on the pan and looks thoughtful. 'How strange,' he mutters.

'It isn't really. I'm Joanna's best friend,' I reply, wondering where he's going with this. What could Joanna have told him about me?

'As I said… strange.' Picking up the bottle of wine, Mark carries it over and refills our glasses. He places it back on the glass coffee table, sits on the leather settee opposite me, and leans forward so that his elbows are resting on his knees. It feels like he's studying my face, and I wonder what he's seeing. Small, pale grey eyes fringed with lashes so fine even mascara makes little difference, a high forehead and the delicately sculpted lips that are my only redeeming feature.

Flustered under his scrutiny, I take a sip of my wine. 'Dinner smells nice. Joanna will be missing out. Do you normally cook for her?'

Mark leans back in his seat and crosses his long legs. 'Sometimes. It's not very exciting, I'm afraid – just sauce from a jar. I like cooking, but I've been too busy to shop, and I wasn't exactly expecting your arrival.' He smiles.

'I don't mind. Really,' I reply.

He doesn't say anything else but observes me from over the top of his wine glass. The huge warehouse space is silent, except for the tick of an old station clock on the furthest wall. I can't meet his eyes but look beyond him at the tiny pinpricks of light in the distant buildings across the river.

Eventually, he speaks, but it's only my name he says. 'Alice Solomon.'

The way he says it, it's as though he's trying out the name to see how it fits. Pronouncing each syllable carefully as you might a foreign word. He says no more but drinks again, and I'm relieved when the timer on the oven trills.

Mark stands. 'Please, you go and sit down at the table, and I'll bring it over.'

The dining table is at the far end of the room – a hunk of dark wood the same colour as the floor. Pulling out a high-backed chair covered in the same purple velvet as the settee, I sit down and wait.

Eventually, Mark joins me with two steaming bowls of spaghetti. He places one on the slate mat in front of me, then goes back for the sauce. He has a tea towel across his arm as though he's a waiter. I want to laugh, but he's deadly serious.

'Say when,' he says as he pours the sauce directly from the pan, wiping the edge of my bowl with the cloth, where some has splashed, before pouring the rest onto his own.

As we start to eat, my nervousness returns. I'm in a strange apartment in London's Dockland with a man who I've never met and who, until a week or so ago, I'd never even heard of. A man who has just put down his fork to light the stubby candle in its stone holder that sits between us on the dining table. Self-consciously, I start to eat. Twisting the spaghetti around my fork. Biting the inside of my cheek in embarrassment when it slips back onto my plate. I battle on, thankful that Mark doesn't seem to have noticed.

I wish Joanna was here. It's not the first time I've met one of her boyfriends, but it's certainly the first time I've met one on my own. It feels odd.

As though reading my thoughts, Mark lifts his fork and smiles. 'So what do you think then?'

'I'm sorry...?'

'About me? That's what you said you came to do, isn't it? Suss me out. It reminds me of when I visit a new property, when the owners are away, to fill out a snagging list. Only it's not a building that's being vetted... it's me.'

I take a gulp of wine. 'It's not like that.'

'No, of course not. I'm just teasing you. I only hope you approve.'

He gives me a sidelong glance and smiles. It makes his eyes twinkle, the creases at the corners of his eyes more defined. I realise that I like him.

'Well, you're certainly an improvement on some of the guys Joanna's hooked up with in the past.' I hope she doesn't mind me telling Mark this. 'She always seems to pick men with issues.'

Mark raises his eyebrows in amusement. 'Issues?'

'Yes, problems with alcohol or drugs. Guys with little or no prospects... that sort of thing.'

'Oh dear.' He points to the half-empty wine bottle. 'Maybe we shouldn't have any more of this then.'

My cheeks start to burn, and then I see by his face he's joking. I laugh. 'Believe me, you're nothing like them.'

Before long, we lapse into silence. With no television or music, it's just the sound of forks on china. The clink of a glass on the slate coaster. I feel tongue-tied struggling to find a topic I can share with this man I know nothing about.

Mark finishes his pasta before me. Putting down his fork, he wipes his mouth on the linen napkin beside his bowl. 'You don't need to look so worried. I don't bite. In fact, I'm fully house-trained and fit for civilised society.'

Feeling foolish, I force a smile. 'I'm sorry. I'm not being very good company. It's just odd to be here without Joanna.'

I put my fork down, my plate still half-full. Not wanting to appear rude and yet not wanting to continue eating with this man watching me.

'Is there anything you'd like to ask me?' He looks at me, amused. 'Now you're here?'

There are so many things I want to know. What attracted him to Joanna, what her parents thought of him… why she hadn't told him about me. I choose the safest one. 'How long exactly have you and Joanna been together?'

I know she told me in her message, but I can hardly believe it.

'Not long. Just over a month.'

'Is that all?'

'We knew straight away that it wasn't going to be just a flash in the pan, and I asked her to marry me pretty much straight away. Got down on one knee on the quayside and that was that.' He rubs imaginary mud from his left knee. 'We went and chose a ring that very afternoon. There didn't seem any reason to wait to get engaged as from the moment we met, we both knew it felt right. Does that make sense?'

I don't know if it makes sense, but it is incredibly romantic. It took years of encouragement to persuade Drew to ask me, and I remember what Sally said about her own husband. My fingers slide to my bare ring finger, and I have to force down my jealousy.

'In fact,' Mark continues, 'I've never met anyone like her before. She's intriguing. Full of life.'

I think of the fun Joanna and I had at university. Falling into our halls of residence drunk after a night out. Holding each other up and trying not to wake anyone as we stumbled along the corridor to our rooms. Playing music at full volume until the girl in the next room thumped on the wall.

'Yes. She is.'

He twists the stem of his glass between finger and thumb, then puts it down and leans back in his chair, his eyes betraying his amusement. 'Anything else you'd like to know?'

It's strange to be here at the table with Mark, asking him questions. In the past, my first meeting with Joanna's boyfriends would be in some noisy pub or club while the two of them flirted and sparred. I'd sip my drink and watch them, all the while, trying to think what I'd say to Joanna when later she'd ask the inevitable question. *Well, what did you think of him? Will he piss the parents off?* And it would be impossible not to feel sorry for the guy. Knowing he was just an amusing distraction for her, and that in a few weeks' time he would, in all likelihood, be cast off for someone even more unsuitable.

This is the first time I've ever had the opportunity to really get to know someone and that's because Joanna's not here.

I've been looking at the congealing strands of spaghetti, but now I raise my eyes to Mark. 'This place… the area. It's so strange. So sad. What made you and Joanna choose it?'

Mark throws his napkin on the table and pours himself another glass of wine. His mood has suddenly changed. 'New Tobacco Wharf is a fucking joke.'

I'm shocked at the vehemence of his words. The feeling behind them. It's the docks I'd been talking about, not the development.

'But this building… the apartment. It's magnificent. I've read the brochure and seen how the area will look when the re-development programme is finished. Surely, anyone who could afford it would give their right arm to live here.'

'Only they wouldn't.' It's said with bitterness.

'What do you mean? Why not?'

'We thought we'd got a new St Katharine Docks here, but we were wrong.'

As he speaks, his face darkens, and I notice, for the first time, the shadows under his eyes. He looks older again.

'Why?'

He pushes his chair back. 'Anyone who bought up land here found they'd timed it badly. The rush to buy the apartments never came. There was discussion of new transport links to the area, but right before they should have been confirmed, when we'd already bought the land, they were cancelled… delayed indefinitely. Once the early buyers realised it would be years before the area became the next big thing, as they'd been promised, they cut their losses and left.'

It's properly dark outside now. Despite the steel uplighters that Mark turned on earlier in the corners of the room, the living space seems dark too. The minimal furniture overshadowed by the large expanses of bare exposed brickwork. The iron columns casting shadows across the wooden flooring.

With no carpet or curtains, the air feels chilly too. I give an involuntary shiver and hope Mark hasn't noticed.

'So how many people live here?'

'In New Tobacco Wharf or in Black Water Dock?'

I twist the stem of my glass, watching the candlelight catch its cut-glass surface. 'Both.'

Mark turns his head to look out of the window. 'Black Water Dock is more or less a ghost town. You saw the new developments further along, I presume? The ones that look like fucking great liners. They never got finished. Ran out of money. It's the same story throughout the docks. The whole place is languishing in redundancy. Maybe if it had been a little closer to Canary Wharf…' He tails off, and I see genuine sadness in his face. 'It had such great potential, but now it's just a no man's land somewhere between ruin and recuperation.'

'And this building? Are many of the apartments occupied?'

He shakes his head. 'Just this one and a couple of others. There's a woman who lives in the apartment two floors down and another belongs to a couple who come down from the country on the odd weekend. The others were bought to let out.'

I'm finding it hard to get my head around it. There must be at least forty apartments in the warehouse. Apart from the ones Mark's mentioned, could they really all be empty?

'That's sad.'

Mark stands and walks to the window. 'It is for those of us who invested. A downright tragedy. No one wants to buy here as it's too expensive. I told them...' He turns suddenly. 'But you don't want to hear all this.' Moving back to the table, he pours me more wine. My head is getting muzzy. 'Tell me about yourself. How did you and Joanna meet?'

'We met on my first day at boarding school.' I smile at the memory. Remembering how Joanna had saved me from the loneliness that threatened to overwhelm me. 'She'd already been there a term and took me under her wing.'

He raises his eyebrows. 'I wouldn't have you down as a boarding school type.'

'I wasn't, but I was good at music. My parents could only afford to send me there because I won a scholarship. They were both clever in their own ways but came from families where expectations weren't high. Neither achieved much at school and ended up in jobs that bored them. They wanted better for me and when they discovered I had a talent, they made sure they did everything they could to give me the best chance to use it.'

'And did you? Use it, I mean.'

I think of the place where until recently I was teaching and realise just how much I'm going to miss it. 'Not in the way my parents hoped. I think they imagined me as a classical pianist at the Royal Albert Hall or something. A teacher wasn't exactly what they'd had in mind, but I do love teaching – especially those moments when you realise you've made a difference to someone's life. I used to have my own class, but I also took all the music lessons, so maybe the music scholarship wasn't wasted after all.'

I stop, remembering how much I'd hated Mum breathing down my neck. If she wasn't checking I was practising, she was inviting the neighbours in to hear me play. I used to cringe with embarrassment, but now I'd do all of it again just to have her back.

'Your parents must be very proud of you now.'

His eyes are on me, but I look away. 'My mother's dead, actually.'

I feel my eyes prickle at the thought of her and turn away, not wanting to cry in front of him.

Mark blinks. He leans forward slightly. 'I'm so very sorry. I shouldn't have presumed.'

'It's all right. It happened a long time ago.' I think of the clues I'd missed. The way Mum changed the subject whenever I rang her to ask how she was. Saying her recent tiredness was probably due to the extra shifts she'd done at Asda, the muscle aches just a symptom of the cold she'd not managed to shake off. Then she'd turn the questions back on me: was I enjoying my final year at school? Had I made up my mind what university I wanted to go to?

As always, the guilt rushes in. I should have read between the lines when she said that Brighton had a perfectly good music course… that I could live at home. How I wish now that I had followed her suggestion rather than applying to go to the same university as Joanna – a five-hour train journey away. That I hadn't been having too much fun to come home as often as my parents would have liked.

'And your father?'

'My dad lives in Corfu with a girl half his age. He's set up a bar and grown his hair. I went to visit him to see if we could build some bridges, but it's hard to do when he's sitting with a pint in his hand, watching the sun set over the sea and gloating over how lucky he is to have been able to pull someone young enough to be his daughter.' I hear the bitterness in my voice. 'He shacked up with her soon after Mum died. I can't forgive him for that.'

'I'm sorry. I can see how that distresses you.'

There it is again. That old-fashioned turn of phrase. I wonder if he's just being polite.

'I can't help it. He says he was lonely and thinks that makes it all right, but it doesn't.'

Mark looks puzzled. 'Yet you say your mother passed away some time ago. This relationship isn't new any more.'

'I know that, but it's not something I can forget. It's like he's taken Mum's memory and stamped all over it. Joanna understood.' I steer the conversation back to safer waters. 'When I got the scholarship to St Joseph's, it was like stepping into another world, but Joanna made it all right. She chose me to be her friend.'

Mark looks amused by what I've said. 'Chose you?'

'Yes, there were two other new girls. When the head teacher asked the class for someone to befriend us, Joanna picked me.'

While I've been talking, Mark has got his phone out. He checks it before putting it back in his pocket. 'That sounds like her.'

Unable to tell whether he thinks this is a good thing or not, I plump for the former. 'Yes. From then on we were inseparable.'

I smile to myself, remembering what it was like to bask in her attention. Her way of making you feel like you were the centre of her world, if only for a few minutes. 'I was over the moon when Joanna's mother invited me to stay for part of the summer holidays. It was meant to be just a few days, but Joanna persuaded her to let me stay a whole week. I loved it there. From her bedroom window, you could see right across the fields to where they grazed the horses. I'd never known anyone with a horse before, and they had three. The only pet I'd been allowed to have was a rabbit.'

'Did Joanna ever stay at yours?'

I try to imagine it. Wondering what she'd have made of my little bedroom with its view of the side of next door's pebble-dashed house or the living room with Dad's socks drying on the radiators. We'd have had to eat off plates balanced on our laps as the table was always piled with the stuff Mum planned to sell on eBay to make some extra cash. And where would I have taken her? The rec at the end of the road? Burnside Shopping Centre where half the shops stood empty, and the ones that were left, I knew Joanna would hate?

'No, she never came to mine.'

How could I have introduced her to the friends I'd had in junior school before I moved to St Joseph's? What would they have had in common? I burn with shame at how I'd dropped Kylie, my best friend since playschool. And Chelsea. And Tanya. It wasn't that I'd preferred the girls at the boarding school, in fact some of them had been mean to me that first term, picking up on my accent and laughing when I couldn't play tennis. No, it was just that I had Joanna now.

'We realised we didn't need anyone else,' I say, even though I haven't voiced my thoughts. 'Having each other was enough.'

Mark clears his throat. 'I see. But things change. I'm proof of that.'

My smile slips. His words have dragged me away from a time when I felt stronger. Funnier. Invincible. 'Yes, of course. I'm not talking about now, I'm talking about when we were kids. She was the one who comforted me when I was homesick in the first few weeks. The one who told the girls who picked on me to fuck off.'

I see the amusement in Mark's eyes. 'That sounds like her.'

'She was pretty fearless. Told them they were stuck up and only did it because they were jealous of my hair.' I place a hand self-consciously to my head. 'It was very long then, even though I had to keep it tied back most of the time.'

Mark smiles. 'I can see why. It's a beautiful colour.'

'Thank you.'

Embarrassed by this unexpected compliment, I stand and pick up the plates. I take them into the kitchen and stack them in the dishwasher, my head still full of Joanna.

Tomorrow I will be going back home to my empty house and my empty life. It's a darker place without Joanna in it.

CHAPTER ELEVEN

It takes me a long time to get to sleep. I shouldn't have let Mark refill my wine glass, and I have a raging thirst. Also, with no curtains to close, just the horrible electric blinds, the tall warehouse windows are backlit by the moonlit sky. Squares of light from the small panes, patchworking the wooden floor. My bed. My face.

As I lie awake, I think of what Mark told me and imagine the empty apartments in the building. Layer upon layer of corridors where no one walks. The subterranean vaulted car park, with its hundreds of empty spaces, where my car waits in the darkness. What did Joanna think about when she slept here? Did she ever think of me? Why was our photo on the fridge? Had she just recently moved it there? After she texted me, perhaps?

In the other bedroom, Joanna's fiancé sleeps beneath her naked picture. Or maybe he's lying awake too, wondering how he's ended up with a stranger in his apartment. Thinking of what he'll say when Joanna gets home. How he'll describe the ordinary-looking girl with the red hair who's in the guest bedroom. Will he quiz her about me? Or will I be forgotten by the time she gets home? It's only now I realise I never asked Mark what course she was on.

At one point, I think I hear footsteps on the wooden boards outside my door. The sound of the front door opening, then closing. Distant voices on the quayside outside my window. But when I get up to look, there's nothing to be seen except for the moon reflected off the dark water. The silhouette of a crane.

Shaking the pillow to plump it, I lie on my back, letting the phosphorescent moonlight wash over me. Hearing Joanna's words in my head. *I'm never getting married. What's the point?* Something had made her change her mind. Made her decide to marry a man she'd only known a few weeks. What was it about Mark Belmont? Was it money? Was that her motivation?

I think of the school holidays I spent at her parents' large gabled house in the country. The gravelled driveway with the separate double garage that housed their expensive cars. Joanna's bedroom that looked over the paddock where she kept her pony. Drifting off to sleep in the bed next to my best friend's, I'd pretend that it was *my* house, imagine her glamorous mother and her handsome father were *my* parents. And as I listened to Joanna's gentle breathing, I'd try to think of ways to put off going home.

CHAPTER TWELVE

I'm woken by a knock on the door. Sitting up, I look at my phone and see that it's nearly nine.

'I didn't know if you drank tea.' Mark's voice comes through the door. 'There's a mug out here for you. Or maybe you'd prefer coffee?'

'No, tea's fine,' I call back. 'Thank you.'

Pulling a jumper over my nightdress, I go to the door and open it a crack. Mark has left a tray on the floor outside, on which is a mug of tea. He's nowhere to be seen. I pick up the tray and take it back to my room, then sitting cross-legged with my back against the headboard, I phone Joanna's number. It rings once. Twice. Three times. Then the voicemail clicks in just as it did before.

'Joanna. Where are you? I'm at your apartment. Mark says you're on a course. Did I get the wrong weekend? Are you back tonight? When you get this message, please ring. If your course ends today, maybe I can delay going home until you get back.'

Taking my clothes with me, I open the door to the en suite and go inside. I hadn't paid it much attention last night, but now I realise how white it is – in total contrast to the bedroom. White ceiling. White tiles. White bath and toilet. Even the square bidet that projects from the wall is white.

Leaving the door ajar, I turn on the shower. While I wait for it to heat up, I lean towards the mirror, the lights positioned around its edge, reminding me of something you might see in an actor's dressing room. My face stares back at me, and I'm surprised at how tired I look, how drained, tension showing itself in the fine lines around my eyes. I turn my head from side to side trying to gauge what Mark would have seen when I'd appeared on his doorstep. My appearance certainly wouldn't have knocked him out. In fact, no one would give me a second look if it wasn't for the colour of my hair. That's something that's always been commented on.

As I stare at my reflection, I feel again the deep-seated shame. The humiliation. Remember how Joanna had turned me away from the laughing girls in our dorm. Hear her voice. *Ignore them, Alice. You don't need them anyway.*

But I'm not that thirteen-year-old any more. I'm a grown woman.

The glass door makes no sound as I slide it open and step inside the shower cubicle. The showerhead is huge, a stainless steel disk that drenches the white tiled floor with rainforest-like water. I don't use my own meagre toiletries but unscrew one of the little bottles that are lined up on a glass shelf. I read the labels: shampoo, conditioner, body wash. They smell of jasmine. They smell of spa days and expensive holidays, not that I've had many. Most of all, though, they smell of Joanna.

Flipping open the lid of the body wash, I squeeze some onto the palm of my hand and lather my body. The shower cubicle fills with a scent that's exotic and heady. The fruity undertones sweet and warm. It's like Joanna has wrapped her arms around me, and it's comforting.

By the time I've showered and dressed, scraping my hair back in a band as I don't want to ask Mark if I can borrow Joanna's hairdryer, the enticing smell of bacon is coming from the other room. When I open my door, I see Mark, a striped apron around his waist, a spatula in his hand.

'Hope you're not a vegetarian.'

I shake my head. 'No. I was once, but I lapsed.'

A picture comes into my head of Joanna wafting a bacon sandwich under my nose in the kitchen of the flat we shared and how, suddenly, the bowl of muesli I was eating tasted of cardboard in my mouth. It was a week after I'd broken up with someone and was feeling down. She'd cut the sandwich in half to let me share, and I swear nothing had ever tasted so good. I never was good at resisting Joanna. I expect she knew that even then.

'Good because bacon's about all we've got. Oh, and some tomatoes.' He places two rashers on a plate, adds the tomatoes and hands it to me. 'Hope that's okay. There's some bread and butter on the table.'

I look at the triangles of neatly buttered bread, then back at Mark. He looks tired, the circles I saw under his eyes last night more pronounced, his skin pale beneath the dark stubble on his chin.

'Are you all right, Mark?'

He frowns. 'What do you mean?'

'I just thought you looked…' I don't know how to continue without seeming ill-mannered.

'I didn't sleep well.' He puts bacon and tomatoes onto his own plate. 'I've a lot on my mind.'

He seems out of sorts. Swearing under his breath when he realises there's no tomato sauce left in the bottle. It's unsettling and, just as I did last night, I feel as though I'm an intruder. My idea of staying a little longer melts away. I wanted to wait to see if Joanna returned today, but now I feel like I should leave.

'I'll eat this, then go. Your Sundays must be precious. I'm sure there are things you want to do.'

He looks up sharply. 'There's nothing.'

I stand with my plate in my hand, wondering what on earth I'm even doing here. 'Even so. I'll leave when I've had this.'

'No, don't go. Not yet.' Taking off the apron, he takes his plate to the dining table and places it on the slate mat. I follow him.

I think of the breakfasts Joanna and I used to eat when I stayed with her when we were children. Her mum would be out seeing to the horses and her dad would have long since gone to work, so we had the place to ourselves. Joanna would raid the fridge and the cupboards, placing a random assortment of food on a tray: cold sausages, a carton of yogurt, crisps, leftover apple pie, a slice of Battenberg cake. Then she'd carry it up to her bedroom and place it on the bed where we'd eat the feast with our fingers, Joanna's duvet bunched up around our chins.

As we chewed on the sausages and dipped our fingers into the white bowl of the yoghurt pot, Joanna would tell me stories of the things she got up to when her parents were out. Stealing cigarettes from her mum's drawer. Drinking her dad's whisky straight from the bottle. I, in turn, would confide in her my worries. How Mum always looked tired, the double shifts at the supermarket taking their toll. How Dad had lost yet another job. How, sometimes, my life was unbearable.

She'd put her arm around me, her fingers sticky with cake and whisper in my ear. *I know what will cheer you up.* Stealing into her parents' huge bedroom, the thick shag pile carpet warm beneath our bare feet, she'd pick up the receiver of the white telephone beside the bed. *Your turn to go first*, she'd say. *Who shall it be today? Rhona or Charlotte? They both need taking down a peg or two.*

Later, as we lay on our backs on her parents' king-sized bed, we'd not be able to contain our laughter. Joanna always knew how to make me feel better.

'I thought you might like me to show you around, now you're here.' Mark's voice breaks into my thoughts.

'Are you sure?' I take a seat opposite him in the same place as last night, facing the tall windows. As I watch, the clouds roll back, bringing the city across the river into view.

'Of course. It will give me something to do.' Cutting his bacon into neat batons, Mark spears them with his fork before putting them into his mouth. 'In fact, it will take my mind off things.'

'Then I'd like that. Thank you.'

We eat the rest of our breakfast in silence. When I've finished, he waves away my offer of help, carrying the plates to the kitchen and putting them in the dishwasher.

I put on my shoes and fetch my bag from the bedroom, then wait in the corridor as Mark checks all the windows, then locks the front door. Checking once, twice, to make sure it's secure. Considering the warehouse is practically empty, it seems an unnecessary ritual.

Before Mark can suggest taking the lift, I make for the door that leads to the stairs, surprised when he follows. Six flights later, we're in the large atrium, and I try to imagine what it would be like if the fountain in the centre was playing. If the reception desk was manned by a beautiful girl or handsome young man in uniform. Instead, it's empty. Dead. Like a stage set with no actors and no audience.

Mark stops. 'If you don't mind waiting here a second, I'm going to pop in and let Derek know you're here. Just in case he's wondering.'

'Derek?'

'Yes. He's the guy we employ to make sure the place runs smoothly.'

'What does he do?'

'All sorts. Security mainly, but he also organises the cleaning and does some of the maintenance. One of the conditions of sale is that the building is kept in proper order.' He shakes his head in dismay. 'Even if there are no damn people living here.'

Striding over to a door near the reception desk, Mark knocks, then opens it. Inside the room is a large desk, on which stands a computer and several black and white monitors. The man sitting at it has his back to us, but as he turns, I take in his thin pale face, narrow shoulders and the freckled nicotine-stained fingers that rest on the mouse pad in front of him.

'Everything okay?'

Derek nods. 'Yes, sir.'

'Just so you know, I have a friend staying. A friend of Joanna's to be perfectly accurate. I didn't want you thinking anything, well—'

'Of course not.' The man looks directly at me. The way he stares, reminding me of a doorman at a club. 'Thank you for letting me know.'

'Alice's car is the white Mini that's parked next to mine. Keep a good eye on it.'

'Oh, I will, sir.' He swivels back to face the monitors. 'Will that be all?'

'Yes.' Mark gives a formal nod. 'Have a good day, Derek.'

'You too, sir.' There's a hint of obsequiousness in Derek's tone, but if Mark notices, he doesn't care. Or at least he doesn't say anything.

I thank Mark when he lets me go through the door first. 'How long has Derek worked here?'

The doors slide silently closed behind us.

'He's new. The last guy, Saul, left one day without saying why. Can't say it bothers me, Derek is very thorough. Very reliable.' He points along the quayside in the opposite direction from which I arrived yesterday. 'We'll go this way. It's more interesting.'

Yesterday, the tide had been high, but today, it's lower, revealing the weed-covered sides of the dock that would normally be hidden by the waterline. The quayside is overgrown with grass. Keeping to the uneven path, we pass a couple of metal storage units and more empty warehouses, remnants of Black Water's former glory, and I'm filled with a sadness I can't explain. There are more derelict buildings, more shells of naked brickwork filled with rusting scrap metal and old roof tiles, and I'm just wondering why Mark has brought me here when he stops suddenly and points.

'This is it.' His voice is filled with a passion I haven't heard before. He's not looking at me but into the distance. He opens his arms to accommodate the scene. 'This was my dream.'

From where we stand, the skyscrapers and glass towers of Canary Wharf glitter in the distance, but when I turn and look in the other direction where Mark's pointing, I can also see Tower Bridge, just beginning to open to let a ship pass through.

'I thought this was what people wanted. To breathe life into something that's died. It's not just the money, you know.' He's staring at me again with those piercing blue eyes behind his glasses. 'It's about regeneration for the future. Creating something better... or at least as good.'

His phone rings, and he takes it out of his pocket and looks at it. Without answering it, he shoves it back without a word.

'Was that Joanna?'

He looks startled. 'Joanna?'

'Yes. I thought she might be letting you know when she'd be back.'

'No. It wasn't Joanna.' I think I see his eyes film, but then he blinks and they're clear again, leaving me wondering if I imagined it.

He turns back to the brown river. 'You know they say this place is haunted?'

'Really?' I look around me as though a ghost might suddenly appear.

'Oh, yes. Two hundred years ago, the Thames was crammed with shipping. Wharves lining both sides of the river from Lambeth to the Tower. Hard to believe, isn't it?'

As he speaks, a couple of barges covered in tarpaulin and a red and white tug slide past. On the other side of the river, I can just make out the commentary from a Thames Clipper as it rumbles by, its decks packed with people.

'That was until the docks started to close.'

'Why's that?'

'They weren't deep enough for the larger ships.'

I think of the black and white photograph I'd seen. The tall-masted ships, the bustling quayside and compare it to the wasteland I'm standing in. He's right. It's hard to imagine it now.

'See there?'

Mark leads me to the edge of the water. Next to a black bollard a series of stone steps lead down to the water. They're ancient. Mildewed and slippery where the Thames laps at them. Either side, embedded in the stone, metal rings that would once have been used for mooring boats drip.

'Sometimes, the past is wiped out but, if you look closely enough, some of it remains. They call them The Devil's Staircase. Over the centuries, it's where many people have lost their lives. Accident. Misadventure. Suicide. The locals say a few have come back to settle their scores.'

A dark cloud has rolled over the sun, and I turn away. Wishing he hadn't shown me. Not wanting to think of the lives lost. The lives wasted. Subconsciously, my hand slides down to my stomach.

'And further along the river, at Execution Dock, there's an old scaffold. It was used as an execution site for over four hundred years.' He points to where the river bends. 'Mutineers. Murderers. Smugglers. Pirates. Any crime committed at sea. The admiralty made sure the bodies were visible from the waterfront in case anyone was getting an idea to do the same. They were left hanging there until three tides had ebbed and flowed over their heads.' He runs his hand across his neat dark hair. 'Brutal.'

The ground tips and sways.

'Would you mind if we go back? I'm not feeling too good.'

Mark stops talking, his face creased in concern. 'Yes, of course. You should have said. I have a habit of getting carried away. Ask Joanna…' He turns away, his lips pinched together. 'Anyway, we should be getting back. It looks like it's going to rain.'

We walk back along the quayside and, as New Tobacco Wharf comes back into sight, I wonder whether Joanna ever walks this way. What she makes of this strange place and what her life is really like? I glance back at the steps covered with green mildew.

Does she feel the ghosts of those who have lost their lives on the slippery stones as keenly as I do?

As Mark holds the door of the warehouse open for me, I can't rid myself of the feeling that something's not right. But, it's only as I start the climb to the sixth floor having left Mark at the lift, that I realise what it is. It's as if by taking me to the quayside, he's been trying to tell me something.

But what that might be, I have no idea.

CHAPTER THIRTEEN

I'm packing away my wash things in preparation to leave when I hear the sharp buzz of the intercom. Thinking it's Joanna, I run into the living room to find Mark with his finger on the button. He looks at me and smiles before pressing it.

'Hey, beautiful. Good course?'

At the thought of seeing Joanna, my heart quickens. 'She's back,' I say, under my breath.

'No, Mark. It's not Joanna.'

The voice that fills the room is a woman's, but it's not Joanna's. It belongs to someone older, and although I haven't seen her in years, I recognise whose it is. It's Denise, Joanna's mother.

Mark releases the button as though it's given him an electric shock, and steps back. 'Bugger. What do they want?'

'Mark, what's wrong?'

He's gone ashen. He's massaging his temples with the tips of his first two fingers.

'Tell me, please.' I pull at his arm, making him look at me.

'It's just not a good time for them to come.'

I look around, thinking it's because he's worried he hasn't had time to tidy up, but the room is immaculate. 'Then tell them it's not convenient. Ask if they'll come another time.'

'I can't do that. Fuck.' He paces, his hands in his pockets. 'Did you ever meet them?'

'Yes, a few times, but I haven't seen them in years.'

'Then you'll know how difficult it is to put them off.'

He presses the button on the intercom again. 'Denise. Gary. How lovely. I'll put the kettle on. Come on up. There's someone I want you to meet… or someone you haven't seen in a while.'

Turning to me, he takes me by the arms. 'Help me out with them, Alice. You must know what they're like.' His worry startles me, but then it's the same sort of thing Joanna used to say. She always had to live up to their expectations. 'Alice, I can't do this on my own. I'll explain properly later.'

I remember how Denise was when Joanna and I were teenagers. Her narrow face perfectly made up. Her hair expensively highlighted. Gary was just a shadowy figure in a suit. The man who made Joanna cry when he sat her down to discuss her school report, just as he might an underling at work who he was going to fire. I'm intrigued to know what they're like now.

'All right.'

He rubs his hands up and down the top of my arms. 'Thank you. Just follow my cues.'

Before I can ask what he means, there's a buzz on the door and Mark opens it.

'Denise. Gary. Good to see you.'

He shakes the man's hand and kisses the woman's cheek, then steps back to let them in. 'You remember Alice?'

I don't move but wait until they come into the room. It's Denise who sees me first, quickly hiding her surprise. Composing her voice. 'Is that really you, Alice? How lovely.'

I nod, becoming again the thirteen-year-old girl who longed to be part of their family. 'You look well, Mrs Maitland. In fact, you've hardly changed.'

She hasn't. She's hardly aged at all. Gary, on the other hand, has put on weight, the buttons of his shirt straining against his stomach.

He holds out his hand for me to shake, then turns back to Mark, leaving me wondering if he even remembers who I am.

'Came over to talk to you about the photographer. There's a guy in Vauxhall who will do the lot for three thousand. Before, during, after. The works. Taken some society shots. Knows his stuff. Also, the manager of the band we wanted for the evening has said they'll cancel their other gig to fit us in.' He rubs finger and thumb together. 'Didn't take much persuading.'

Going over to the leather settee, he sits, his legs spread. Denise joins him and, after a moment's hesitation, I sit opposite on the crushed velvet one, feeling like I'm about to be interviewed.

'Don't worry about the kettle,' Gary shouts over to Mark, who's filling it from the slim tap. 'I'll have a scotch.'

Mark takes a bottle of wine from the fridge. 'Ladies?'

I shake my head. 'No, thank you. I'll be driving.'

'So, where's Joanna?' Gary sounds like a head teacher summoning his pupil.

Mark hands him his scotch. 'She's on a course. Sorry, I thought I'd told you. Maybe we should talk about the photographer and the wedding some other time. When she's here.'

'Strange. She didn't say.' Denise looks at me over her glass as she takes a sip of wine, her red lipstick leaving a crescent on its surface. 'And you, Alice. I have to say, I'm surprised to see you here. I didn't realise you and Joanna were still friends.'

The words burst out of me. 'Of course we are. Joanna wanted me to come here to talk about the wedding.'

Gary's looking at me now. 'I don't recall your name being on the guest list?'

The air in the room seems to contract. Everyone's eyes are on me. As their faces start to swim before my eyes, I grip the edge of the settee to anchor myself.

How can I tell them? How can I admit that they're right? I want to feel that Joanna is still my friend, but the truth is very different.

I look behind me, and Mark is busying himself getting glasses out of the cabinet.

The truth is that I haven't actually seen Joanna in ten years. All I have is the memory of how we used to be and a message on my phone reaching out a hand of friendship.

But they don't know that.

Inside, I'm squirming with embarrassment, but Mark comes to my rescue. He must have heard what Gary said. 'There are so many people on it, you probably don't remember half of them.'

'You're right there.' Gary gives a bark of laughter. 'The list keeps getting longer.'

I watch the scene play out, feeling more and more awkward. The conversation moves from the photographer, to flowers, to what the ushers will be wearing. I've never felt such a spare part. As they talk, I watch the clouds move across the skyline, breaking apart to reveal patches of blue.

Mark's speaking to me now, but I've been so lost in thought that I haven't been listening. 'Sorry, I was miles away,' I say, coming back to the conversation.

Mark fixes his eyes on me. 'I was saying that you thought so too when you saw Joanna yesterday. That's right, isn't it?'

Joanna's parents are looking at me now, waiting for me to reply. I feel out of my depth and wonder what it is I've missed. What is he asking me?

'Yesterday?'

'Yes, before she left.' He angles towards me, his intense blue eyes levelled at my face, and I find I can't look away. 'She was a bit out of sorts.'

'Yes.' I hadn't meant to say it, but there's something hypnotic in the way he's looking at me. 'She was.'

Gary links his fingers together. 'Odd. Very odd. She's usually so upbeat about everything.'

Mark's eyes slide from my face to the window, where a perfect cloud is caught between the metal-framed panes of glass. 'I've found, in my humble opinion, that people can be multi-faceted. Joanna included.'

'Don't be such a pompous arse.' Gary downs his scotch and places it back on the coaster, folding his arms across his stomach.

A shadow passes over Mark's face, and I'm aware of a tension between the two men that, until now, they've managed to hide. But, just as quickly, his mouth forms into a smile. Why has Mark asked me to lie for him?

'You're right, Gary. It's that bloody public school I went to. Can't erase the damage.'

Gary laughs and the atmosphere in the room lightens again.

Thankful the conversation has moved away from me, I think about the drive home to my sad little house. My half-written application forms. My empty life. The thought of going back there is horrid, but something doesn't feel right here in Joanna's home.

Denise isn't going to let me get away that easily. She's looking at me as though trying to work me out.

'What made you come to visit the weekend Joanna was going away?'

It's too late to change my story now. Tell Joanna's mother I didn't know she was going away. That I haven't even seen her.

'Alice is helping to organise Joanna's hen night.' Mark breaks off from the conversation he's been having with Gary. 'She thought it would be easier to do so from here as she could get a feel for the area. Look into places they could go… what they could do.'

I pick at my nail. 'Yes, I didn't want to do it while Joanna was here as it would spoil the surprise, so she suggested coming this weekend… when she was away.' I tail off, aware of how unlikely this sounds. Surely, that would be the chief bridesmaid's job. I feel a stab of hurt at not having been given that role.

'I see.' Denise finishes her drink. 'Come on, Gary. It makes more sense for us to come back another time when Joanna is here.'

Picking up her bag, she gives a tight smile and stands, gesturing to her husband to do the same. I watch them as they walk the length of the living area to the front door, relieved that soon the charade will be over.

Mark lets them out, then comes back to me.

Instead of sitting down, he stands with his hands on the back of the settee, his forearms tensed. 'Thank you,' he says to me.

I turn to look at him, confused by what's just happened. 'Why couldn't we have just told them the truth?' I ask him. But what is the truth? That Joanna forgot she'd invited me to stay? That she doesn't give a damn about me? I realise that I might have cared enough about the friendship Joanna and I had to come down here, but that text might not have meant as much to her.

But Mark doesn't reply. It's as if he isn't listening. He's leaning forward, staring at the window, his jaw set.

'Tell me what's going on,' I say, trying to get him to pay attention. 'Something's not right. Something you're not telling me. Where is Joanna, Mark? Where is your fiancée?'

I don't know what I was expecting, but it isn't this. As I watch, his thin face changes. Everything I've seen up until now disappears. Gone is the self-assured man so passionate about his dream, the public schoolboy with impeccable manners. In his place is one whose eyes are filled with anguish.

He doesn't change position, just grasps the back of the settee harder, turning the purple velvet white.

'I don't know where she is, Alice. I don't know where the hell she's gone. Joanna is missing.'

CHAPTER FOURTEEN

I stare at him, hardly able to believe what I'm hearing. Joanna missing? I search Mark's face for clues, but he's not meeting my eyes. It's something he's not done before and it's worrying.

'But you said she was on a course.'

'I know what I said.' Mark slumps onto the velvet settee and drags his fingers through his hair.

'Are you sure she didn't say? Might you have just forgotten?'

He shakes his head. 'No. Everything gets written down in the home diary, otherwise we wouldn't have a clue what each other were doing.' Getting up, he goes over to the kitchen island and picks up a book with a shiny grey cover. Coming back with it, he flicks through the pages until he comes to the week we've just had.

He runs his finger down the page. 'See. Nothing. Just a note of my meetings.'

I see there's no mention of my visit in there either. Had she just forgotten to write it down? 'It's only been a couple of days. I'm sure she'll be back tonight, and we'll be laughing about how forgetful you both are.'

'No.' Mark's brows pull together. 'It hasn't been two days. I haven't seen Joanna since Thursday evening.'

There's a hollow feeling in my stomach. 'Thursday?'

'Yes. She was here when I went to work that morning. I kissed her goodbye as usual, but she wasn't here when I came home.' He drops his head into his hands. 'Christ. Where do you think she could be? If anything's happened to her…'

I place a hand on his arm. 'Nothing will have happened to her, Mark. There'll be some logical explanation. How did she seem when you saw her that morning?'

His head jerks up sharply. 'What do you mean?'

'I just thought if I could picture her mood the last time you saw her, it might help me have a better understanding of what's going on.'

'She was fine. A little subdued, maybe, but fine. We were planning a wedding, for Christ's sake. We were happy. We were in love.'

I look around me at the warehouse apartment with its tasteful, carefully chosen furniture – a room out of a magazine with no heart or soul. Everything reduced to its common denominator of bare brickwork and wooden flooring. A storage area. Nothing staying in it for very long before moving on again.

'You've got to think, Mark. Where might she have gone? Might she be staying with friends?' I think about the wedding she was planning. 'What about her bridesmaids? Maybe she's with one of them.'

'She doesn't have many friends – not proper ones. The bridesmaids were going to be a couple of cousins on her mum's side. She hardly knew them. Oh, Christ. I don't know where she is.'

With a shock, I see he's weeping. No sound, just silent tears that make my heart clench in sympathy. I've never seen a man cry. Not my father. Not Drew. My heart goes out to him, but I have no idea how to react. It's not as if I know him.

I stand awkwardly and put a tentative hand on his shoulder, feeling his muscles tense under his shirt. 'I'll make us a drink and then we can think what to do.' I get up, then sit back down again. Something's bothering me. 'Don't you think you should have told her parents? They have a right to know.'

'And say what?' He twists round, his eyes red. 'It's lovely to see you and, oh by the way, your daughter's gone missing. Can you believe it! No, Alice. I can't tell them. Not yet.'

Taking out a white handkerchief from his pocket, he blows his nose. 'Christ, I'm sorry. It's not like me to be so weak, but you can't imagine how dreadful it's been keeping this to myself. I didn't realise how worried I was until I told you.'

Going over to the window, I press my hands against the cold glass and look down. Below me is the Thames. Brown. Sluggish. Dotted with tugs and a larger cargo vessel. To the left, hidden by the bend in the river are the slippery steps that will now mostly be hidden as the tide is high. I remember the story Mark told me about them, and my heart beats a little faster. I know what Mark said, but what if Joanna was depressed? She was always one to act first and think later. What if she'd called me because there were things she wanted to tell me?

Once I would have been there to listen. Guilt twists in my stomach.

'I think I should stay,' I say, turning to him. 'Just until she gets back or at least until we know where she is.'

Mark draws his hand down his face. 'I can't expect you to do that. What about your job? It's Monday tomorrow.'

'I'm a teacher. I've broken up for the Easter holidays. But anyway, I have no job. The school closed... went into receivership.'

He looks shocked. 'That's terrible. I'm very sorry.'

'I suppose, looking back, I shouldn't have been surprised. Pupil numbers had been dropping for a while.'

I remember how we'd been summoned into school, even though it was the beginning of the holidays. How we'd sat on the red plastic chairs the children used, watching as Trevor, our head, walked onto the stage with a man in a dark suit. The gathered staff all knew something was wrong – I could see it in their faces and hear it in the snippets of their conversations: *Why do you think...? Have you heard...? What the hell...?* Next to me, Sally had struggled to control the toddler on her lap. As he kicked out at the chair in front with his sandaled feet, she'd tapped him sharply on the leg, making him grizzle.

We were all on edge, waiting to hear the news, and when at last Trevor had made his announcement, I was numb with shock. I wasn't to know that this was only the beginning of my troubles.

'But what about family,' Mark continues. 'A husband. Partner.' I see his eyes lower to my hand, registering, probably, the lack of a ring. 'Won't you be missed?'

'No,' I say quickly. 'There's nobody.'

'Then, if you're sure you don't mind, I'd be very glad of the company. As you say… just until Joanna gets back.'

I'm surprised but also pleased by what he's said. He seems uneasy, and I wonder if it's because he doesn't want to be alone. I'm glad my being here will help.

'She'll be back soon. I know she will.' It's nothing but a gut instinct, but there are things Joanna wants to talk to me about. I'm sure of it.

'I expect you're right.' Getting up, Mark collects up the glasses and walks the length of the room to the kitchen area.

'But, Mark.'

He hesitates, then carries on walking. 'Yes?'

'If Joanna isn't back by the end of tomorrow, I think you should notify the police.' It's not that I think she won't be back by then, but if it happens, we need to do the right thing.

He pauses, as though thinking about what I've said. 'Yes, of course,' he says. 'Of course, that's what I shall do.'

But there's something in that hesitation that makes me wonder if he would if it wasn't for me being here. Whether, despite his tears, he cares as much about Joanna as I do.

CHAPTER FIFTEEN

The next day, Mark goes into the office and I'm left alone in the apartment, wondering how on earth I'm going to fill my time waiting for him to get back or for Joanna to finally return. I start by unloading the dishwasher and putting the crockery away in the plate racks inside one of the sleek wooden cupboards. Looking around for something else to do, I wipe down surfaces that are already clean, then search the cupboards for a vacuum cleaner to hoover the vast expanse of wooden flooring. The place is like a show home. Echoey. Clinical. Not exactly a love nest.

When I've finished, I get my book from beside my bed and open the wooden double doors between the industrial-looking windows. If I'd expected to find a Juliet balcony, I'm disappointed. Instead, when I've drawn the bolts and pulled back the doors, there's nothing between me and the overgrown quayside below but three wrought iron bars, running from one side of the doorframe to the other.

Taking one of the dining room chairs, I place it in the opening and put my feet up on the middle bar, the spring sunshine casting stripes of shadow onto my legs. But I can't concentrate. I'm thinking of Joanna. Wondering where she is. Wondering when she'll return.

What if I read Joanna's message wrongly or misinterpreted it? Half expecting to find that I've made a mistake, I check my messages, looking for the conversation I had with her. There it is: her invitation for me to visit. She'd almost begged me. Said she couldn't get married without her best friend's approval. Nothing ambiguous about that. The warmth I felt when I first read her message returns. It's wonderful to be needed again. Wanted. Different halves of the same whole – that's what we were. Complementing each other. Balancing each other.

Then, just as quickly, the warmth ebbs away as I remember that she's not here. That neither Mark nor I know where she is. I ring her number, and when I hear the request to leave a message, I almost shout into the phone.

'Joanna. It's not a joke. Ring me.'

My battery's low. I forgot to put it on charge last night. It must have been because I was in a strange room. A strange bed, with a pillow that smelt faintly of Joanna. Going to the bedroom I search in my bag for my charger before realising I've left it in the car. I could go down to the underground car park to get it, but something stops me. Whether it's the thought of having to climb all those flights of stairs back up to the apartment or whether it's the memory of the metal shutter that stands between the cars and the daylight, I don't know, but, whatever it is, I decide to wait until Mark is back.

Joanna used to sleep in this room. Not sure what exactly it is I'm looking for, I start to investigate. Opening drawers and kneeling to look under the bed. Hoping to find something that will give me a clue to Joanna's life: a hint of why she chose Mark over everyone else.

I pull open the double doors of the fitted wardrobe, half expecting to find some of Joanna's clothes still hanging there. There's nothing though, just a half dozen hangers on a rail. A single wardrobe door next to it elicits a set of drawers. The top one is empty. The next one is too. The third though, refuses to move when I pull it and it's only when I crouch and see the small keyhole that I realise it's because it's locked. I pull it again but, of course, it doesn't budge. Frustrated, I close the door again. What would Joanna need to keep locked away?

And then it dawns on me what I'm doing and I'm ashamed. The drawer may contain passports, birth certificates, medical records. Whatever's in there is private. Pushing myself up, I leave the bedroom, annoyed with myself for being so nosy. Even if the drawer had been unlocked, the contents are a part of Joanna's life. Not mine.

I find a couple of eggs in a wire-framed basket and hard-boil them, eating them with some tomatoes and salad I've found in the fridge. Then, when I can't stand the silence any more, I take the spare key Mark's left me and let myself out of the apartment. I need to get out; I'll get my phone charger after all.

As the apartment door shuts behind me, I stand and listen, hearing nothing except my own heartbeat in my ears. Out here, the sweet musty smell is stronger, and I wonder if it could be the tobacco I'm smelling. Decades of storage allowing the distinctive odour of its leaves to permeate the wooden floors. The huge beams. The bare brick walls.

Taking the stairs, I walk down two flights, but instead of continuing to the basement, I stop at the fourth floor and look through the rectangular glass panel of the door into the corridor. Somewhere on this floor is an apartment belonging to one of the few other residents of Tobacco Wharf.

Feeling a strong urge to meet this woman, I push open the door and step into the corridor, looking to the left and right. Who knows, with so few people living in the warehouse, she and Joanna might have been friends. We might be friends.

Trying not to let my shoes make too much noise on the wooden floorboards, I choose a direction at random and walk down the corridor, surprised when I'm rewarded straight away. Music is coming from the first door I come to, something folky, and without thinking of what I'll say if the door is opened, I press the buzzer and wait.

When no one comes, I ring again, and this time the door opens. There's a chain attached, and through the small gap, I can make out a nose, an eye, a flash of dark hair. At first, I think it's Joanna, but when the chain slides back and the door opens wider, I see the woman is nothing like her. Only her hair bears a resemblance, shiny and black – though of course I have no idea what Joanna's hair looks like now. For all I know, she could have cut it. Dyed it. Shaved it off.

'Hi.' I feel awkward now. Wondering what she'll make of this stranger who's pitched up on her doorstep.

'Yes?' Behind her, a small dog yaps, and she turns and shushes it. 'Did you want something?'

The woman is around the same age as me and, now the door is fully open, I'm shocked by her appearance. Her eyes are huge in her pinched face, the dark circles under them barely disguised by the heavy make-up she's applied. She's wearing a gossamer fine, baby pink top that has slipped from one shoulder revealing a sharp-edged collarbone. Seeing me look, she pulls it back up with long thin fingers, the silver bangles on her arm jangling.

Under her hollow gaze, my confidence ebbs away. 'I'm sorry to bother you, but I'm a friend of Joanna's. The woman who lives upstairs.'

Her thread thin eyebrows raise slightly. 'I see.'

She says nothing more, just appraises me with her dark eyes. Behind her, I see that the living area of her apartment is almost identical to Joanna's. The only difference being that her wooden floor is covered in a variety of patterned rugs, and the two large, red settees can barely be seen beneath the colourful scatter of cushions and Indian throws that adorn them.

When my eyes return to her, the woman is frowning. 'Did you have a message from her? Joanna?'

I shake my head. 'No. I just thought it would be nice to meet someone else who lives in the warehouse.'

'You live here?'

'Well, no, not exactly. I'm just visiting, but being on my own here is creeping me out a bit.'

'Tell me about it. Is it any wonder people don't want to live here? Think it's bad now? You should try it in winter. The wind howls around the building. It's like living in a bloody mausoleum overseen by Big Brother.' Seeing my puzzled look, she expands. 'I'm talking about Derek. I presume you've met him.'

I think of the man I'd seen in the room next to reception. The way he'd looked at me. How uncomfortable he'd made me feel. 'I met him yesterday. Does he work here full-time?'

'Yes, but it seems like he's always on duty. Doesn't matter what time of day or night I come in; he always seems to be here. Coming out of that grubby little room of his to stick his nose in where it's not wanted.' She cocks her head at the far wall of the corridor. 'We've been told that the cameras on each floor are just for show and aren't connected, but I'm not so sure. How would we know?'

I look at the little white camera that points down the corridor, imagining the two of us framed on one of Derek's screens. It's not a comfortable thought.

The little dog is at the door now. Running forward before retreating again, its bark an angry yip.

'Take no notice of Pixie. She thinks she's bigger than she is.' She scoops the dog up in her arms, tiny lines forming around her dark red lips as she puckers to kiss her silky head. 'Small dog syndrome. I think Derek has the same problem.'

I laugh, but even as I do, my eyes are sliding again to the cameras. Maybe we shouldn't be talking like this, just in case.

Eventually, the woman puts the dog down. 'What did you say your name was?'

'I didn't, but it's Alice. I'm staying in Joanna's apartment.'

I study her face to see if there's any reaction to this, a clue that she knows Joanna isn't here. There's nothing.

'I'm Eloise. Are you staying long?'

It's strange to be conducting a conversation outside her door. The corridor stretching away from us, the security camera at the end. I'd rather be in her apartment. Unlike Mark and Joanna's, it looks bright. Welcoming. It makes me want to see more of it, but without an invitation, I have to stay where I am in the corridor with its strange smell.

'I don't know. It depends.'

'How is she?' Eloise leans against the doorframe, her hands in the pockets of her black culottes. The thin legs that show beneath them displaying the nobs of her ankle bones, ending in long, slender feet encased in strappy gold sandals.

I force my eyes away. 'Joanna?'

'Yes.'

'Why do you ask?'

'No reason. It's just that I used to see a lot of her and now...' She hesitates. 'I guess she's just busy with the wedding and things. When she told me she was getting married, you could have knocked me down with a feather. Never had her down as the marrying type.'

It doesn't look as though it would take much of a feather to knock this woman down. There's no substance to her. No permanence.

'I didn't think so either. But Mark seems nice.'

'That's what people say.' She looks away. 'Tell Joanna I said hello.'

She crouches to stroke the dog, and I take the opportunity to look at her better. The bottom of her blunt cut hair razor sharp, her eyelashes long and spiky, coated in black mascara which does nothing to enhance her gaunt appearance. But despite this, there is an odd haunting beauty to her.

Abruptly, she stands. 'I have to go now. I've things to do.'

'Of course. It was nice to meet you. Maybe you'd like to come up to ours for a drink sometime.'

Eloise looks at me curiously. 'To yours?'

I correct myself quickly. 'I mean to Joanna and Mark's.'

'Thank you, but I don't think so.'

Before I can reply, she's shut the door, and after a couple of seconds, the music becomes louder. With no alternative but to leave, I go back to the staircase deciding when I reach the door to the reception to get some fresh air before going down to my car.

I push open the door, seeing again the polished marble floor and empty fountain. Derek's door is open. He's looking at one of the monitors, his grey-uniformed back to me. As I move closer, I see that on the screen is the black and white image of a car. My step falters. If I walk past, he might see me, and I don't want to have to talk to him, but equally, if I go down to the underground car park, he'll be watching me.

Turning, I walk quietly back the way I came, relieved that Derek hasn't seen me. I go back to Joanna's apartment and let myself in. But not before I've glanced at the security camera on the wall. Shivering as I remember Eloise's words.

CHAPTER SIXTEEN

It's dark when Mark comes in, a bag in each hand. Having failed to locate the TV controller, I'm sitting in a corner of the velvet settee looking as if I'm reading, but in reality, I'm thinking about Derek. Wondering what it is about him that makes me uneasy. It shouldn't matter that he watches the comings and goings of the wharf on his monitors, in fact it should make me feel safer. It doesn't, though. It just makes me nervous of leaving the privacy of Joanna's apartment.

'Any news?' I ask.

He puts the bags down on the island, looking puzzled. 'News?'

'Joanna. Has she contacted you?'

I watch as he takes the shopping out of the bags – a slab of some sort of meat in wax paper, tiny new potatoes and giant shiny red tomatoes.

'No,' he says, placing a tomato on the marble chopping board in front of him. 'Nothing.'

Sliding a kitchen knife from out of the stainless steel knife block, he starts to slice with smooth, precise movements of his hand. He looks distracted. Energy running through him like an electric current. 'I thought we'd have steak tonight. Nothing fancy. There's a nice bottle of Cabernet Sauvignon in the wine rack that will go beautifully with it. Could you open it, please?'

I put down my book. 'Don't you think we should—'

'There's a corkscrew in the drawer over there if you need it. Do it now so it can breathe.'

Bridling at the command, but wanting something to do, I go over to the wine rack. Row upon row of metal tubes embedded in the brick wall – most of them containing a bottle.

Mark looks over his shoulder. 'The second one on the left. Third row down. Do you know anything about wine?'

I think of the beer that Drew kept in the fridge and shake my head. 'No, not really.'

'That bottle's quite young, but I'll cook the steaks rare, and it will lessen the tannin. Should be the perfect accompaniment.'

Relieved to find that, unlike last night's, the bottle has a screw top, I open it and leave it on the side. Mark has his back to me again. He's put the tomatoes on a plate and is now trimming the steak on a different chopping board.

'The glasses are up there.' He indicates the cupboard to my right, and I open it, taking out the two nearest the front. 'No, not those... they're for white. The ones for red are to the right of them.'

Feeling the colour rise up my neck, I get out the right ones and fill them, remembering just in time that I need to leave some space at the top to let the wine breathe.

I place a glass in front of him. 'Is there anything I can do?'

'No. You're my guest.'

It's the second time he's said this, and I'm not sure how to respond for technically I'm Joanna's guest, not his.

I lean my elbows on the steel worktop. 'I met a woman today.'

Mark stops trimming the meat and looks up at me, his knife glinting in the light of the pendant stainless steel lamp that's suspended from the ceiling above the island. 'A woman?'

'Yes, the one you told me about. The one who lives on the fourth floor.'

Looking down again, Mark edges the tip of the boning knife under the membrane of silver skin on the underside of the steak. Loosening a corner, he pulls at it, using the flat of the knife to help separate the skin from the meat. The movements quick. Professional.

'I thought you said you couldn't cook.'

'No, I said I don't get much opportunity. Believe it or not, I might be a property developer, but I'm actually not a bad cook. The two things aren't mutually exclusive.'

I laugh. 'That's good. Drew never used to…' I stop. For a moment I'd forgotten that Drew is no longer in my life.

'Drew?'

I draw in a breath. 'He's my ex. I'd rather we didn't talk about him, actually.'

'Of course.' He reaches out a hand to me, then realising it's got blood on it from the meat, draws it back again with an apologetic smile. 'I'm sorry for asking.'

'It's fine. He cheated and I know now I'm better off without him.'

He nods. 'You sound very definite about that.'

'Oh, yes.' I think of my dad and his little floozy. 'I certainly am.'

The wine is tart but delicious on my tongue. It's nice chatting to Mark as he prepares the meal, companionable, the high-ceilinged warehouse apartment feeling warmer now he's back in it. I wonder if he feels it too, but even if he does, we both know it can't last. For the dark cloud of Joanna's absence is hovering over our heads and, at some time tonight, we are going to have to address it. Besides, she could be home any minute. At least I hope she could be.

Picking up the steaks, Mark transfers them to a plate next to the convection hob and empties the trimmings into the shiny metal bin under the counter. It reminds me of another time, another kitchen. Watching someone else who was also in love with Joanna.

I push the thought aside.

'So what did she have to say? This woman on floor four. I presume you're talking about Eloise.'

He asks the question purposefully as if he's trying to appear casual and doesn't care about my answer.

'Not a lot. I don't think she really wanted me there. She didn't even ask me in.'

'That sounds like Eloise.'

I wonder how well he knows her but don't want to ask.

'She asked how Joanna was.'

He looks at me sharply. 'And you didn't tell her?'

'No. No, of course I didn't.'

The nod Mark gives me signals his approval. 'Good girl.'

'But we need to talk about it, Mark. You said that if she hadn't come home by tonight, you'd call the police.' I look around the bare apartment. 'I don't think we can ignore it any more. She's been missing for four days now. I don't like the feel of it. It's not like her. I'm worried.'

Mark moves away from the hob. He stands opposite me, across the kitchen island, his stature making me feel small. When he speaks, there's a chill in his voice. 'How would you know what is or isn't like her, Alice? As far as I'm aware, you haven't seen Joanna in a while, otherwise she would have mentioned you.'

'I know,' I stutter. 'But I was her best—'

He holds out his hand as though fending off my words, a muscle twitching just above his jaw. 'Please, just don't say it. Have you forgotten who I am?'

We stand looking at each other, locked in a battle I don't really understand. I take in Mark's thin face, the narrow nose, the neat dark hair and heavy-framed glasses. It's the face of a scholar or a model for an upmarket men's clothing range.

I'm the first to back down, dropping my gaze and seeing how his long fingers grip the edge of the worktop – as though if he lets go, he might float away. 'I'm sorry. Of course, you're right. You're her fiancé.'

His shoulders relax. Reaching up a hand, he pinches the bridge of his nose between thumb and forefinger. 'And if I am, this only goes to show how little she thinks of me. God, I'm worried sick.'

'Then ring the police.'

'I will. But please… I can't tell them she's been missing for as long as she has. I should have notified them sooner, I know I should, but I thought she'd be home by now. They'll think it odd – will look at me as though I've done something wrong.'

'No, they won't.'

'Oh, believe me, they will. They'll make me feel like shit. Like I'm to blame in some way.' He leans his arms heavily on the metal worktop and rests his forehead against his fists. 'I can just see the way the cops will look at each other when I tell them. Judging. Fucking judging – when all I've ever done is loved her.' Reaching out a hand, he places it on top of mine. 'Please, Alice.'

'I won't tell them she's been on a course if she hasn't.'

'No, no. I don't expect you to tell them anything except what really happened. That you arrived on Saturday expecting her to be here, but she wasn't.'

I'm struggling to understand. 'But why not just tell them the truth, Mark, that you haven't seen her since Thursday morning? I expect Joanna wanted time out from the stress of organising a wedding. Okay it's strange she didn't tell her fiancé, but it won't be the first time it's happened, I'm sure.'

Mark looks at me sadly, shaking his head as though he's my teacher and I've got a simple sum wrong.

'It might not be strange she didn't tell her fiancé,' he breathes in deeply, 'but it's strange that she didn't tell her husband.'

'Her husband?' My brain feels dull. Uncomprehending.

'Yes. Her husband.' Mark looks bone-tired. Defeated. 'You see, Joanna and I are already married.'

CHAPTER SEVENTEEN

I take a step back from the island. Everything has been turned on its head, what I believed and what I have just been told at odds with each other. It must be how Alice in Wonderland felt when she fell down the rabbit hole. I look around the living space as though expecting the white rabbit to suddenly appear, and when it doesn't, I force my eyes back to Mark.

'What do you mean married? You can't be.'

Mark raises his eyes to mine. 'It's true. We tied the knot last week.'

I search the room for reasons. My mind trying to make sense of everything. 'But she would have said. She would have told me.'

'Well, clearly she didn't.'

'But why would she have said what she did in her message if it wasn't true?'

He shrugs. 'You tell me?'

'Who knows… apart from me?' Pulling out one of the white plastic chairs from beneath the island I sit, scared my legs will give way.

'Nobody. You're the only one I've told. We just went and did it.'

'But her parents…' I think back to the conversation we had yesterday about photographers and bands. 'They think there's still going to be a wedding. They're still planning it, for Christ's sake.'

'And therein lies the problem. Joanna couldn't cope with it all. They were putting pressure on her for a big wedding. You know the sort of thing – marquee in some stately home or other, a designer dress, hundreds of guests we've barely even met. I reckon it would have been just a showcase for her father, to be honest. A chance to talk about his latest project. Get people to sink money into more schemes that have a sod all chance of making any money.'

I want to tell him that the wedding he's describing is exactly the kind I'd have imagined Joanna having, if she'd ever wanted to get married. Exactly the kind of wedding *I'd* like to have given the chance.

'They wanted to pay for it all too.' He grimaces. 'Jesus, it was humiliating. Still, I would have gone through with it for Joanna's sake. Put up with everything.'

Seeing I've finished my wine, Mark tops it up, and I thank him.

'But it wasn't what she wanted after all?'

He shakes his head. 'She hated it when her parents told people that it was them who had got us together. That it was their idea we should get married. I told her it didn't matter as I would have loved her no matter how we'd met, but she had a bit of a bee in her bonnet about it. Said it would be romantic to just go ahead and do it. Not tell her parents or anyone until we had to. I think she wanted to see the look on their faces.'

Did she want to see the look on mine when I found out? If she did, she's missed it.

'Congratulations.' It's all I can think of to say. 'I hope you'll both be very happy.'

'Thank you.' It's said stiffly, and I realise how stupid that must sound under the circumstances.

'But if Joanna doesn't come back, the police will have to know. You won't be able to keep it quiet for ever.' I'm not sure why it bothers me so much that he tells them. It's none of my business after all.

'Oh, Jesus.' Mark draws his fingers through his hair. It's clear he hasn't thought of this. 'Yes, I suppose so.'

'They'd find out soon enough once they started digging. Ring them now, Mark. Just get it over with.'

'Yes,' he says. Taking his phone out of his back pocket. 'You're right. I'll do it now.'

He turns away as he punches in the number, pacing the kitchen as he gives brief details to the person on the other end who I presume is a desk sergeant. Yes, the person missing is his wife. No, he hasn't seen Joanna since Saturday morning. No, she doesn't take drugs. No, she hasn't a mental illness.

When the conversation is over, Mark takes the phone from his ear and puts it on the worktop. He looks at me.

'They said they'd send the next available uniformed patrol over to talk to us, but it's more likely to be tomorrow than today. Look I've got to pop down to see Derek. There's a problem with the air con in one of the apartments, and I've a prospective buyer looking over it tomorrow. I won't be long.'

'Do you need to go now?' I look at the slabs of red meat beside the hob, waiting to be fried. Realising that my appetite has left me. 'What about the steaks?'

'I'm sorry, I meant to speak to him earlier. I'll cook them when I get back.'

'Oh, Mark. While you're down there, I don't suppose you could go to my car and get my charger cable for me? I left it in there, and there's not much charge left on my phone.'

'Of course.' Mark holds out his hand. 'Keys?'

I fetch my bag from the bedroom and unzip the front pocket. Taking out the keys, I hand them to him. 'Thank you.'

'You're welcome.'

He pockets them and lets himself out of the apartment, leaving me alone with my thoughts. Tomorrow the police will be here, and I feel nothing but relief. The only way I'd feel better is if Joanna would come home.

CHAPTER EIGHTEEN

I'm awake. Lying in the pitch black, my eyes wide open searching for the tiniest scrap of light. Sitting bolt upright, I clutch the duvet in my fists, knowing it's a dream. Willing myself to wake.

But I don't.

I open my eyes wider, but there's still only darkness. Heavy. Claustrophobic. My heart thumping in my chest, I turn and look in the direction of the tall warehouse windows. Last night, their curtainless panes had shown up pale grey against the brickwork, but not tonight. Now there's nothing – only the darkness pushing in on me.

It's terrifying. Like a different room.

Swinging my legs out of the bed, I reach my arms in front of me into the pitch-blackness. Walking forward until I reach the brick wall, I work my way along it like a mime artist. After what seems like an age, I find the door and grasp the handle, relief flooding through me. But when I press down, it doesn't give.

I'm trapped. Trapped in this room with no windows. The blackness pressing against my eyeballs. Fighting for air. Fighting to breathe.

A sob escapes me. And then I'm hammering against the door, again and again, before sliding to the bare boards. Sobbing uncontrollably.

'Joanna,' I scream. But Joanna isn't here to save me. Not this time.

*

The door opens. Light floods into the room. Arms are lifting me, laying me back on the bed, but I don't want to lie down. I want to get away from the room. From whoever is in here with me. I kick out at them as they try to hold me still.

'Alice. For goodness' sake. It's me, Mark. Stop it.'

My hair is stuck to my face, my nightdress twisted around my legs. As my eyes focus, I see that Mark is standing over me in navy blue pyjama bottoms and a grey T-shirt.

He rubs at a scratch on his arm. 'Jesus, your nails are sharp. What's the matter? You'd wake the neighbours, if there were any.'

'I was scared. I panicked. I couldn't see,' I say feebly. 'It was so dark.'

'It would be. The blinds are closed.'

Looking at the windows, I see that he's right. Across each one, from nearly floor to ceiling, are horizontal metal blinds, their grey louvres tightly shut.

'But I didn't shut them?' My breathing is beginning to return to normal. 'They were open when I went to sleep.'

Mark looks unconvinced. 'Are you sure?'

I nod unhappily. 'Of course I'm sure. I don't even shut my curtains at night in my own house.'

'Well, let's get them open for you.' He walks to the bedside table. 'Where's the remote?'

'I don't know. I haven't seen it.'

'We usually keep it next to the bedside light.' He looks at me. 'Why didn't you turn it on if you were scared?'

I look over at the light, embarrassed. 'I don't know. I panicked and didn't think. I just wanted to get out.'

Mark's hand is fishing between the bedside table and the mattress. After a moment or two he holds the remote aloft like a prize. 'Here we are. You must have knocked it off the table when you turned over and activated it.'

'But it wasn't on there when I went to bed. I would have noticed.'

'You were tired.' He smiles. 'We'd also had rather a lot of wine.'

He points the remote at the window, and the horrible blinds slide back up into their housing. Outside, the sky is dotted with stars. The tall buildings on the other side of the river brightly lit. If I went over to the window, I know I'd see their silver reflections bringing the dark water of the dock to life.

Mark puts the remote back on the table. 'Are you all right now?'

I want him to leave, but equally I want him to stay. A glance at my phone shows me it's only three in the morning. Switching on the bedside light, I nod. 'Yes. I'm fine now. It probably didn't do me any good eating the steak so soon before going to bed. I'm sorry for waking you.'

'It doesn't matter. It was thoughtless of me to expect you to eat so late. I should have waited and seen Derek in the morning. Please forgive me.'

'Honestly. There's nothing to forgive.'

'I'll say good night then.'

Mark closes the door, and I lay back on my pillow, my eyes fixed to the grey squares of windowpane between the thin metal frames. What happened has brought back a terror from my childhood that I've tried to forget. Joanna and I had been in the grounds of her parents' house playing dares. She'd dared me to touch the electric fence around the paddock, that thankfully turned out not to be turned on, and I'd dared her to ride one of her horses, the piebald, bareback. Her final dare, though, had been something that had put fear into my heart. *I dare you to go into the garage and shut the door, then count to ten.* She knew I hated the dark but said it would help me face my fears.

I hadn't wanted Joanna to think me a baby, and she had, after all, completed all my dares without hesitation. How could I not? With thumping heart, I'd gone into that garage, now empty as her dad had taken the car to the golf course, and standing on tiptoe, I had pulled the door closed. I'd thought that there would have been some light coming under the door, but there wasn't. It was pitch black.

I hadn't got to ten. I hadn't even started to count. The suffocating darkness pressed in on me until I knew, with absolute certainty, that I'd gone blind. That my fear was slowly shutting down each part of my body, and I was going to die. Not caring that I'd failed the dare, I pushed at the lower part of the door, thinking that it would swing up, but it didn't. I banged on the door, screamed at Joanna, and she'd tried too, but it wouldn't budge. Eventually, she'd run to get her mum, and when eventually the door opened, I was sobbing like a five-year-old.

It's horrible being alone in this room with my fears, and for the first time since I found out what a snake Drew was, I miss him. Reaching out to my phone, I draw it towards me and press the button to bring it to life, wanting to see the screen saver of the two of us. The one we took last Christmas when we were happy. Not caring that it will be painful. Was it true what he said when he came to pick up the last of his things? Had I really been pushing him away?

I'm just about to switch the phone off again, when I notice the battery symbol in the top right-hand corner of the screen is red. The number beside it showing twelve per cent. Last night I'd plugged my phone into the cable Mark brought up from my car, but clearly it hasn't been charging. I pull out the cable, then push it back in again. The zigzag sign that shows it's charging properly doesn't appear. Maybe the wall socket isn't switched on. Leaning over the side of the bed I check it, but the switch is down. I don't understand. The phone was fully charged when I arrived here on Saturday, so the charger must have been working properly in the car.

A wave of anxiety washes over me again. My phone is my link to the outside world. It's a funny expression to use, but that's how I feel. For at this moment, New Tobacco Wharf, with its musty corridors and empty apartments, feels a million miles from anywhere.

And, despite the fact that Mark is in the bedroom on the other side of the apartment, I've never felt so alone. Or so desperate to see Joanna.

CHAPTER NINETEEN

The two police constables sit side by side on the leather settee. A woman and a young man who looks barely old enough to be doing this job, acne scars still gracing his cheeks. They've introduced themselves as PC Rose and PC Jameson. We sit opposite them, the coffee table between us, and I'm feeling decidedly underdressed in my jeans as Mark's in his tailored suit. After they've gone, he'll be going into the office.

All the time Mark's been talking, giving the basic details – Joanna's age, description and what she was wearing the last time he saw her, the policewoman has been scribbling in her notebook. Now, she looks up, her pen tapping at the page. 'And you say you've been married how long, Mr Belmont? Or are you happy for me to call you Mark?'

Mark purses his lips. 'Mark is fine. We got married just over a week ago. Last Thursday week actually.'

PC Jameson looks up. 'Congratulations.'

'I don't think at this precise moment there's much to be congratulating me about, do you?'

The young man lowers his eyes, the red that's creeping up his neck evidence of his embarrassment. 'No, I suppose not.'

PC Rose narrows her eyes slightly at him, then carries on. 'Thursday. That's not your usual day for a wedding.'

'I think you'll find that all depends on what your priorities are. It's not unusual if the only thing you care about is marrying the person you're in love with. If the only person's wishes you want to take into account are theirs.'

As he speaks, Mark rubs circles on the pinstripe fabric of his knees. Round and round. I'm mesmerised by it, and when I see the policewoman has noticed too, I wish he would stop.

Raising her eyes to his face, she gives a brief smile. 'Yes, of course.'

She flicks back a page in her notebook. 'Now, you said that no one else was with you at your marriage. Just the witnesses. And they were...'

'I don't know their bloody names.' Mark throws up his hands in frustration. 'I told you, I'd never set eyes on them before. We wanted their signatures, not their life stories. What's this got to do with anything?'

I try to signal with my eyes for him to stay calm, but he's not looking at me. So instead, hoping to break the tension in the room, I clear my throat.

'Mark's been under a lot of pressure... at work. And now his wife is missing. You can't blame him for being upset.'

I think about how he must be feeling: his dream project here at Tobacco Wharf failing and now his wife gone.

The policewoman glances at me, then at her colleague and writes something in her notebook. 'Yes, of course. I'm sorry, Mark. I know that this must be very tedious and upsetting, but we just want to get a better picture of what happened.'

Mark leans his elbows on his knees and rests his forehead against the heels of his hands. 'No, I'm sorry. I didn't mean to shout. I'm just worried something might have happened to her, that's all.'

The policewoman closes her notebook. 'Of course you are, and it's understandable, but try not to worry. From what you've told us your wife isn't vulnerable. You've said she doesn't have a problem with depression or her mental health, and she doesn't abuse alcohol or drugs. So, in all likelihood, she'll be just another adult who, for whatever reason, has decided they need a break.'

'But Joanna wouldn't—' I stop, wishing I hadn't said anything. Not wanting to get involved. Up until now, I've done nothing but give my name and explain who I am. I've let Mark answer the few questions the policewoman has asked, but now her attention has turned to me again.

'Miss…' She runs her finger down the page. 'Solomon. Remind me again why you were visiting Joanna?'

'You can call me Alice.' I glance at Mark. 'She wanted me to meet him. Meet Mark… to find out what I thought,' I finish lamely.

'What you thought of the man she'd already married.' Despite the ironic smile, her tone is scrupulously polite.

'Yes.'

'And do you still have this message?'

I nod, realising as I hand my phone to her, that I've been economical with the truth. I haven't mentioned that, as far as I knew, they were still planning the wedding.

She reads the message and makes some more notes before handing my phone back.

'And this was the last message you received from her?'

'Well, no. Not the last. There were a couple of others after that.' I find them and show her, listening to the scribble of her pen on the page. 'She was excited. Happy.'

'But that was the last you heard from her?'

'Yes. I thought it was odd that she hadn't replied to my messages.' I turn the phone off quickly to conserve what little battery I have left.

'And yet you came all the way to Black Water from the south coast to see her, even though you hadn't made any specific arrangements. That was quite impulsive, Alice. Was it because you were worried about her?'

'No, I wasn't worried. Why would I be? Joanna could be like that sometimes… distracted. Scatty. I expect she forgot she hadn't replied to me. My life had just been turned upside down, and I wanted to see her.'

PC Rose nods and smiles, but even to my ears, the way I've tried to excuse Joanna sounds feeble. 'Look, I'd just lost my job. Split up with my fiancé. My life was coming apart, and I knew Joanna would understand. She's helped me through some difficult times in the past and was the obvious person to turn to.'

'Of course.' It seems to be her stock phrase.

'So the last time you saw Joanna was when?'

I bite my bottom lip and look away. 'I haven't seen her for a while.'

I can feel her eyes boring into my head. 'How long exactly?'

Colour flushes up my neck. 'Ten years.'

Mark's head snaps up. PC Rose looks from him to me, then back down to her notebook. 'Ten years,' she repeats as she writes it down. 'And do you mind me asking why you haven't seen each other in all that time?'

Knowing I have to pull myself together, I raise my chin and look her in the eyes. 'We've both been busy. Our lives have taken us on different paths. It's not necessary to see someone to still be in their heart. And it's not a coincidence that it was me Joanna contacted to meet Mark. She's always valued my opinion.'

'I see.' PC Rose turns to Mark again. 'And you say that nothing is missing. Her passport? Clothes?'

'No. She's taken her bag that would have her purse and phone in. To be honest, I wouldn't know if there were any clothes missing.' He looks towards the bedroom. 'She has rather a lot, you see.'

'And you say your wife is a life coach? What exactly does that entail?'

'She helps people make changes that put them back in charge of their lives.'

'And she works for a company?'

'No, she's self-employed.'

'Does she have an appointments book? Something that would give us an idea of who she might have seen over the course of last week.'

Mark shakes his head. 'We have a home diary where she jots down if she's working, but the details of the appointments she keeps on her phone.'

PC Rose makes a note. 'Do you remember if she said she had an appointment with anyone on Saturday? Does she work at weekends?'

'Sometimes. But I don't know if she was seeing anyone. There was no record of it in the diary.' He's starting to sound defensive again. 'We don't live in each other's pockets.'

'No, that wouldn't be a good thing.' PC Rose puts the notebook into her pocket. 'We'll need to see the diary, Mark, and I wonder if you'd mind us searching the apartment.'

'Will that be necessary?' He swallows hard, his Adam's apple dipping. 'You can see she isn't here.'

PC Jameson scratches his head. 'You'd be surprised how often missing friends and relatives are found safe and sound in their own homes. Sometimes, people have been known just to be hiding.'

Mark looks incredulous. 'Are you seriously expecting me to believe that my wife is simply hiding in the wardrobe? This isn't a joke, you know.'

'No, of course not. I didn't mean it to sound like that.' The young policeman looks awkward, and I wonder how long he's been doing this job.

PC Rose stands. 'If you'll excuse us, we'd like to start in your wife's bedroom, if you could just show us which one it is.'

Looking relieved, PC Jameson stands too. 'It shouldn't take long.'

Mark indicates the door, and we sit in silence while they conduct their search. After a while, he looks at me. 'Is it true you haven't seen Joanna in ten years?'

'Why would I lie?'

A smile hovers on his lips. 'The same reason you fabricated the truth from the police and didn't tell them Joanna's been missing for longer than they think. You like to please.'

I'm taken aback. 'That's not true,' I say, prepared to explain myself.

There's a movement in the doorway of Joanna's bedroom and PC Rose comes out, followed by PC Jameson. I close my lips, scared they'll hear. The young constable was right; it hasn't taken long to search the apartment as, despite its size, it's clear Joanna isn't here.

PC Rose comes over to us. 'Could you please tell me which is Joanna's toothbrush? I'd like to take it back to the station with me as it will contain her DNA.'

Mark tenses. 'Yes, of course. It's the yellow one.'

She disappears back into the bathroom, then returns with the toothbrush in a sealed plastic bag. 'We also need a list of your wife's friends and a recent photo. One that's a good likeness.'

'I'll try to find one.' Mark gets up and goes over to the cupboard under the television. Sliding open a drawer, he takes out an envelope containing a few photographs and looks through. 'Will this one do? We're not really ones for taking pictures.'

I'd somehow expected it to be one of their wedding, but it isn't. Instead, it's a photograph of Joanna taken in the apartment. She's leaning against the iron balcony railings, her back to the river. The heavy wooden doors a perfect frame for her tall slim body.

'Yes, that's fine. If you find a head and shoulders one, you can always send it through later.' PC Rose picks up her hat and places it on her head. 'At the moment your wife isn't a priority, Mark, but that doesn't mean we won't be starting enquiries. We'll be in touch but, in the meantime, if you think of anything, anything at all, let us know straight away. With any luck, she'll be home soon.'

Mark stands as well, his long arms hanging by his sides, his fingers curled into fists. It's hard to read his expression. 'But what if you're wrong? What if something's happened to her?'

'The likelihood of a missing person being the victim of serious crime is fortunately low, but as I say, if your wife still hasn't returned of her own accord in a few days, or if anything else comes to light, do please let us know.' PC Rose walks to the door, the young police constable following at her heels. When she reaches it, she turns back to the room, her eyes moving from one end of it to the other, and I wonder if she's seeing it as I am. A soulless place. No plants to break up the spaces. No pictures or objects to reflect the personalities of the people who live here.

'One last thing, Mark. You say you're the property developer for Tobacco Wharf, along with your wife's father. Do you or Joanna have access to any of the empty properties?'

Mark folds his arms. 'I do, but the keys are kept at the office. My wife doesn't have access to them.'

'I see. Thank you, you've been very helpful, and as I said, try not to worry. We have all we need at the moment, but, in the meantime, if you can think of anyone at all who your wife might have seen in recent weeks, do please contact them. It's surprising how often they can provide the missing link.'

Mark opens the door to let them out. The policewoman walks through, but the young man hovers in the doorway. In the forty minutes they've been here, except for his faux pas with the badly timed congratulations, he's been very quiet.

'Just one further thing, Mark.'

'Yes?'

'I was just wondering… has anything like this ever happened before?'

'What do you mean?'

'Has your wife disappeared before?'

Mark draws himself up. 'Don't you think I would have told you if it had?'

The young man nods. 'Of course, you would. Sorry to have asked. We'll be in touch.'

We wait at the door as PC Jameson joins his colleague at the lift. With a ping the doors slide open, and he pulls back the concertina inner door, dragging it closed again once they're both inside. As the metal doors slide shut, I shiver, thinking of the small airless space inside.

Mark has already gone back inside. He's in the kitchen opening a bottle of wine as though we have something to celebrate. Even though he'll be driving.

'What are you doing?'

'What does it look like I'm doing?'

He pours half a glassful and downs it in one. 'Want some?'

'No. It's only eleven.'

Ignoring what I've said, he pours me some and pushes the glass across to me. 'Live a little. I just want to say thank you for not saying anything.' He smiles. 'It's the second time I've said that in two days, isn't it? Are you always this obliging?'

Heat burns my cheeks. 'I'm doing it for Joanna.'

'No,' Mark says. 'You didn't do it for Joanna. You admitted yourself that you haven't seen my wife in ten years. You did it for me.'

I wonder if he's right. There's something about Mark, but I don't know what it is. Something that makes me want to help him. Despite this, I wonder if I've done the right thing.

CHAPTER TWENTY

Mark picks up his keys and is just leaving when I remember my phone.

'The charger you brought up from my car isn't working.'

'Not working? Did you plug it in properly?'

'Yes, but I've checked it in other sockets just to be sure.'

I unplug the charger from the wall beneath the kitchen cupboards and plug the toaster back in. 'The battery's practically dead, and I don't like being without my phone.'

Mark takes the charger from me and looks at it. 'It didn't charge at all?'

'No.'

Picking up my phone from the counter, he plugs it in and wiggles the cable. 'There's nothing obvious. And you say it was charging all right on your way here?'

'Yes. It was working all right then.'

Getting his own mobile out of his pocket, he holds it out to me. 'Do you want to use mine? Is there someone you need to ring?'

I take it from him. The phone is expensive. The latest model. 'Thank you.'

But now the phone's in my hand, I realise there's no one I want to contact. I hand it back to him. 'Don't worry. I can do it later. I've still got a bit of charge, so could you give me your number just in case I need it? Just write it down as I don't want to make you later than you already are.'

Mark scribbles his number on the writing pad that's next to him, then pockets his phone. 'I'll tell you what. I'll buy another charger for you when I get out of the office later.'

I smile. 'That would be great. Thank you. Oh, and Mark?'

'Yes?'

'My car keys. You didn't give them back to me yesterday.'

'Didn't I?' Mark frowns and digs deep into his pocket. 'Oh, no I didn't.' He brings out the bunch of keys and hands it to me. 'Sorry.'

'Don't worry. I'm not planning on driving anywhere. Not today, anyway.'

'That's all right then. I'll see you later. What have you got planned for the afternoon?'

'I thought I might invite Eloise up for a cup of tea.'

He breathes in through his nose. 'I don't think that's a good idea.'

'Why not?'

'I just don't think we should complicate matters at the moment. Not after what's happened to Joanna.'

'But we don't know what's happened to her.'

He fixes me with his blue eyes. 'Precisely and that's why we don't want to muddy the waters with idle gossip.'

Straightening his tie, Mark goes to the front door and lets himself out. 'I'll see you later, Alice.'

'Yes. Have a good day and don't forget the new charger.'

'I won't.'

'Bye then. Try not to be too late home.'

From the way he turns his head, two lines deepening between his brows, I know that I've said the wrong thing. I'm mortified.

'I… I'm sorry. It's a habit. I used to say it to Drew when he went out in the evening. He was a music promoter. I could never get to sleep until he'd come home and—'

'You don't need to explain. I understand perfectly.'

The door closes, and he's gone, leaving me wishing the earth could open up and swallow me.

Crossing the room to the black wooden doors, I open them and look out, hoping to get a glimpse of Mark's car as he drives around the front of the building. I'm just about to give up and go back inside when I hear it. As he drives past the neat box trees in their pots, I wonder if he'll look up, but he doesn't and soon the Lexus has turned the corner and is out of sight.

Did Joanna lean on this black railing and raise a hand to Mark as he left for work? Did my friend mind being left alone in this warehouse, the only company the tall abandoned cranes on the dockside and the gutted buildings full of rusting car parts and scrap metal? Did she count down the hours until his return, as I know I will?

I laugh out loud. Of course not. Joanna was an independent woman. Chances are she'd have left the apartment before him, driving away from Black Water Dock to meet her clients. Sitting in bars in Canary Wharf. Having fun. I lean on the black railing for a moment, straining my eyes to see the towering office blocks, hazy in the distance. She must be fine, just like the police said. Perhaps she left of her own accord. There's nothing to be worried about.

There's a movement below me, and I look down. It's Derek the security guard. He's standing with his hands in the pockets of his black bomber jacket, looking in the direction in which Mark has just driven. Slowly, he turns his head and looks up to where I'm standing, and I step back into the room out of sight. I know he's seen me, though.

I close the doors and lock them, my skin prickling. Why *did* Joanna leave without a word or a note? Was she unhappy? Could Mark be having an affair? Or maybe she was.

I think of what Mark told the police officers. Is it really possible she could have taken clothes without him knowing? Or did she have reason to leave in a hurry? Deciding to leave everything behind including New Tobacco Wharf with its luxury apartments no one wants to buy.

I think of Mark in his serious pinstripe suit. The neat beard. The preppy glasses. Then I think of his meticulous manners and how upset he was when he told me Joanna was missing. Yet here he is today, driving off in his flash car as though he doesn't have a care in the world. But looks can be deceiving, and it's not as if I've always been the best judge of character.

I'm glad I'm not driving home today. After my terrible night, I'd found it hard to get back to sleep, even with the bedside light on and the blinds up. Every time I closed my eyes, I felt the darkness pressing in and had to open them to the light again before my panic could take hold. But eventually my body had given in to the weight of tiredness, and I'd slept a bit, waking to welcome sunlight shining through the windowpanes.

Has Joanna ever been scared living here? Has she lain awake in her magazine-perfect bedroom with its Egyptian cotton sheets, the ceiling fan turning slowly above her head? Cooling skin bathed in the sweat of intimacy. Mark beside her.

Not that I've seen that room properly, only the glimpse afforded that first night. I look at the closed door and it's as if invisible hands are pulling me. Before I'm aware of what I'm doing, I've crossed the wooden boards to the door in the far wall. Hesitating only a second before opening it and peering inside.

The room is bigger than the one I've been sleeping in but, unlike mine, its brick walls have been painted a stark white. The metal shutters are the same as the ones at the rest of the windows, but, in this room, they've been partially opened, a strip of brown Thames visible between them and the white floorboards.

Joanna looks down at me from her picture. She's on her side, the fingers of one hand entwined in her hair, her other hand flat on the ground supporting herself – her thumb dimpling the skin of her small round breast.

I turn away from the rose-pink nipple, my cheeks flushing pink. Imagining Mark's hand cupping those breasts, his own fingers in her dark hair.

In the half-light of the bedroom, I open the huge mirrored wardrobe that spans the width of the room. Biting my bottom lip as my hand touches the smooth sleeve of a midnight blue silk blouse. The satin strap of a halter neck evening dress. Some clothes with their labels still attached.

Would Joanna have been able to afford all these clothes on the money she got from being a part-time life coach? It seems unlikely, but, then again, I can't imagine her allowing Mark to fund her lifestyle. The girl I used to know would have scoffed at the thought. But then I think of Joanna's old room in her parents' house: the wardrobe of clothes by London designers I'd never heard of, the new computer by the window overlooking the field of horses and the diamond studs she'd got for her sixteenth birthday. Clearly, her scruples hadn't extended as far as her parents.

I try to remember if she'd ever mentioned a trust fund. It wouldn't surprise me. It would be the perfect trade-off for the lack of interest they took in her when she was growing up. A way to appease the guilt – if they felt any.

Before I can question what I'm doing, I've slipped the blue blouse off its hanger. Laying it on Joanna's bed, I pull off my T-shirt, then slip my arms into the sleeves and do up the buttons. The material is whisper-soft against my skin, and when I look at myself in the full-length mirror, I see how the colour sets off my hair, turning it a richer shade of auburn.

It feels strange to be wearing Joanna's clothes even though it's what we used to do at university. Back then we'd swap tops we were bored with. Something old becoming new again on a different body. Not that there was much Joanna wanted to borrow of mine.

Lifting the lid of an antique wooden jewellery box, I see inside its velvet lining a wide gold bracelet such as Cleopatra might have worn. A tiny black box next to it offers up a pair of tiny diamond studs. Could these be the same ones I coveted all those years ago?

After a moment's hesitation, I lift one of the earrings and push it through the hole in my earlobe. I do the same with the other, pushing on the butterfly clips to secure them. It's only as I close the lid of the jewellery box that I see the tiny drawer at the front, hardly visible against the marquetry of the wood.

I slide it open, expecting to see more jewellery, but there's nothing inside except for a small key. Taking it out, I rub the shiny metal with the pad of my thumb. I wonder? Might it be? Quickly, I slide the drawer back into place and go out of Joanna's white bedroom, shutting the door behind me.

In my own room, I open the wardrobe door and, crouching down, attempt to slip the key into the lock, biting my lip in frustration when it slips out of my fingers and onto the floor. My second attempt is more successful, and my heart beats faster as it slips into the lock and turns easily. I won't allow myself to feel guilty; I'm doing this for a reason. There could be something inside that will help me discover where Joanna is.

The drawer slides an inch or so, then stops. The space inside is jammed full of paper, and something is caught at the front, stopping it from sliding on its runners. Easing my fingers into the small gap, I prod and probe at the contents until, at last, I'm rewarded for my efforts. The drawer slides open, and I'm able to see why it got stuck. It's packed full of photographs.

But they're not just any photos. With a gasp, I sit back on my heels, the blood draining from my face.

They're all of me.

Every single one of them.

CHAPTER TWENTY-ONE

Emptying the photographs onto the floor, I see that they span the years from when I met Joanna at the age of thirteen to the last time I saw her when I was twenty-one. Some of them are just of me but, in others, Joanna is there too. In one, we're sitting on Joanna's bed in her parents' house, giving a thumbs up to the camera. In another, we're in the field with the horses, my hand raised to the soft neck of the piebald.

So many of them, crammed into this small locked drawer. No wedding photos. None of Mark. Just of me.

I'm looking through them all when the buzzer goes in the living area. It's not the front door intercom, but someone at my door. Joanna's door.

The buzzer goes again. Wondering if it could be Eloise, I shove the photographs back into the drawer, pressing them down with my hand and pushing it closed. I'm pleased at the thought of seeing her again as, even though I only met her briefly, she intrigued me. I'm also hoping she might tell me something of interest about Joanna. Pushing myself up from the floor, I hurry over to the door and look through the spyhole. But it's not Eloise who's standing there, it's someone else. Someone whose face is level with my eye, knowing that I can see him.

Derek.

I step back from the spyhole, my heart thumping. Why is he here? Leaning my shoulder against the door, I'm just trying to decide whether or not to open it when the buzzer goes again, making me jump. If I don't let him in, what will he think? With his panel of monitors, he must know I haven't left the building. Must know I'm here.

I tear at a nail, a habit I haven't had since I was at school, and wait. Maybe he'll tire and go away. But it doesn't happen. Instead, the buzzer goes again, a long high-pitched drone that grates. It's clear he's not going anywhere.

Leaving the chain in place, I open the door a couple of inches. 'Hello?'

He nods at me, his face impassive. 'If it's not too much trouble, I need to access Mr Belmont's apartment.'

'Is anything wrong?'

His voice is a study of patience. Slowly, he runs the flat of his hand across his ginger crew cut, and I notice how fine the hair is. Like a child's. 'I'll be able to explain better if you take the chain off.'

After a second's hesitation, I reluctantly slide it out of its track, forcing a smile to cover my discomfort.

Derek rocks back on his heels, fixing me with his small, light blue eyes. By his feet is a back holdall full of tools. 'Mr Belmont asked me to take a look at the air con unit. One's been playing up in another apartment and as all the units came from the same supplier, he's worried they might all have a fault.'

Is it Eloise's apartment he's talking about? As far as I remember, no one else is living here permanently.

Picking up his bag, Derek takes a step forward. 'You don't have any objection, do you?'

There's a sheen of sweat on his forehead despite the fact the air in the corridor is cool and he wipes it away with his sleeve. I hate the thought of this man in the apartment, but I don't have much choice. It was Mark who asked him to come up, and it's his apartment after all.

The fingers of Derek's right hand absentmindedly stroke the word *security* that's stitched onto the breast of his black bomber jacket, and I can't drag my eyes away from them.

'So it's all right if I come in?'

The corridor is empty. No one here except the two of us. I don't like the thought of Derek being in the apartment with me, but I feel powerless to refuse. My fingers make contact with the mobile in my back pocket, tracing the hard edges. I could call Mark, but I want to save what little charge I have left.

Reluctantly, I step back. 'Of course.'

'Thank you. I just need access to the condensing box. It's in the smaller of the two bedrooms.'

Moving past me, he walks confidently across the long, open stretch of bare wooden floor towards my room. Unlike Mark, he's not tall, but his lean frame looks hard and muscular.

As he disappears into my room, I'm wishing I hadn't left my nightdress draped over the iron bars of my bed and can't help wondering whether I've left my bag open, displaying my clothes and underwear.

'How long are you likely to be?' I call after him.

I hear a cupboard door being opened. 'As long as it takes, miss.'

There's the squeak of floorboards, the sound of something heavy being moved. A metallic clang. I want to go in and see what he's doing, but the bedroom is too far from the apartment door. Instead, I sit on one of the white plastic stools in the kitchen area and wait.

After twenty minutes or so, he reappears. He's undone his jacket and the tight-fitting black T-shirt he wears underneath accentuates the tautness of his stomach muscles.

He stands with his feet apart. 'The air con seems to be okay.'

'That's good. Thank you for checking.'

I wait for him to leave, but he doesn't. Instead, he walks to the windows. Putting his holdall on the floor, he looks out. 'Staying long?'

I want to tell him it's none of his business, but I don't want to rile him. If I'm genial to him, he might leave quicker. 'I haven't decided.'

He turns and surveys the room, his hands in the pockets of his uniform trousers, pulling them tight across his taut buttocks. 'Know how much these cost?' When I don't answer, he carries on. 'Close to three million. Do you have three million?'

I shake my head, not trusting myself to speak. I want him out of here, not talking about things that don't have anything to do with him. He runs his hand over the back of the leather settee.

'New Tobacco Wharf. What a cliché. Hankered after by rich bitches with more cash than sense.' He gives a dry laugh. 'Not that there are many of those around at the moment willing to dig deep into their pockets. It's just a warehouse after all. Just a fucking great empty tobacco warehouse. Mark Belmont must have seen her coming, got out his fishing line. Another rich wife to help recoup his bloody losses.'

I can't listen to any more. 'I'd like you to go now.'

Derek looks at me as though suddenly remembering I'm here. Picking up his bag again, he walks over, stopping in front of me. He's so close I can smell stale coffee on his breath, and I instinctively lean back, my back making contact with the sharp edge of the metal worktop.

He touches a finger to the end of my hair, making my skin crawl. 'Though it looks as though she might have some competition.'

From my seat on the high bar stool, our eyes are at the same level. He's looking at me curiously, and I can't think straight. If I shout for help, who would hear me? If I run for the door, he'd be there before me.

My fingers grip the plastic edge of the seat. 'I don't know what you mean.'

Reaching out, he rubs the collar of the blue blouse between thumb and finger. 'Don't you?'

I pull back, and he laughs. 'The police were here.'

'Yes.'

He strokes his chin, the stubble rasping under his fingers. 'Now I wonder what they could have wanted?'

I don't want to tell this man anything. Why should I? 'I don't know. It was Mark they wanted to see, not me.'

As though someone has flicked a switch, Derek steps back and smiles. 'Thank you for your time, Miss Solomon. I'll let Mr Belmont know that there's nothing to worry about. That the air conditioning unit seems to be working fine. I hope you enjoy the rest of your day. Please don't get up, I'll let myself out.'

With a strange little bow, he walks away, and I don't move until I hear the click of the apartment door as it closes. I wait a moment, then slip down from the bar stool and run to the door, sliding the chain into its slot with shaking fingers. Then I press my ear against the door, not breathing until I've heard the metallic clunk of the lift's inner door as Derek pulls it open then shut again.

When all is silent once more, and I've double-checked the door, I let the air out of my lungs. Derek's visit has rattled me. Has he got something to do with Joanna's disappearance? Does he know where she went? I no longer want to be here, and I decide I'll get my things together and go.

I stop at the door of my bedroom and look in. Even though nothing seems out of place, now I know Derek's been in here, the room feels defiled. Grubby. Forcing myself to go in, I pick up items of clothing and stuff them into my bag, then go into the bathroom and take my washbag from the glass shelf above the sink.

Coming out again, I check the bedside drawers and the wardrobe to make sure I haven't left anything, hesitating when I see the drawer that contains my photographs. A part of me wants to look at them again, but I know that if I do, the reminder of how we once were might make me want to stay.

Quickly, I turn the key, but instead of returning it to Joanna's jewellery box, I leave it in the lock. I don't want to go back into the room Joanna and Mark share. I feel guilty at leaving when I don't know what's happened to her, but Joanna isn't my responsibility. She has a husband now. Someone else to take care of her.

It's only when I touch my finger to my ear and remember I'm still wearing Joanna's earrings and blouse that something Derek said comes back to me. Something I don't understand.

Carefully, I twist off the butterfly clip and cup the diamond studs in my hand. I've changed my mind. I'm going to wait until Mark gets home because there's an important question I need to ask him.

CHAPTER TWENTY-TWO

We sit at the dining table as we have the previous evenings, a bottle of wine between us. We've eaten the thin, tender spears of asparagus, which were our starter, and the pan-fried duck breast Mark has just served me, along with some new potatoes and tender broccoli, which smells delicious.

I've told him about Derek's visit, but not about how uncomfortable he made me feel. Nor what he said about Joanna, though why I haven't, I'm not sure.

'Derek's a lifesaver. To be honest, Gary and I don't know what we'd do without him as he'll turn his hand to anything. Used to be in the army, would you believe. Not sure why he left, but their loss is our gain.'

It doesn't surprise me. I can imagine him in his soldier's uniform, an automatic machine gun in his hand, darting between buildings in some war-torn country, searching out an unseen enemy.

'My brother's in the army.'

'Really? Where's he stationed?'

'Last time I heard he was in Cyprus.'

'Last time you heard? You're not close then.'

'Not really.' I don't say any more. I know that it will sound childish if I tell him I haven't forgiven my brother for siding with my father. For telling me *life goes on* even though, just a few months earlier, life had stopped for my mother.

I cut a small piece of duck and put it in my mouth. 'You don't think he's a bit,' I try to choose my word carefully, 'strange?'

Mark draws his brows together. 'Strange? No, not at all. He's reliable. Civil. Committed to his job. Not easy to find people like that these days. What made you say that?'

I think of his coffee breath. How he made my skin crawl.

'It doesn't matter. I just found him a bit familiar, that's all. It's probably because I don't know him well enough.'

Mark frowns. 'That doesn't sound like him. Would you like me to have a word?'

'No, no. Please don't say anything. I don't want to cause any trouble.'

I put my knife and fork down. 'Did you get the new charger for my phone? You said you'd do it on the way back from the office.'

Mark hits his forehead with the heel of his hand. 'Damn. I completely forgot. I'm really sorry. Can it wait until tomorrow?'

'I suppose so.' The two glasses of wine I've drunk has put paid to my idea of going home tonight anyway.

'The offer's still there to use mine if you want to.'

'No, it's fine. I'll go and get one tomorrow. But there was something I wanted to ask you. Something Derek said that neither you nor Joanna mentioned.'

Mark looks at me, his blue eyes fixed on mine. 'Yes.'

I want to look away but can't. For some reason, it seems important to know the answer, but asking him outright seems rude. I have to, though – the answer might be the missing piece of the puzzle I've been looking for. The reason Joanna's not here.

'It's just that Derek said you'd had another wife.' I fiddle with the stem of my wine glass. 'You never said.'

The precisely cut piece of pink duck breast, which Mark has speared on his fork, hovers an inch from his lips.

'And why would I? I hardly know you.'

'I know, but Joanna and I... I just thought...' I stop, wondering what it is I'm trying to say.

Mark puts his fork down, the meat untouched. 'I'm not sure why it's of interest, but yes, I have been married before.'

It's said without emotion, but I notice how a small pulse jumps at the corner of his eye. I want him to say more, but he doesn't, and it's left to me to break the silence. Embarrassed, I find myself babbling.

'I know divorces can be hard, but you've got Joanna now.' I stop, realising the stupidity of what I've said.

There's a sharp scrape as Mark pushes back his chair. Picking up his unfinished plate of food, he takes it to the bin and scrapes it into the dark interior.

I get up too. 'Mark, I'm sorry I didn't...'

'She's dead.'

For one awful minute I think he's taking about Joanna. My throat constricts, and my voice comes out in a whisper. 'Dead?'

Mark wheels round, the metallic clang of the bin lid as it closes echoing in the cavernous room. 'Her name was Tanya.'

Realisation dawns, and I'm weak with relief. 'It's your wife who died?'

'Yes.' He turns suspicious eyes on me. 'Who did you think I meant?'

I recoil from the chill in his voice. 'Nobody. I wasn't thinking.'

'It was Joanna, wasn't it?' His voice is icy. 'You think Joanna's dead?'

'No. No, of course I don't. When you said she'd died, I thought you meant—'

Tears spring to my eyes, and Mark's face softens.

'Yes, I see now how the misunderstanding came about. I'm sorry I was sharp, it's just that it's still a bit raw.' Gathering himself, he gives a thin smile. 'Please, sit down. Finish your meal.'

I do as I'm told, but the duck has grown cold on my plate, and I've no longer any appetite for it. 'I'm sorry for upsetting you.'

Joining me at the table again, Mark refills our glasses. 'It wasn't your fault. She was a wonderful woman, and it was only two years ago… maybe I'm not over it yet.'

I'm not sure how to respond. If he's not over her, then where does Joanna fit in?

Mark takes a large mouthful of wine, his Adam's apple rising as he swallows. He looks at me over the top of his glass. 'I suppose you want to know how she died?'

'No. Please, you don't have to talk about it if you don't want to. I should never have said anything.'

'It's all right. Really, I don't mind. In fact, it's nice to have someone to talk to about her. My wife, my first wife that is, died in a car accident. It happened one night when I was away on business. The police found her car in the ditch.' His head is in his hands now, his fingertips leaving tramlines in his thick hair. 'She'd hit a tree and there was nothing they could do to save her.'

'Oh God. I'm sorry. That's awful. Do they know how it happened?'

'No. It was late so there were no witnesses. The likeliest thing is that she was driving too fast. Lost control.'

'What was Tanya like?'

'Sweet. Kind.' There's a catch in his voice. 'She was only thirty-nine. That's too young to die. Too bloody young. And now Joanna…'

There's a hollow feeling in my stomach as I realise something. 'You didn't say anything about Tanya to the police when you told them Joanna was missing. Why not?'

The thump of his fist on the table makes me start. 'Because it's none of their damn business. Joanna's disappearance has nothing to do with the past. With me. Besides, I couldn't face another interrogation.'

'Interrogation?'

'Questions. Questions. Bloody questions. Where were you? What was your marriage like? Which one of you was in charge of servicing the car? As if I was in some way to blame. It was a simple accident. And now you know why I was in no hurry to go to them about Joanna until I really had to. I just couldn't face having the whole business with Tanya dredged up again.'

'But if Joanna doesn't come back soon, they're going to be asking more questions. And if there was an investigation into Tanya's death, they'll soon make a connection to you as her husband. They'll find out eventually, Mark.' I look at him, exasperated. Remembering how he hadn't wanted to tell them about his whirlwind marriage to Joanna. 'You can't avoid it forever.'

'It's not going to happen. She'll be back by then.' He finishes his wine. 'She'll come back, and then things can get back to normal.'

'And if she doesn't?'

'I don't like you talking like that.'

'But we have to face facts, Mark. Joanna is gone, and we have no idea where she is.'

He closes his eyes briefly. 'We'll cross that bridge if and when we come to it.'

Although it shouldn't be, the word *we* is comforting. It makes me feel like we're in this together. But then I remember the hidden photographs in the bedroom. Imagine Joanna taking them out one by one when Mark is out of the house. Looking at them. Would she have been remembering the fun we had when we were together? Our special friendship?

The part of me that has never got over being rejected by my father... by Drew, responds. Despite our years apart, Joanna has never forgotten me. The proof is in that locked drawer. Maybe there is no *we* after all. Just *me*.

I look at Mark's profile. The thin, slightly hooked nose. The high forehead and long face with its neatly trimmed beard. He's a man who's been married twice. One wife is dead, the other missing. I shiver. Does he know about the photographs? Something makes me sure he doesn't, and I'm glad.

In this cold apartment in a dock that feels abandoned, it's a small secret... but one that warms me. Joanna wants me here for a reason, and I'm not leaving until I find out what it is.

CHAPTER TWENTY-THREE

I'm sitting at the kitchen island, eating my breakfast and mulling over everything that's happened since I've been here. How Joanna and Mark have married in secret. The way Mark has kept it from her parents and would have kept it from the police if he'd had the chance. His previous marriage and how it ended in tragedy. The drawer in my bedroom stuffed full of photographs… all of me.

I dip my spoon to my bowl, my appetite dwindling. Where on earth could Joanna be?

Mark is at the counter, making a fresh cafetière of coffee. With all that he's concealed, I should feel nervous around him, but how can I when I know how shocked he was when he mistakenly believed I thought Joanna was dead. I could leave him here to deal with it alone, but with each day, my worry for my friend intensifies. Joanna invited me here for a reason, and I owe it to her to stay and figure out what that might be.

Mark brings the coffee over. He pulls out a stool and sits before clearing his throat. 'I have to go away for a couple of days. I was wondering whether you would mind staying and keeping an eye on the apartment for me.'

I raise my head from my muesli, realising that all the time I've been at the breakfast bar, Mark's eaten nothing. The whites of his eyes are bloodshot as though he hasn't slept well. 'You're going away? Is that a good idea when Joanna is missing?'

'I have no choice. I've got to work.'

'When are you going?'

Mark pours himself another coffee from the cafetière in front of him. 'Later this morning and I'd be happier if someone was here in case she comes back. Please, Alice, I wouldn't go, but Gary wants me to check on one of our properties in Manchester.'

'Can't you ask him to go instead?'

He shakes his head. 'They've gone to Dubai.'

'Dubai? They never said anything when they were here.'

'That's because it's no big deal to them.' His voice has a bitter edge to it. 'They're away more than they're here.'

I've no doubt he's right, but something has been troubling me. 'I think you should have told them about Joanna before they left. She *is* their daughter after all.' Despite their strained relationship, I'm certain they wouldn't have left the country if they'd known she was missing.

'I will when I get back. I promise.' He takes a sip of his coffee. His voice is level, but I can see the effort it takes to keep it that way. 'Anyway, we don't want to spoil their holiday.'

'Jesus Christ, Mark. You make it sound as though Joanna going missing is an inconvenience.'

'I'm sorry. I didn't mean for it to sound like that.' He rubs a hand down his face. 'It's just that everything's so… up in the air at the moment. So unsettled. Please, Alice, I'll be back tomorrow evening at the latest.'

I put down my spoon. Unsettled seems rather an understatement. 'I don't know. I really ought to be getting home.'

Mark stands. He picks up my bowl and mug and takes them over to the dishwasher, the metal tray rattling as he closes the door. 'To what? You have no job. You have nobody who will miss you.'

I stare dumbly at his back. Doesn't he realise how insensitive he's being. It might be true, but it's hardly polite to say it.

'Thank you for pointing that out,' I say eventually.

He straightens up. 'Oh, Jesus, I'm sorry, Alice. It's just that I'm worried sick. What if Joanna comes back and finds I'm not here?

What if she thinks I don't care – packs her things and goes for good?' Coming back to the table, he sits down then leans across and takes my hand. 'Please forgive me. It's just that everything is such a bloody mess. I'll beg if I have to.'

I pull my hand away. I want to say no, pack my bag and go, but my loyalty to Joanna stops me.

'If I did stay, what would I do with myself?'

'Do?'

'Yes, I can't just sit here for two days.' I think of my dead phone. The book with only one chapter left to read. And then it occurs to me that it's already Wednesday. I've been here since Saturday evening and, apart from that initial walk along the quayside with Mark, I haven't left the building. How has that happened?

Mark pinches the bridge of his nose, then looks at me. 'There *is* something. We've had a small staffing problem recently. Our cleaner, Rosetta, handed in her notice, and we haven't been able to find a replacement. Maybe you'd consider covering for a few days, or at least while I'm away. There won't be a lot to do. Just the corridors. You don't even need to do the reception. Derek has that in hand, as well as the outside.'

Seeing me hesitate, he carries on. 'I'd pay you well for the inconvenience, and it would give you something to do.'

'And food? There aren't exactly any shops around here.'

'You don't need to worry about that. Last night, after you'd gone to bed, I placed a food order from Waitrose. I didn't know what you liked, so I had to take a guess. It will arrive later today.'

I stare at him. How did he know I'd say yes?

Sensing he's made a mistake, Mark reddens. 'Please, Alice, I wouldn't ask you if it wasn't important.'

'All right, just a couple of days, then I really must get back.'

Mark reaches across and pats my hand. 'Good girl.'

*

I'm standing outside the lift on the first floor, my finger on the call button, waiting for the number above the door to change from six to one. At last it pings, signalling the lift's arrival, and the metal doors slide open. I pull aside the concertina grill and drag out the vacuum cleaner, feeling pleased with myself for devising a way to get the heavy contraption from one floor to another without actually taking the lift myself.

I wonder what Mark's doing now. Earlier, I'd watched from the window as his Lexus had disappeared around the corner of the warehouse. Then when I could no longer hear the throaty rasp of its engine, I'd turned and viewed the apartment. Imagining what it would be like if it were mine. Thinking of how I would make it more homely: what paintings I'd hang on the long bare walls, what coloured rugs and throws I'd buy. But then I'd pulled myself up short. This was Joanna's world, not mine. And maybe it was no longer hers either.

Now that I'm outside the apartment, I'm feeling the building's isolation more keenly, and as I plug the vacuum cleaner into the socket on the wall, I can't help picturing the empty warehouse spaces behind the closed and locked doors that run the length of the corridor. Spaces that have lost hope of ever being filled with furniture or the sound of voices.

More unnerving than that, though, is the image I have of Derek in his small room off the entrance hall, his pale eyes fixed to the monitors. I glance up at the camera, wondering if he's watching me, and shiver.

Making sure the setting on the cleaner is for hard floors, I make my way down the corridor. The high-pitched whine cutting through the silence. The sweet, musky tobacco fragrance teasing my nostrils. As I guide the metal nozzle along floorboards that have barely had any feet walk their length since the warehouse was completed, it occurs to me that no one will even see my efforts.

When I reach the end, I stop and turn the vacuum cleaner off. On this far wall is an arched window and through it, I see the warehouse next to this one, its side clad in scaffolding. Leaning my elbows on the sill, I look down at the cracked paving below. It's choked with weeds that don't quite manage to hide the wheels of the upended shopping trolley that's been left there despite no shop being near.

As I watch, a gust of wind slaps a sheet of newspaper against the broken wire fencing, beyond which the Thames continues its journey to the sea, not caring that I'm here alone. That Joanna could be out there somewhere. Unhappy. Lost. Or worse.

My thoughts turn to Mark. How horrible it must be for him living in this deserted place with Joanna gone. At least with his first wife, he knew what had happened. *Tanya*. I saw how his eyes had softened when he said her name and can't help but wonder if he was over her when he married Joanna.

I'm lost in thought when a noise behind me makes me turn, one hand to my heart. It's not a loud noise, but a faint click like a door opening or closing. I hold my breath and listen. Mark said this floor was unoccupied.

It's only as I'm beginning to think I've imagined it that I hear the noise again. This time there's movement too. A few steps away from where I'm standing, the door of one of the apartments opens. Long thin fingers, the insides of the first two stained with nicotine, grip the doorframe.

'Joanna?' a male voice asks.

A face looms from the darkness within. Peaked. Sallow. Someone of around nineteen or twenty.

He blinks in the light of the corridor. 'Is that you?'

I hear the urgency behind the words. The underlying relief.

Pressing my back against the cold brick wall, I shake my head, the shock of seeing him striking me dumb. The boy's hollow eyes meet mine, and it's then he sees me properly. Realises his mistake.

'Fuck.' He spits the word, and then the door closes as quickly as it opened.

I don't move. Scared that he might come out again. From his reaction, it's clear he's not supposed to be here. But he knows Joanna. Called her name.

Leaving everything where it is, I tiptoe along the corridor and press my ear against the door. There's no sound. Nothing. I raise my hand to knock and then drop it again. What would I say? I don't know this person. For all I know he's a squatter, off his head on drugs. I could ask Mark of course, but my phone is dead in my pocket.

Trying not to think of my unnerving encounter, I wind the cable around the vacuum cleaner and place it, along with the box of cleaning products I've been using, inside the lift. Then I climb the stairs to the next floor and press the button to summon it. Moving down the corridor as I did on the previous floor.

But the guy's face keeps floating into my head. Who is he and why is he living here? Those sharp cheekbones, the indigo shadows under his eyes – they bring to mind a boy Joanna hooked up with when she was eighteen, a casual worker on a neighbouring farm. It was a time when she'd have done anything to shock her parents. But I'd been shocked too.

How does the boy I saw know Joanna? Could he have seen her in the corridor or on the stairs and fallen for her? He wouldn't be the first and had clearly been expecting her… Might he be the key to where she is?

My imagination is running wild, and I have to force myself to stop thinking about it. What good will it do, suspecting everyone I meet? Instead, I try to empty my mind and finish the work I've started.

By the time I've finished all the floors and have put everything away, I'm starting to feel hungry, and the thought of the Waitrose delivery has grown appealing. When, later, the buzzer goes, I throw the door open, expecting to see the green plastic boxes filled with food.

It's not the delivery man.

CHAPTER TWENTY-FOUR

As soon as I see who it is, I try to shut the door, but he's too quick, his dirty trainer blocking the gap. I push harder, but he leans into the wood, forcing it back open.

'What the fuck are you doing in Joanna's apartment?' He spits the words out, saliva flecking his chin.

Despite my fear, I stand my ground, scared he's going to come into the apartment, but he doesn't. Instead, he looks at me, his haunted eyes beneath the black beanie hat, unnerving. What little I can see of his hair is greasy, so fair it's almost white, a flap of it falling across one side of his gaunt face like a curtain that hasn't been opened properly. He pushes it aside irritably.

'I asked you a question.'

My heart is thrumming against my chest, but I know he mustn't see how scared I am. I force my voice not to quaver. 'Tell me what you want, or I'll call the police.'

Hoping he won't notice the blank and useless screen, I slide my fingers into my pocket, but just as I'm bringing the mobile out, his hand shoots out, snatching it from me.

His eyes dart to the screen, then back to my face again. He waves the phone in front of my face. 'Really?'

I take a step back. 'Look, I don't know what you want, but if it's money...'

'I don't give a shit about money. Did Joanna ask you to come up and clean the place? Answer me... did she?'

As he speaks, he wraps his arms around his body as though he's cold. He sounds less sure of himself now and, up close, there's something vulnerable about him, his stained hoodie and dirty jeans hanging off his thin frame.

I glance behind me. 'No, she didn't. I'm not the cleaner.'

'Then what were you doing when I saw you earlier?' Behind his south London accent, there's a hint of public school.

'No, you've got it wrong. I'm just helping Mark out.'

He eyes me suspiciously. 'If you're not the cleaner, who *are* you?'

'I'm Alice. Joanna is… used to be… my best friend. She asked me to come and stay.'

The youth peers behind me. 'So where is she then?'

I hesitate, wondering what I should say. I decide to stick to the lie. 'She's been on a course. She'll be back soon.'

'She never said. She would have told me.'

His attitude is starting to annoy me. 'I'm sorry, but I've told you who I am. Who exactly are *you*? I was told only Mark, Joanna and Eloise are living in the building.'

His face closes. 'It doesn't matter.'

'It might matter to Mark that someone's been calling at his apartment when he's at work.'

He looks uncertain now. Younger. A muscle works in his jaw. 'Don't tell him.'

He rubs at his eyes with the heel of his hand. The whites look bloodshot, the rims red too. It's unnerving him being here, but he looks so sad, so lost, that the words come out before I can stop them.

'Do you want to come in?'

His face pinches with suspicion. 'Why?'

'I just thought there might be something I could help you with… as Joanna's not here.'

He glances down the corridor, and my eyes follow his, alighting on the security camera.

'Are you worried Derek will see?'

'Not really. I saw him leave the building before I came up. There's no one here but us.' He takes a step forward. 'You got any food?'

'A little. There's an order that should be arriving... from Waitrose.' I stop. He's not going to care about that. 'I'm sure I can find something.'

He follows me inside, and I close the door behind us, wondering if I've done the right thing. He doesn't sit but stands in the middle of the open space, his fingers plucking at the seams of his grubby jeans. He's clearly agitated.

'She didn't tell me she was going anywhere. Why wouldn't she tell me?'

I shake my head. 'If it's any consolation, she didn't tell me either.'

I don't want him to know the truth – how worried I am about Joanna. His erratic behaviour is unnerving, and I'm scared of saying anything that might tip him over the edge.

Leaving him, I go into the kitchen area. I lift the lid from the bread crock and take out the half loaf that's in there, then look in the fridge. 'Ham okay?'

'I don't care. Anything.'

I butter the bread, trying to make my voice conversational. 'How do you know Joanna?'

'She's my stepdad's girlfriend.'

'Your stepdad?'

'Mark.' He says the word as though it's got a nasty taste.

I lift my head in surprise. 'Mark's your stepdad?'

'Surprise, surprise. He hasn't mentioned me.'

'Well, no, but then...'

'Don't make excuses for him, he's an arsehole.'

I cut the sandwich in two and take it over to him. 'I don't think you should talk about him like that.'

'Why not? It's true. After Mum died, he made it clear he didn't want me. I was sixteen and had just failed most of my GCSEs. He thought I was a layabout, said that if I didn't get my finger out, I would amount to nothing.' He looks down at his stained hoodie. 'I guess he was right.'

'What's your name?'

He takes a large bite of the sandwich, and I look away as pickle drips down his chin. He wipes it with his sleeve. 'Nathan.'

I sit opposite him. 'I'm trying to understand. Who looked after you then if Mark didn't?'

Nathan swallows his mouthful. 'He sent me to my gran's. She did her best, but I was a mess after Mum, drugs and stuff, and she didn't know what to do with me either.'

'That must have been hard.'

He looks at me over the top of his sandwich. 'The only one who cared a toss about me was Joanna. I moved back with Mark for a bit and she was there. I thought I'd mind seeing him with someone else, but she was fucking awesome. Gave me the number of a counsellor. Put me in touch with someone who would help me get clean. Not many people would do that for someone they hardly knew.'

As he lifts his arm to take another bite, I see the threadlike tracks on his skin. Seeing I've noticed, he yanks at the sleeve of his sweatshirt with his free hand, his glare accusing. 'I'm not using now, if that's what you're thinking. Though it's fucking hard.'

I drag my eyes away. 'What happened then? Why aren't you living with them now?'

'Mark couldn't cope with me. All he was interested in was his business.' He turns away and bites his lip. 'When he moved in here with Joanna, I was going to come too, but then he went and fucking got rid of our dog – said it wasn't fair to keep her in an apartment and that there'd be no one to walk her.'

I think of Eloise's little dog. Wonder how she manages. 'He might have had a point. New Tobacco Wharf isn't exactly pet-friendly.'

'Then he shouldn't have moved here.'

'Maybe Mark didn't—'

He cuts me off. 'Don't make excuses for him. Shona was Mum's dog. She loved her. I loved her. Anyway, we got into a fight about it, and Mark threw me out.'

He sniffs and looks around the apartment, and I wonder how many times he's been here.

'What did you do?'

'Fucking hell, you're slow. You've seen where I doss. Joanna got me the keys to the empty apartment on the first floor. My stepdad has keys to all the unoccupied apartments, and it wasn't difficult for her to make a copy. If it hadn't been for her, I'd be on the streets.'

It all makes sense now. 'Does Mark know?'

He looks at me as though I'm mad. 'Of course, he doesn't. I'm not an idiot.' He takes off his woollen hat and scratches his head. 'Joanna brought me food and stuff, and the idea was she'd give me the nod if someone was going to look round with a view to buying. They never have, of course. No one wants to live here. It's why Mark has no fucking money – except what should be mine. Most of that has gone too, though.'

I'm confused. 'What do you mean?'

'Mum left everything to him… in her will. I got fuck all.' He slams his plate down on the coffee table. 'Wouldn't put it past him to have forced her into it. Scheming bastard.'

I try to marry up the Mark he's telling me about with the one with whom I've spent the last few days. 'You don't know that.'

'And you don't know *him*.'

'No, I suppose I don't.' I change the subject. 'Don't you get lonely, living there by yourself? I thought the same when I met Eloise. It's so isolated here. So desolate.'

'Who the fuck is Eloise?'

'I suppose she's Joanna's friend. I got the impression when I saw her that they see a lot of each other. Lives on the fourth floor… I'm surprised you haven't seen her around.'

'Seen her around? It's not fucking *Neighbours*.' He lifts his feet in their filthy trainers onto the coffee table and crosses his ankles. Daring me to object. 'Anyway, I don't go out if I can help it.'

'No, of course not. I'm sorry.'

'Why are *you* sorry? I'm not your problem.' His anger has flared suddenly. 'Why are you here anyway? What do you care?'

Getting up, he forces the beanie hat onto his head and strides across the room, stopping only when he gets to the door.

'When Joanna gets home, tell her I asked after her. I tried to warn her about Mark, but I have to keep my distance. Last time I tried to help I learnt the hard way.' His face pinches. 'You and that woman on the fourth floor might think you know Joanna, but you don't. None of you do... not really. But you know what, I don't give a damn any more. You...' He points a finger at me. 'You'd better keep your nose out of my life.'

The loud slam echoes in the carpetless room, making the metal ladles and spatulas that hang from the rack in the kitchen swing. The encounter has shaken me. Quickly, I go over to the door and lock it.

But being shut in does nothing to lessen my unease.

CHAPTER TWENTY-FIVE

That night I sleep fitfully. I'm not sure whether it's due to the steak that came with the food delivery, when it eventually arrived, or the wind that's got up and is rattling the small-paned windows. Whichever it is, the hours are passing slowly. Lying in Joanna's old bed, watching the moon slip in and out from behind the dark clouds, it's hard not to remember the night when the heavy metal blinds shut out all light. My paralysing fear.

I lie awake, thinking of what Nathan told me. How Mark is his stepdad. How the money Tanya left in her will has been spent on money-draining new developments like New Tobacco Wharf. Most of all, though, I think of Nathan's attachment to Joanna, and all she's done for him in the short time she's known him. Did Joanna want me to know all this? Is this why I'm here?

Reaching out a hand, I feel for the controller that works the shutters. When my fingers make contact with it, I push it to the furthest side of the table, so there'll be no danger of it dropping onto my bed again. Of me operating it by mistake. Then I close my eyes and listen to my heartbeat until its steady rhythm lulls me back into sleep.

The scream, when it comes, is bloodcurdling, sending me shooting bolt upright, bedclothes clutched to my chin. The sound hasn't come from inside the warehouse but from outside, somewhere further along the dock. I wait and listen, but there's nothing. Just the silence, broken only by the occasional shake of the window.

Pulling the cover up over my head, I tell myself it's nothing, try to sleep, but I can't. I've never been afraid to be on my own before, but now I wish desperately that Mark was here. Will someone else have heard that awful sound?

I wonder if Eloise is looking out of her window or Mark's stepson Nathan. If I was back home, I'd dismiss the sound as just some drunken kids on their way back from a party... but here? Who even lives here amongst the scrap metal and abandoned cranes except us?

When the scream comes again, I think my heart will leap out of my chest. It's worse than before. High-pitched. Desperate. Throwing back the covers, I run to the window, the floorboards cold beneath my feet, and look out. I'm terrified of what I might see, but it's worse not to know. Have I imagined it?

The moon shivers a band of silver across the black river, picking out the tiny white crests that the wind has whipped up, but the quayside is empty. A sheet of clear plastic flaps against a broken window. A door from a roofless building swings on its hinges. I strain my eyes to see if there's someone out there but find nothing.

Suddenly, the scene in front of me lights up, as though the quayside's a stage, and a performance is about to begin. Something has activated the security light. And that's when I see a movement – something light-coloured against the dark bulk of the warehouse next to this one. I hold my breath, too scared to move.

The scream comes again, louder this time. Impossible to ignore. Someone is in trouble. What if it's Joanna? Pressing my cheek against the cold glass, I make myself look, my shoulders sagging in relief when I see what it is. A vixen disappearing around the side of the building, her mangy fur the same shade of red as my hair.

Back in bed, it takes a long time for my heart rate to return to normal. The incident has made me realise how isolated I am.

Tomorrow I will go to Eloise's apartment and see if she has a phone charger I can use and, failing that, I'll take the car and find somewhere to buy one. I can't carry on staying here with no means of communication. Besides, Joanna may be trying to contact me.

I lie awake, staring at the windows, not moving. Even though I know what made that terrible sound, sleep still won't come. Finally, knowing it's not going to happen, I force myself to get up and go out into the living area. When I was a child and couldn't sleep, Mum would make me a milky drink and its warmth would help me drift off. Hoping it will this time, I pad across the cold floorboards to the kitchen and bend to look in the fridge.

I'm just taking out the milk when I hear something. *Tap tap.* It's not loud but loud enough that I know I'm not imagining it. I freeze, the carton clutched to my chest. It's three in the morning, and someone is knocking on the front door. Who would be outside the apartment at this time?

Not knowing what to do, I do nothing, just stare in the direction from which the tapping is coming. I brace myself for the sound of the buzzer, but it doesn't come. Just the quiet knock again. Once… twice more. I can't move. I'm rigid with fear. Who's out there? What do they want? If it was Mark, he'd use his key. If it was the police, they'd press the buzzer. Is it Mark they're after or maybe Joanna?

Or do they know neither are here, and it's me they want to open the door?

Then a thought comes to me. What if it's Joanna who's outside? What if she's come back and hasn't got her key? Wishing I'd put on my dressing gown, I put down the carton of milk on the island and force myself to walk to the door. When I get there, I push aside the brass cover of the spyhole and look through.

There's nothing to be seen, just the empty corridor, but as I stand there, my forehead pressed to the cold wood, I hear a faint clunk and a hum.

I know that sound.

Whoever it was has given up. They're taking the lift back down to wherever it is they've come from.

CHAPTER TWENTY-SIX

When morning comes, and I open my bedroom door onto the vast living space, everything seems so normal it would be easy to think the happenings of the night before were a dream. Sunlight shines through the large arched windows filling the room with light, and through their panes, I can see vessels on the Thames: a rusty barge laden with yellow containers being pulled by a tugboat. A sleek Thames Clipper leaving a white wake behind it.

The fridge is filled with good things. Greek yoghurt and cheeses. Bacon. Local sausages. I don't have any of this, but instead, take a croissant from the packet I left on the side, warming it through and eating it with the Cornish butter and mixed berry conserve that also came with the delivery.

When I've finished, I let myself out of the apartment and make a start on the cleaning, starting at the first floor as I did the day before. When I reach the apartment where Mark's stepson is squatting, I stop and listen. I know what he said, but I can't just leave him. Without Joanna, how will he eat? How will he survive?

I've brought a bag of food with me: a leftover croissant, a large bag of vegetable crisps and some fruit. I'd planned on leaving them by the door for Nathan to find when he next ventured out, but I have to know if it was him who knocked on my door last night.

Bracing myself, I press the buzzer.

When the door remains shut, I lift my finger to the buzzer and press it again, but this time I don't release the pressure. I can hear it echoing in the empty room – a sound to send anyone mad.

Suddenly, the door flies open. Nathan storms out and whacks my hand away from the buzzer.

'What the fuck are you playing at?' He looks worse than he did when I last saw him, the skin of his cheekbones and around his nose red and flaky. His eyes watery.

I take a step back. 'Are you unwell?'

He glares at me but doesn't answer. Just scratches at his arms. 'What do you want?'

I hold up the bag of food. 'I brought you this. I thought you might be hungry.'

Snatching the bag from me, Nathan looks inside, then throws it back at me. 'I don't want your leftovers.'

I feel myself redden. 'I'm sorry. It's just that you said Joanna…'

'You're not Joanna.'

'I know I'm not, but Joanna's not here and I didn't know if you had any money for food. Look, why don't you let me come in rather than talking in the corridor?'

Nathan takes a step back, one hand either side of the doorframe, blocking my way. 'Get lost.'

'I just thought…'

'What? That you'd be a do-gooder. What is it? Does it make you feel better about getting your feet under Joanna's table? Fucking her husband.'

As if it has a mind of its own, my hand shoots out, striking Nathan's cheek. The slap, echoes in the empty corridor.

Nathan raises his hand to his cheek in shock, then levels his gaze at me.

'Fuck. You.' The words are drawn out, his index finger jabbing at my shoulder as he says them.

I want to apologise, but before I can, he disappears back inside, the slam of the door echoing down the corridor. I stare at it, thinking of all the things I should have asked him. What Mark and Tanya's relationship had really been like? How the Mark I've got to know in my few days here, differs from the one he used to live with? But even if he'd let me ask the questions, I doubt he would have answered them.

By the time I've finished the cleaning and got back to my own floor, it's nearly midday. It's as I push open the stairwell door that I see I'm not alone. Two people are standing outside my apartment, one with their finger to the buzzer. I stop, too scared to go any further, recognising their uniforms. It's the police constables who were here two days ago.

My heart jumps. Maybe they've found Joanna.

PC Rose sees me, but when I reach her, she's not smiling.

'Hello, Alice. You're still here then.' It's a statement rather than a question.

'Yes.'

'And Mark? Is he in? We tried his office number, and he wasn't there. He's not answering his mobile.'

'No. He's away… looking at some properties,' I add, as an afterthought.

The policewoman's eyes are probing. Searching my face. 'You don't sound too sure.'

'I am sure.' There's something about her manner that makes me flustered. Makes me feel as though I've done something wrong. 'It's definitely what he said.'

'Could we come in?'

'Yes,' I say. 'Yes, of course.'

Opening the door, I let them in. 'Would you like something? Tea? Coffee?'

'No.' PC Rose looks around her. 'Thank you. We were wondering, have you heard anything from Joanna?'

'Joanna?'

She gives me an odd look. 'Your friend? You reported her missing on Tuesday.'

'Yes, yes, of course. I'm sorry, I didn't sleep well last night. The foxes…' I tail off. 'No. We haven't heard anything.'

'I see.' She looks at her colleague. 'It's just that something has happened that I thought you, well, Joanna's husband, should know about. Just in case it's connected.'

We're all standing in the middle of the floor like extras in a play. I want to sit down, but the officers show no interest in moving to the settee. I have a sick feeling my legs might not hold me when I hear what they have to say.

Are they wondering why I'm still here? After they've left, will they discuss how odd it is that I'm still hanging around the apartment even though Joanna isn't back? I consider telling them the truth, that Mark has gone away, and I'm staying just in case Joanna comes home, but before I can, PC Rose speaks.

'I need you to know that what we've come to tell you is just a theory… a hunch. It might mean nothing at all.'

'What's happened?'

'A body has been washed up onto a small beach a few miles downriver. It hasn't been identified yet, but from the description you gave, we have reason to believe that it could be Mark's wife.'

My hands rise to my mouth in shock. 'Dear God.'

I think of the depth markers on the dock wall, the tide lapping at the steps of the Devil's Staircase. Did Joanna descend those steps? Can she really have wanted to die?

But the policewoman's words crush that theory. 'There's an injury to her head. It might have been caused by an accident, but we can't rule out the possibility of foul play.'

I pull out a stool from the island and climb on to it, not trusting my legs. 'Foul play?'

'Yes. I'm sorry, but it's something we have to look into. Of course, we might be wrong, and it might not even be Joanna, but we're going to need someone to make an identification.'

I stare at her wide-eyed. 'I can't do it.'

The thought of seeing Joanna's bloated body fills me with horror. Her lovely hair braided with weed. Silt engraving the creases of her skin.

'I haven't seen her for ten years,' I stammer. 'What if I'm wrong?'

'We wouldn't expect you to be the one to make the identification. It needs to be someone who's seen her recently. Mark, or maybe her parents. There are some distinguishing marks on the body that we've photographed and should be easily recognisable to someone who knows her well.'

She hasn't volunteered what the marks are. I try to think – is there something on my friend's flawless skin that would single her out? If there is, I can't remember it.

'We'll be doing DNA analysis, but the results can take up to seventy-two hours,' PC Rose continues. 'You'll understand that we want to make an identification as soon as possible.'

'What about her parents?' I stop, remembering they are in Dubai. With a lurch of my stomach, I also remember that they know nothing about Joanna's disappearance.

'We haven't been able to get hold of them either,' is all she says, and I decide not to say any more. If anything's happened to their daughter, it's better they hear it from Mark.

'Mark will be back later today,' I say. 'I'll get him to call you as soon as he gets home.'

PC Jameson scratches his cheek. 'You don't have a contact number for him, other than his mobile number?'

I shake my head. 'No, he didn't give me one.'

The two officers look at each other. 'I see. Well, when he comes home, please ask him to come into the station or give us a ring.'

'I will… of course.'

'And if anything happens, or you hear from Joanna, please let us know immediately. As I said, there's always a possibility the body we found might not be hers.'

I see them to the door, waiting until they've got into the lift before going back into the apartment. It's only when I stand at the window and watch them walk to their panda car that the enormity of what they've just told me sinks in. A wave of nausea floods through me, and I clutch my stomach, the other hand pressed against the glass, to stop me from falling.

'Oh God. Joanna.'

Suddenly, I have an overwhelming need to share what the police just told me with someone. Anyone.

In the past, it would have been Drew I confided in, but why would he care when he didn't even know Joanna? He'd be polite, would ask me questions, but I know that, after everything that's happened, he'd be desperate to get off the phone. Maybe he'd even tell his new girlfriend that I'd rung.

No, the only person who will understand the pain I'm feeling after hearing what the police told me, is Mark.

CHAPTER TWENTY-SEVEN

I'm wrong, though. There is someone else I can talk to.

Knowing I have to share the burden of what I've just been told or go mad, I let myself out of the apartment and take the stairs down to the fourth floor. Reaching Eloise's apartment, I press the buzzer once. Twice. When there's no answer, I raise my hand and bang with my fist on the door, the noise echoing in the corridor.

'Eloise, are you there?'

There's no reply. But why would there be? It's a Thursday and, chances are, she'll be at work. As I wait, I try to remember if she mentioned a job but can't. When was it I saw her? I count back in my head… it was a Monday, I'm sure of it. Three days ago. Can it really be? Despite having done little since arriving at New Tobacco Wharf, the time is flowing by as quickly as the Thames outside my window. Or, should I say, Joanna's window.

Pressing my ear to the door, I listen for sounds of Eloise's little dog, Pixie – a scrabbling at the door or her high-pitched yaps. There's nothing. That will be it; she'll be walking her. Maybe, at this very moment, she'll be following the path that runs alongside the river. Passing the abandoned cranes, the units to let… the weed-covered steps. It makes me think of Joanna, and I shiver.

Stepping away from the door, I glance at the arched window at the end of the corridor where, beyond the buildings, I can see patches of blue sky combed through with white cloud. The Wharf and Black Water Dock is so cut off from everything that the thought of the outside world is becoming strange. Remote.

With a sense of unease, I realise I haven't been outside the building in five days and the thought of being back in the real world is making me anxious. I have to get a grip – being cooped up in this warehouse isn't good for me. What I need is to get out.

Get some air.

Get back to normality.

In the empty corridor, I make a decision. I'll take my car and find somewhere that sells phone chargers. Anything to get me out. Checking I've got my car keys, I head back to the stairs. When Mark gets back later, I'll tell him I'm leaving. That it's time I was getting back home.

Home.

The word conjures up some faraway place, making me feel like Dorothy in the *Wizard of Oz*. Only in Black Water Dock there's no yellow brick road – just one made of tarmac covered in chippings, its weed-tangled verges studded with rubble and broken bottles.

Without warning, the terrible reality comes crashing in, making me grip the stair rail. How can I leave Mark when in a few hours he will discover Joanna is dead? Another griping pain hits, and I stop until it subsides. I can't think of it or I will fall apart. One step at a time. I'll get myself back in contact with the world, and then I will think how I can support Mark when he finds out the truth.

I've reached the ground floor, curiosity making me stop and look through the glass panels in the door. Through them is the lonely atrium. The expanse of marble floor. The fountain that never plays. On the reception desk, there's a large vase of tall, red and purple spikes of gladioli, and I wonder who they're meant to impress. Who will ever see their showy display?

Derek's door is closed, and I'm glad. Hopefully, he's out doing his maintenance, or whatever it is he's supposed to do. And, if he is, it means that when I get into my car, he won't be watching me. Wondering where I'm going. What I'm doing.

Leaving the ground floor, I take the last flight of stairs to the underground car park, but I don't push open the door. Instead, I stare through the glass, my skin prickling. The space inside is in total darkness.

My heart rate increases steadily until I remember the lights are on motion sensors. They won't activate until I open the doors, but once inside, the fluorescent strips will flood the empty parking bays with light, and everything will be fine.

Breathing in deeply, I press my shoulder to the door. It swings open and, to my relief, the lights come on immediately, illuminating the red brick vaulted archways with their heavy columns. In front of me where I left it is my car, the space next to it where Mark's had been now standing empty. Today, there are no other cars, just the red Mazda convertible I saw on the first day, parked further down the row. It doesn't look as though it's been moved since I arrived on Saturday and, as I look at it, I wonder if it might be Joanna's? Why didn't I think to ask Mark?

I walk over to it and peer through the darkened back windows, scared that there will be some trace of her. Something to confirm this car is hers. I want to think she's taken her car, driven somewhere to be on her own or maybe to stay with friends that Mark doesn't know. She doesn't know where I've been living, so she wouldn't have gone there.

But then I realise my stupidity. Even if it is Joanna's car, what would it prove? She could have taken a taxi somewhere. Or been picked up in someone else's car. It doesn't mean she walked to the river. It doesn't mean she never left. That she took her own life at those slippery steps.

Or slipped.

Or fell.

Or was pushed.

It doesn't mean she's dead.

The hot lump that's been in my throat since the police visited rises. Mustering all my willpower, I swallow it down, knowing I must stay calm. I have to, for Joanna's sake. For Mark's. For mine. I mustn't give up hope.

The car is empty – just the black leather seats and a dashboard and trim that look showroom-new. No empty crisp wrappers stuffed into the cup holders or crumbs on the passenger seat. Nothing to give away anything of the owner.

I stand for a moment, my hand caressing the shiny red bonnet. I don't want to believe it's Joanna they dragged off the silted river beach. Can't contemplate that she might be gone.

Slowly, I walk back to my own car, get in and turn on the engine, the sound echoing in the high-ceilinged space. Not letting myself cry, I drive between the empty parking spaces towards the solid metal roller door that will take me back out into the world. When I reach it, I rummage in my bag for the door remote and press the button.

I wait, but nothing happens.

Winding down my window, I reach my arm out and point the remote at the door, pressing the button again. Still there's nothing.

I look ahead of me, scanning the door surround for something that will manually raise it. A button. A lever. There's nothing though, just the smooth metal panel that's between me and the daylight. What's wrong with it? Why won't it open?

Unease builds inside me. I could leave the car and walk, but if I did, how long would it take me to get from Black Dock to civilisation? It didn't seem that far in the car, but on foot, I've no idea. It's not just the distance that's putting me off, it's the labyrinth of derelict buildings I'd have to walk through, their bricked-up entrances covered in graffiti. I'd have to navigate my way between the empty metal units and the abandoned cranes. And when I'd left them all behind, there would still be the wasteland to cross. Maybe it's better to wait until Mark comes home.

Reversing into a bay, I turn the car round and drive back to the space I came out of only a few minutes ago. Getting out, I walk to the door that leads to the stairs and push it with my hand.

It doesn't move.

At first, I think it's just stiff like it was on the day I arrived, but when I use more pressure and it still doesn't budge, a ball of fear forms in my stomach. Instead of pushing, this time I pull at the handle, my hand slick with sweat. Still it won't open. I shake the door once then again harder, knowing, even as I'm doing it, that it's futile. It's locked.

As I stand in the vaulted tomb, I force myself to think. There must be some kind of electrical fault that would explain why the metal garage door wouldn't raise. Why the door to the stairs have locked too. I grip the handle of the door tighter and look around me. If that's the case, then I'm trapped… the only way out is the lift.

I mustn't let my panic take control. Derek might be back by now. He will have seen there's a problem and will probably at this very moment be sorting it out. All I have to do is be patient. Wait until someone comes or force myself to take the lift. I look at the shiny silver door, trying to imagine what it would be like to step inside. It's years since I've done it, but just thinking about it makes my hands clammy. My heart rate increase. Could I even bring myself to step inside?

Taking a step back, I look at the camera in the corner of the car park and a terrible thought occurs to me. What if it's not a fault? What if it's Derek who's done this?

The only thing I'm certain of is that I can't stay down here, in this echoey brick space under the warehouse, with no windows. No light except for the artificial whiteness of the fluorescent tubes that run along the rows of empty spaces.

Knowing I have to face my fear, I step up to the lift, trying not to think of what it will be like to step inside. How I'll manage when the metal doors slide shut and it's just me and the four walls. I'm just about to press the button to summon it, when I see that the lights above the lift are already moving. I don't know what number it started at, but it's already at 2 and soon it will be here.

It must be Derek. As quickly as it arrived, my relief fades. I don't want to be alone in here with him, and the lift is the only way up to the warehouse. Backing away, I wonder if I can hide in my car. Pretend I'm not here. Only, he will know. He'll have seen me. There's nothing for it but to lock myself inside it. The lift is at 1. I spin round ready to run but, in my haste, I forget my weak ankle. It twists under me and the next thing I know, the hard, stone ground is coming up to meet me.

I drag myself backwards towards the nearest stone pillar, my eyes never leaving the lift door. My ankle is throbbing, but it's nothing compared to the pounding of my heart in my chest. Pressing my back against the pillar, I sit motionless, praying that when he comes out, he won't see me. Counting the seconds. Finally, the 1 changes to 0.

I hold my breath.

And that's when the lights go out.

CHAPTER TWENTY-EIGHT

At first, I think I'm in my bed at home, and then I realise that it's not a duvet that covers me but a cashmere pashmina in a pale dove grey. Under my hand I can feel something velvety. I run my finger over it. It's Mark's settee I'm lying on.

'Feeling better? I've put ice on your ankle.' Mark is standing over me. He lifts the shawl, and I feel now the coldness that's penetrating my foot. Bending down, he carefully moves the bag of peas that's pressed against it. 'It's still looking pretty swollen.'

I run my mind back, remembering the underground car park, the press of the cold stone pillar behind my back, my paralysing fear. Nothing more.

'What happened, Mark? How did I get back up here?'

'I carried you. You fainted.'

'Did I?'

'Yes. I came home to find the car park door wouldn't open and was coming down to see if I could work out what the problem was. I could hear your screams as the lift door was opening, but by the time I got to you, you were out cold. You frightened the life out of me. I didn't know what had happened and thought at first you'd been attacked.'

'I'm sorry.' I feel foolish now. 'The lights went out. The easiest way to describe it is claustrophobia… but it's more complex than that. What I'm really petrified of is being trapped in the dark. It makes me feel I'm going to die.'

Mark sits on the settee opposite me. 'That explains the other night then… when the shutters closed.'

'Yes, and it's why I won't go in the lift. The thought of the lights going out while I'm in there is terrifying.'

He nods. 'I wish you'd said.'

'I didn't want you to think me stupid.'

He leans forward, his elbows on his knees, and pinches the bridge of his nose. He looks tired, ill, but he's looking at me intently. 'And you care that much what I think?'

I don't know if I'm imagining it, but his words seem weighted with expectation. I'm confused. Unsure of what I think. Instead of answering, I let the question go and sit up, gingerly feeling my ankle. Hoping he won't see the telltale flush at my throat. As my fingers make contact with the swollen flesh, I give a yelp.

'Sore?'

'Yes, it's pretty tender.' I put my hands in my lap and tap a rhythm on my legs with my fingertips. Something's bothering me. 'When I was in the car park, Mark, I noticed there was another car there. A red Mazda. I just wondered… I was just thinking… is it Joanna's? Because if it is, why didn't you say anything to the police? Surely the fact that it's still in the car park tells us something.' I feel the colour leach from my skin. 'It means something happened to her here.'

Mark's voice is cool. 'You think Joanna's car in the car park is suspicious?'

I nod. 'Very, don't you?'

'And you think the fact that I didn't tell the police is suspicious too?'

I draw in a breath. 'I didn't say that.'

'Oh, yes, Alice. I think you did. The implication was clear. I'm covering something up… is that what you're saying? Because if it is, I want to know.'

It's as if the temperature in the room has dropped a degree or two and I shiver. 'No. That's not what I meant.'

But I know it is. It's what I was thinking when I looked into the dark interior of the car. Saw how clean it was. Mark remains where he is, but beneath his eye a nerve ticks rhythmically. I'm suddenly nervous.

'Maybe I should leave.'

The vertical lines between Mark's eyes deepen. 'When I've said what I have to say, you can make that decision. I'm sorry you think so little of me, but you don't need to worry. The Mazda isn't Joanna's. She sold her Merc a fortnight ago and hasn't managed to find another that she's happy with. Since she's been without a car, either I've been driving her, or she's called a taxi.'

I let out my breath. 'I see.'

'Yet you let your imagination run wild, didn't you? Do you have reason to doubt the people who are good to you? Is it that ex-fiancé of yours who's made you this way?'

'I'm sorry.' I'm rigid with embarrassment. 'It's just that I'm so worried about her, I can't think straight.'

Mark's face softens. 'I forgive you then.'

'Thank you. But if the Mazda isn't Joanna's, who *does* it belong to?'

He points to the floorboards. 'It belongs to Eloise. In any case, I told the police about the car situation when they came round the first time.'

Did he? I don't remember. But I can't worry about it now for the mention of the police has caused my chest to still. It's as though I've forgotten how to breathe. 'Oh God, Mark. How could I forget? Something awful has happened.' Mark doesn't say anything, and I think he hasn't heard. 'Mark. This is important. The police were here earlier.'

His head snaps up. 'The police? Again? What did they want?'

'They've found a body. It was washed up further along the river.' My stomach twists at the thought of what I'm going to say next. 'They want you to make an identification.'

Mark stiffens, the colour draining from his face. 'Why me?'

'Because they think it could be Joanna. I'm so sorry, Mark. You should ring them now and let them know you're back. That you'll go straight away.'

He doesn't move. Just sits, staring at the coffee table.

'Mark?'

'Yes. Yes. Of course. I'm just shocked, that's all. Why do they think it's Joanna?'

I try to remember what they said. 'She fits the description. Is it possible it could be her?'

He doesn't meet my eyes. 'God, I hope not.'

He sounds helpless and my heart goes out to him, but then I remember his stepson. The things he said. Should I tell Mark about his visit? Before I can, his hand slams down on the table, making me jump.

'Why couldn't she have just been satisfied?'

What does that mean? I don't like him like this. He looks different. Edgy. As though someone has rubbed the polish off him. I want to ask what he means, but I'm afraid. Turning to face him, I try to put my foot on the floor, but the pain makes me raise it again.

'Here let me.'

Coming round to where I'm sitting, he takes one of the cushions and positions it on the coffee table. As he gently places my foot onto it, I'm aware of the warmth of his hands. I look at his long slim fingers and, for one ridiculous moment, I imagine the feel of them moving to my ankle. To my calf. My thigh. Hot guilt rises, and I pull my foot away.

'Sorry, did I hurt you?' He sits next to me, frowning, his nearness throwing my thoughts into confusion. 'Looks like you won't be going anywhere for a while.'

'I'm fine. Please go to the police, Mark. It's better we know the worst. The not knowing is just as bad.'

He stares at me. 'How can it be just as bad? My wife might be lying on a mortuary slab dead?'

'I know. I'm sorry. I didn't mean it to come out like that.'

Mark gets out his phone and the card that he was given the day the police first visited. He looks up at me, then back down at my swollen ankle. 'Will you be all right here on your own after what happened earlier?'

As I remember the darkness and the utter certainty I was going to die, the fear hits me again. 'Why didn't the doors open, Mark? What went wrong?'

'I'm sure it's nothing to worry about, but I'll find out when I get back. It was probably just an electrical fault. Derek says everything's working again and will probably have a good idea of what happened by now. I can send him up to talk to you about it if you're worried.'

'No.'

It's said too quickly, and Mark frowns. 'Later then, when I'm back. You really don't have any reason to dislike him, Alice. He came to us with a very good reference.'

I don't say anything. All I know is I don't want Derek in this room with me.

Mark makes the call to the police and as he puts the mobile back into his pocket, I consider asking him to leave it with me before deciding not to. It wouldn't be fair to leave him without a phone while he's driving.

'Here, you'll want something to do.' Mark holds out the TV controller to me. 'I'm not one for watching TV myself, but you might like to. Historical dramas were Joanna's favourite… She used to watch them with Nathan when he was—'

He stops, and his face hardens.

The mention of his stepson was accidental, I'm sure. I take my chance. 'Nathan?'

Mark looks away, and I can tell he's wrestling with himself. Deciding whether or not to tell me.

'Mark? Who are you talking about?'

He keeps his back to me. 'Nathan is my late wife's son. We… I… had a lot of problems with him.'

I keep my face neutral. 'I'm sorry. That must have been difficult.'

'He was only a teenager when his mum died. It affected him badly. Problems with drugs. Hanging out with the wrong people – you know the sort of thing. He had a breakdown and was hospitalised for a while. When he came out, he chose to live with his grandmother rather than me. We would have liked him to come and live with us here, but he made it impossible.'

I shift my position on the settee to make my leg more comfortable. 'In what way?'

'He became obsessed with Joanna. I thought it was because she was a mother substitute but…' He shakes his head. 'It was more than that. I found photos… of her. Ones he must have taken when she wasn't aware. Lots of them. When I confronted him about them, he became upset. Angry. He packed his things and left. I haven't seen him since.'

I stare at him. The story is different to the one Nathan told me. 'Mark, I—'

He cuts me off. 'Look I don't want sympathy. I need to get to the police station.' Getting up, he takes his coat and puts it on. 'Call me if you need me.'

I start to tell him that I can hardly do that without a phone, but he's already out the door, raising a hand to me in a gesture of farewell before slamming it closed behind him. For a few seconds, I watch the door, hoping he might come back again, that he'll have forgotten something, but he doesn't, and I'm left alone with no option but to sit with my foot up as I did after I got back from Corfu.

I look around me, frustrated. With all that's happened, I don't feel like watching television. I'd never be able to concentrate. What did Mark mean when he said that Joanna should have been satisfied? Had he been talking about the apartment? Their life? The place is like a home from a magazine, but there's not a lot to do here, and I can imagine Joanna getting restless.

Joanna.

My stomach clenches. What is Mark going to find when he reaches the police station? I lie back on the cushions and close my eyes, overcome by a great weariness as the stress of the last few hours catches up with me. It's not long before I fall asleep.

I wake to the sound of car keys being thrown onto the kitchen island. Mark's back. Pushing myself up, I twist round on the settee and try to guess from his body language what's happened. As soon as I see his face, I know it's not good.

'You've got to tell me, Mark. Was it Joanna?'

He comes towards me, his face drawn, his eyes dead-looking. He doesn't answer but goes to the wooden doors between the windows and opens them, letting in the cool night. Leaning his arms on the railing, he stares into the distance.

'No. It wasn't Joanna.'

'Thank God.' I close my eyes, releasing the breath I've been holding.

But Mark doesn't look glad. Instead, he looks out at the dark river, his chin cupped in his hand, his fingers pressing the hollows of his cheeks. He looks wretched. 'They showed me items of the woman's clothing. Her coat. Her blouse. At first, I thought it could be her, but then they showed me something else and I knew that it wasn't.'

His lean body hunches over the railing. He looks older. Broken.

'Mark?'

When he doesn't answer, I press him. 'It's good news though, isn't it? It means Joanna's okay. She might come home. We mustn't give up hope.'

Slowly, he turns his head, acknowledging me at last.

'Later I'm going to call the police and tell them I've heard from her. That she contacted me and is fine.' His words are flat. Unemotional. 'I'll say it's all been a misunderstanding.'

My heart leaps. 'My God! Joanna's been in touch? Why didn't you say?'

He looks at me as though I'm stupid. 'Why do you think, Alice?'

'I've no idea.' My head is reeling with the unexpected news. 'She's all right. That's all that matters.'

'I didn't say that.' He locks eyes with me as if by force of will he can get me to understand, rather than having to tell me. 'It's simply what I'm going to say to them.'

At last, the penny drops. 'Please don't tell me you're going to lie to them. For Christ's sake, Mark, why?'

Mark looks at me, then sighs heavily. 'Because of this.'

Taking his wallet from his pocket, he opens it and from where he keeps his bank notes, pulls out a folded piece of paper. He places it on the settee next to me. I look at it but don't touch it. Too afraid of what it might say.

'Just tell me.'

Mark leaves the window. He comes over to me and sinks back onto the other settee, his hands over his eyes.

'Someone has got her, Alice. And they're asking me for money.'

CHAPTER TWENTY-NINE
Joanna

It was dark. Darker than anything I'd ever experienced before… and so cold. I lay on my side on the thin mattress, feeling the scratch of the sacking that covered me, the concrete floor beneath making my shoulder ache.

I tried to move, but I was so drowsy it was as though my muscles and nerves had a life of their own and I fell back down again. My head hurt, my wrists too. Lifting my hand, I felt the skin. It was tender and sore, as though at some time my wrists had been bound. I lay still, my heart beating a tattoo in my chest. Trying to make sense of everything.

I remembered walking along the quayside, stopping only when I reached the Devil's Staircase. For a few minutes, I'd looked at the stone steps lapped by the brown water, wondering if I had the nerve to walk down them. If I had the courage to let the river take me to a place where I could be at peace. I knew I didn't, though; I wasn't that brave.

It was as I stood staring out at the sluggish water, that I'd thought I'd heard my name being called. Maybe it was my imagination or just the wind playing tricks on me. Blowing through the broken windows of the empty warehouses. Rattling the doors on their hinges.

I'd turned, my foot slipping on the slimy stone, the blue sky tipping and filling my sight as I fell backwards. I remembered nothing more and when later I came to, it was as if I'd awoken in hell.

'Hello?' The voice that came out wasn't like my own. I was used to sounding confident. In control. This was the voice of someone weak.

The only sound was a scratching somewhere behind me. Rats? I pressed my face into the sacking.

'Please. Is anyone there?'

My words echoed. What was this place? Lying very still, trying not to give in to the fear that was enveloping me, I forced my brain to make sense of things. There had to be a reason why I was here. Reaching out my arm, I dragged my hand across the floor, feeling nothing but the rough concrete beneath my fingertips. I tried again to sit up, this time taking it slowly. Managing to get onto all fours, I crawled forward, my hand outstretched, stopping only when my fingers made contact with a wall. Cold overlapping metal sheets that rang dully when I slapped the flat of my hand against them. Where was I?

I banged again, my fingers bunched into fists, the sound echoing in the empty space, like the tolling of a bell. The hollow sound only accentuated how alone I was. Not caring that my knuckles were smarting, I carried on, unaware that they were sticky with blood. I didn't care about the pain. I just needed someone to hear me.

It was exhaustion, not pain, which eventually made me stop. My hair was stuck to my face, my breathing coming in gasps. Why didn't anyone come? I sat with my back against the wall, my knees pulled to my chest, the blackness pushing in.

I'd never felt so alone. I wasn't used to it. All my life I'd had someone by my side who needed me. Where were they now?

In the pitch darkness my husband's face came to me, and I reached out my hand as if to touch it, remembering the first time I saw him. How my parents had presented him at their work gala dinner as though offering me a prize. I saw him as I did then – a bit older than I was used to, tall and slim, his muscles smooth and defined beneath his white dinner shirt. Understated, not showy, like the men I'd met who went to the gym to impress rather than keep fit.

Poor Mark. Unaware he was just a pawn in my parents' chess game. I remember the way his eyes lingered a little longer than they should on mine. The smile that changed his face, making me wonder what it might be like to kiss him.

Knowing the vision wasn't real, I pulled my hand back and leant my head against the wall, wincing as the metal ridges made contact with the tender back of my skull. Gingerly, I touched it. A lump was forming, but thankfully the skin didn't appear to be broken. I wanted Mark now. Where was he? Why didn't he come for me?

The darkness was like a living thing. Images moving out of the black then receding. Taunting me, torturing me, until I wondered if the blow to my head had made me delirious.

As soon as Mark's face began to fade, it was replaced by my mother's. I pressed my fists to my eyes, knowing that if I lowered my hands, she'd be watching me, just as she had at that dinner. My father's face stared out of the blackness too – his lips moving, telling me what a godsend Mark had been. How the company would never have survived had it not been for his input. His great ideas for expansion.

I tried to push their images away. Hating them. But, in the vast, lonely confines of my lockup, the only things I had to keep me company were my memories. They played before me like a film: the starter of lobster bisque the waiter served us; how comfortable Mark seemed and the way he sparred off my father, not letting him get away with his bullshit. Every now and again, he'd look over at me and smile. It made me feel attractive – appreciated in a way I hadn't for a long time. Alice had made me feel that way too. But Mark had been my parents' choice not mine. Why had I been so weak?

While I was trying to work out the answer, I thought I heard a vehicle outside. Maybe someone had found out where I was. Mark. The police. Forcing my wobbly legs to stand, I beat at the wall.

'I'm here. I'm in here!' I screamed.

By the time I gave up, exhausted, my hands throbbing out the rhythm I'd just beaten on the metal sides, there was no longer any sound. Either they'd got out of the vehicle or driven away.

Minutes passed, but there was still nothing.

Sinking my head into my hands, I cried as I hadn't cried since Alice turned her back on me.

CHAPTER THIRTY

Alice

'What do you mean got her. Who? Where?'

'Jesus, Alice. Stop asking questions. How would I know where? It's not as if they're going to tell me, is it?'

My mind's racing. 'You've got to say something to the police. You must. You can't lie to them now and tell them we've heard from her when we haven't.'

'Don't you see I have to? If they think she's still missing, they'll come back. Search the empty apartments. Talk to people.'

I'm struggling to understand. 'But that's good, isn't it?'

'Christ, don't you get it at all?' His tone is sharp. Impatient. 'They'll kill her if the police are involved.' He jabs at the paper. 'You just have to read what they say they'll do. They're sick.'

He crouches down in front of me. Sinks his head into his hands. 'They want money. In cash. I've been doing everything I can to get my hands on it by the deadline: emptied my bank accounts, clawed back money from people who owe me. Jesus Christ, I even asked Gary for a loan, which was fucking hard when I couldn't say what it was for. He suspects something. I know he does. Keeps asking why she's not answering her phone, and I have to stall him. Promise I'll get her to ring later.'

I pick up the letter and read it quickly, my insides churning when I reach the last paragraph where they say what they'll do to her if Mark doesn't find the money. I drop it onto the floor and press my hand to my stomach.

'They can't mean it.'

Mark looks up at me, his eyes red. 'Are you willing to take that risk?'

It's hard to speak, the words sticking in my throat. 'How long have you known? When did you get this?'

'A few days ago. It was why I went away yesterday. To try to get the money.'

'Where is it?'

Mark looks at the door of the bedroom he shares with Joanna. 'It's in a holdall under the bed.'

I look at his face. See written there the strain. The worry. 'You've got to tell me. When is the deadline, Mark?'

'It's tonight at ten.'

'Tonight?'

Getting up, Mark starts to pace, his hands balled into fists. 'There's an abandoned chapel further along the dock, and I'm to leave the holdall in there.'

When he walks back my way, I grab his hand. 'Don't do it, Mark. Tell the police. It's too dangerous to do this on your own.'

He looks down at our joined hands, my fingers clutching at his. 'I'm not on my own though, Alice.'

'What do you mean?'

'Well, there's you.'

'Me?'

'Yes.' Mark kneels on the floor next to where I'm sitting, and although it's an inappropriate time to be thinking it, I can't help wondering if this was where he proposed to Joanna.

I force myself to ignore the bitter taste of jealousy that's formed at the back of my throat. 'How do you mean?'

'I knew you were different the day you first set foot in here. Knew you were trustworthy... call it a gut feeling. I *can* trust you, can't I, Alice? I have to.'

'Yes, but lying to the police again? This isn't a game, Mark.'

'Of course, it's not a bloody game. My wife is in danger, and you imagine I'm treating it like a game of chess?' He shuts his eyes and tips his head back. 'Is that really what you think? What you really, truly believe?'

'No, of course not. It's just…' I turn my body round, so I'm sitting rather than lying, wincing when my foot touches the floor. 'Do you really think this is the right thing to do?'

Mark pushes himself up from the floor. 'There is no other way. Not if we want to keep Joanna safe from harm.'

'But who do you think has her? Why Joanna?'

'It's obvious, isn't it? To anyone on the outside, I must look the perfect target. Successful property developer, smart car, apartment in the next Covent Garden of Dockland.' He mimes quote marks in the air, bitterness creeping into his voice. 'Only they've got it wrong, haven't they? I'm worth fuck all! Lost everything when the bubble burst. The two of us living off Joanna's parents. It's humiliating.'

'I'm sorry.'

'Why are you sorry, Alice? It's not your problem.'

'No, but I know what it's like to have nothing. When I was growing up, my mum had to hold down three jobs just to make sure we ate properly and had a school uniform that wouldn't embarrass us.'

'What about your father?'

I think of the series of menial jobs he won and lost. Nightclub bouncer. Garage cashier. Building labourer. Jobs he'd give up when he got bored. 'He was a loser. It was Mum who held it all together.'

My eyes fill with tears at the thought of her. 'When she died, I lost the person who meant the most to me.'

Apart from Joanna.

I picture her at the funeral, even though I hadn't invited her. Remember how she'd sat with her arm around my shoulders, a packet of tissues in her hand for when they were needed. I'd told myself it was better than having no one.

Don't cry, Alice. I'm here for you.

And for a while, I'd almost forgotten what she'd done. What she'd made me do. It was only when the grief at losing my mother started to lessen, that I let myself remember.

Quickly, I push the thought away. That was a long time ago, and this isn't about me now. It's about Joanna. This time it's she who needs me, just as I needed her all those years ago.

Mark leans over me and places a hand either side of my arms. 'You must tell me, Alice. Are you going to tell the police what I've just told you?'

I can't think clearly. Can no longer feel the breeze from the river through the heavy doors. Instead, the air in the room now seems thick. Suffocating.

I try to stop my thoughts from racing out of control. 'What if they don't let her go? What if it's just a trick and they ask for more money? You know that could happen… I've read about it often enough.'

Mark releases me, his hands dropping to his sides. 'If that happens, then we'll go to the police, but it's a chance I'm willing to take. Are you?'

I think of Joanna, the way she'd turned around in her chair, her hand shooting up. *I'd like to look after her, Mrs Talbot.* My relief that someone had wanted to be my friend, despite the fact that I didn't fit in.

'I suppose so, but if anything goes wrong…'

'It won't, and, if it does, we'll tell them, I promise.' He looks at his expensive watch. 'Jesus, the time. It's nearly five.'

'We need to stay calm, Mark. We've hours yet.'

'No. We haven't. I didn't manage to get all the money. I'm about ten thousand short. I've got to go out again. Pull in some favours.'

Going across to the island, he picks up his keys. 'If the police get in touch, say nothing. Tell them I haven't been home.'

'But why would they get in touch? The girl they found in the river wasn't Joanna. You're going to tell them she's no longer missing.'

Mark puts his suit jacket over his shoulder, holding it with one finger. 'That's true but...' He pauses, and I steel myself for what he's going to say. No revelations at this moment are likely to be good.

'What is it?'

'The girl. The one who drowned. I know her.'

The blood drains from my face. 'Who is she?'

He looks at me intently as though waiting to see my expression. 'It's Eloise.'

CHAPTER THIRTY-ONE

Joanna

I had no way of knowing if it was day or night. No way to tell how long I'd been there. I'd pushed my mattress against the wall so that I wouldn't lose it in the cavernous space. Most of the time I sat or lay, but when I felt my legs start to cramp, I'd stand and find the wall, pressing my hands against its cold surface. Working my way to the far corner, then back again.

I'd discovered that there was a door at the far end of the unit, had felt the frame with the tips of my fingers and run my hand down the ridge where the door slid shut. Desperately trying to open it before realising that with no handle on the inside, nothing to grip, it was impossible. Eventually, I'd given up trying, screaming into the darkness in frustration.

In time, my eyes had started to adjust to the darkness, and I'd begun to make out shapes. Crates and boxes that offered up objects that, without full sight, I had no hope of recognising.

My empty stomach rumbled. It must have been hours since I last ate – a small tray of sushi from M&S that I'd bought for my lunch along with food for the weekend. All the things I knew Alice would like: salmon, wild rice, nectarines and Greek yogurt. The type of food we used to eat at the small kitchen table in the house we rented when we were at uni. Food we wouldn't have been able to afford had it not been for the money my father put into my bank each month. Guilt money for being an awful dad.

Alice. I pictured her car pulling up outside the wharf, her eyes widening as she took in the impressive brick building. I hugged the thought to me. It would keep me going until they let me go. But who was it that was keeping me here? I looked in the direction of the door, my heart pounding. What did they want with me?

And where were *you*, Mark? Weren't you worried what had happened to your bride?

I twisted the wedding band on my finger, still finding it hard to believe the two of us were actually married, that I didn't insist we wait. I would have been happy to have stayed living together, but I'd given in. Not to my parents – oh no, they'd wanted a big wedding: marquee, a band, a parade of bridesmaids my dad could ogle at. The works. No, it was Mark who'd wanted us to just get on and do it, saying it would be more romantic just the two of us. No fuss. No charade.

In the end, we never told my parents what we were doing, just skulked away like naughty schoolchildren. Me high on adrenaline, Mark high on the cocaine he'd snorted before the ceremony. When I said *I do,* the only ones to hear my words, apart from Mark, were the registrar and two witnesses from the office next door.

But looking back wasn't going to help me.

Was Mark at this very moment looking for me, criss-crossing the passageways between the derelict buildings, pulling open the rotting doors and staring into the spaces filled with car tyres and fallen masonry. Or would he have walked further still? Climbed the fence into the new development – the one that looked like ships washed up on a sea of rubble. Calling my name.

Jez wouldn't have done that. He wouldn't have cared enough. But why was I thinking about him anyway? Jez was ancient history, and it wasn't as if I'd liked him that much anyway. A tear slid down my cheek, betraying me, and I wiped it away with my sleeve. This was what being locked in that echoing metal building did to you; it made time lose all meaning.

A terrible thought came to me then. It was possible that Mark hadn't started worrying yet. After all, it wasn't unusual for me to take off for a couple of days when Mark's attention became smothering or when I needed space and time away from his constant questioning. He'd promise, when I returned, that things would be different. That he'd back off a bit and let me live my life. They were promises he could never keep though, and, after a few days, it would start all over again. Where had I been? What had I been doing? Who had I seen?

A metallic sound brought me back to the present. A scraping over by the door. It was followed by a shaft of sunlight that sliced through the dark, causing my eyes to close. I scrambled to my feet. Blindly stumbling forward.

'Who are you? What do you want?'

But there was no answering voice. Forcing my eyes to open, all I could see was a dark shape against the bright background. The sound of something being pushed across the floor.

'Wait!'

I tried to run towards the light, but it was as if my legs didn't belong to me. As quickly as it arrived, the strip of light started to narrow again until, with a clang, it was gone.

'Don't leave me. Please…'

I pounded on the door, but no one came. And then I heard the thrum of a car engine. Listened, with tears streaming down my face, as it got fainter and fainter. After the few seconds of light, the velvet darkness was heavy. Choking.

Panic made my breathing more rapid, intensified my fight or flight response, but there was nowhere to go. Nowhere to escape the black. I'd made it to the door, and it was then my foot made contact with something. Bending down, I touched it. It was a plastic tray with some food on it. I shoved it away, not caring that I was hungry, then slid to the floor, my back against the panelled metal wall.

I needed to think. I needed a plan.

CHAPTER THIRTY-TWO
Alice

'Eloise?' I press my fingertips to my temples. 'Are you sure?'

'Yes, I'm certain. At the police station, as well as showing me the clothes, they showed me photographs they'd taken of a tattoo on the woman's wrist. It was the Chinese symbol for friendship. At first, I thought it was Joanna's as she has one just like it, but when I looked closer, I realised it wasn't hers. My wife's was smaller; she'd had it done first, but Eloise had got hers done at a different tattoo parlour.'

I'm not sure I can take any more. 'God, that's awful. Poor woman.'

I think of Eloise. Her friendliness the day I went to see her even though I could have been anyone. Her concern for Joanna. I can't believe she's gone.

'Yes, it's a tragedy.' He lowers his eyes momentarily. 'Look, I need to go.'

'You can't. Not yet.' I grab his sleeve. 'I have to know what's happening here.'

'Eloise was…' He looks away as though trying to think of the correct word. 'Thin-skinned.'

'Thin-skinned? What's that supposed to mean?'

'Oversensitive. Took things to heart.' He wrinkles his nose in distaste as he says it. 'She was a car crash waiting to happen. Knew it as soon as she moved in.'

I'm shocked at the harsh way he's said this. The lack of empathy. I remember what the police told me. A blow to the head. Possible foul play. Even if she was sensitive, she was vulnerable living all alone in this place. She'd been hurt. She must have been scared.

Mark drops his jacket onto the back of the settee, his tall frame casting a shadow across my body. 'It's not her we should be worrying about.'

A woman's dead and he's telling me not to worry? Fresh uncertainty nudges in, and I fight to keep my voice steady. 'Do they know what happened? They said she had a head injury.'

Mark shifts his weight, his shadow moving off me. 'They're not sure yet, but the most likely explanation is she slipped and hit her head on the dock wall as she fell into the water.'

'What did the police say when you told them who it was?'

His tone is defensive. 'I didn't.'

I look at him aghast. 'You said nothing?'

Mark leans in close and takes my face between his hands. 'Think about it, Alice. They'd be over this place like a rash and we can't afford for that to happen, not with Joanna in danger.'

I think of Eloise with her shiny black hair. Her thin frame. Her strange haunting beauty. 'But what about Eloise? Won't there be someone who'll miss her? Friends? Family?'

'I doubt it. She never mentioned family and, as far as I know, Joanna was her only friend.'

'But don't you think it's odd, Mark? First Joanna goes missing and now this. Both women who lived in Tobacco Wharf. Women who were friends, who spent time together.'

As I speak, an unsettling thought enters my head. I'm now the only woman living here.

Mark straightens up, his tall body framed by the huge arched window that throws cubes of sunlight across the wooden floor. Their grill-like pattern isn't comforting. His shoulders are rigid. 'You've heard of the word coincidence?'

His tone implies it's not a question he expects to be answered, and reddening under the intensity of his gaze, I search for something else to say that will dispel my fears. 'How well did you know her? Eloise, I mean.'

My tone is light. Frivolous. As though we're discussing the weather rather than a woman who has lost her life.

He shrugs. 'Not well. She was Joanna's friend, not mine. She said that from the day she met her, they had an instant connection. In fact, they were like this.' He crosses the first two fingers of his right hand. 'That's why they got those stupid tattoos. You'd think they were teenagers the way they acted together. Eloise would often be here when I came home from work, the two of them drinking wine, laughing. They'd stop as soon as they heard my key in the door, of course, and Eloise would always leave soon after, as though I'd spoiled the party. Then, one day, she just stopped coming.'

'Did Joanna ever say why?'

'No. Knowing my wife, she probably got bored of her, and to be honest, I didn't care. If truth be told, I found the friendship odd. Too intense. They even swapped keys in case one of them was out when the other called round. It was so they could wait until they got back. I was never comfortable with that, but I suppose it was useful for when Eloise was away, and Joanna fed the dog.'

I look at Mark in horror. 'Oh my God. The dog… Pixie. She'll be in the apartment alone. We'll have to go and get her. She'll be starving.'

'Jesus, I forgot the dog.' Panic is written across his face. 'Look, Alice. I don't have time for this. I've got to get the rest of the money. If I give you the key, could you go down and get her, do you think?'

I stare at him. 'How can I do that, Mark? Look at me!'

Mark looks at my foot. 'I'm sorry that was stupid of me. It's just that I can't think straight. Joanna…' He looks desperate. Anguished.

'It's all right. I'll see if I can walk. Help me up.'

Mark slides his arm around me, taking my weight. With difficulty, I stand.

'How does that feel?'

'Let me try on my own.'

I put my foot to the floor, testing it. If I don't put too much weight on it, I can walk, just about. Enough for me to get to Eloise's apartment anyway. 'It hurts but I'll manage. You go.'

His voice is filled with relief. 'Thank you.'

There's a large bunch of keys hanging from a hook on the wall. Mark grabs it and works one of the keys off the ring. He hands it to me. 'Here you are. I can't thank you enough, Alice. I'll help you to the lift, then I must hurry.'

I look at him in horror. 'I can't. I told you, especially after what happened in the car park.'

'Even if I ride down with you?'

'Look, just go. You're wasting time. I'll be fine.'

Mark looks at his watch. 'Okay but take it slowly.' He holds out his arm for me to take. 'I'll help you to the stairs. God, I hope that poor dog's okay.'

Opening the apartment door, he helps me through, and we walk slowly down the long corridor, Mark's arm around me. At the door to the stairs, I stop. 'I'll be all right from here. I'll go down on my bottom if I have to.'

I give a half-hearted laugh, but Mark's face remains serious. 'Are you sure you'll manage? We don't want any more accidents.'

'I'll be fine.'

'Then I'll go. I'll find the rest of the money, give them what they want and then we can get back to normal.' He looks helpless, standing there, in his work suit. Like a lost boy.

'All right.'

But what *is* normal? It's a long time since anything has felt even remotely that way.

'Try not to worry.' Mark holds open the door and waits until I'm through before letting it swing closed behind me.

I stand alone at the top of the stairs, looking over the banister at the winding flights below. Wondering if I'll make it all the way down.

But more than that, I'm wondering what I'm going to find when I open Eloise's door.

CHAPTER THIRTY-THREE

Joanna

Another day had passed. Well, I thought it was another day. The only way I could judge was by the opening and closing of the door. The slide of the tray across the floor. It made me think of Nathan and the food I used to bring him, knowing that without me his life could slide back out of control.

I remembered how his eyes would light up in his pale face whenever he opened the door to me, grateful for my help. Thankful that he didn't have to ask his father for anything. Not that he would have received any help. Mark well and truly washed his hands of him a long time ago. Happy to take on his wife's money after she died but not her son. Poor kid. What would he do without me? He'd be worrying. Wondering why I'd stopped coming to the empty apartment where he'd made his camp. His loss maybe rekindling his addiction.

From his sleeping bag on the floor of the squat, possibly the only squat with a circular bath and a jacuzzi, he might well have been considering telling Mark everything. About our meetings. How I'd kept him off the streets. I hoped he would, as with two of them looking, there'd be more chance of me being found.

There was something about Nathan that reminded me of Jez. He was about the same age Jez was back in the days when we were together. The way he held his body was the same too – limbs permanently tensed as though waiting for a chance to escape. I hadn't known then it was me Jez wanted to escape from. When he did, he'd left me with a heart torn in two. Left me for Alice.

Ever since the day we'd met in the classroom of St Joseph's, she'd been by my side. The friend I'd always craved. I know the other girls were wary of me, thought me stuck up, but Alice was different... my soulmate. She'd laugh at my jokes and help put the arguments with my parents into perspective. We'd joke that we were sisters, although the lives we'd been born into couldn't have been more different. Wear our hair in the same way. Buy the same tops. And when she came to stay at my house in the holidays, she helped to make life bearable.

I wasn't to know that she would change. How once we'd gone to university, she'd start to put herself first. Lie to me about why she couldn't go out with me in the evenings, saying she was studying in the library. When I'd found out it was because she was seeing Jez, I'd felt as if the rug had been pulled out from under my feet. It had taken me a long time to trust her again.

I forced my mind back to the present. The past was the past and what I needed now was to find a way out of this place. Something told me I wasn't being kept far from home. It could have been the dank smell of the river that came in when the door opened or the cry of the seagulls. More likely, it was the absence of cars and the sound of human life.

Each time the door opened, I'd try to catch a glimpse of my captor, but I never could. The sudden light entering my widened pupils forced them to contract. My eyelids to snap shut. Last night, when the door slid open, I'd pleaded with them to let me go, but my words fell on deaf ears. Why wouldn't they speak? I didn't care what they said. I just wanted to hear a human voice. Anyone's... even theirs.

Something to make me know I was still alive. That I wasn't going mad in that darkness.

CHAPTER THIRTY-FOUR

Alice

After what seems an age, I reach the floor below. Half hopping, I make my way down the corridor to Eloise's apartment. As I reach the door, I listen. Desperate to hear Pixie's high-pitched barks.

There's nothing.

Thrusting the key in the lock, I go inside. 'Pixie?'

The bright, homely apartment is silent. There's no sign of the little dog. I hobble inside, past the red settees with their colourful throws and cushions that I'd seen through the door the day I'd met Eloise, and start to search. The living area first and then the kitchen where I find a blue rubber mat with a faint ring showing where her water bowl would have been. It's not there and there's no sign of a food bowl either, though there's an empty dog food can on the counter. Picking it up, I inspect it. What clings to the sides is dried and crusty.

'Where are you, Pixie?'

Through Eloise's apartment window the sky is leaden grey, rain dulling the outlines of the buildings on the opposite side of the river. From where I'm standing, I can see the ugly metal frame of a harbour crane, its chain swinging in the wind, the cab almost level with the window. At least from the living area of Joanna's apartment, I have a clear view of the river. I haven't seen the wooden gallows Mark told me about on my first morning at Black Water

Dock, but I don't need to: the arm of the crane, with its heavy chain, is reminder enough.

I look around the living area, picking up cushions and putting them down again, lifting coloured throws and moving magazines, hoping to find something that will give a clue as to what happened. A note maybe or the signs of a struggle. There's nothing. No clues and no dog.

It feels wrong to go into Eloise's bedroom, but I have to be sure Pixie isn't hiding in there. Pushing down the handle, I find it's locked, but at least it means the dog isn't in there. The door to the second bedroom isn't locked though and opens to a bright and colourful space. The bare bricks have been painted sunshine yellow, and instead of the wooden boards I step onto each morning, the floor is covered in a carpet the colour of the ocean. Everything is clean and tidy, and I shut the door again.

Knowing it's pointless to worry about a dog that isn't there, I'm about to leave the apartment when something in the kitchen catches my eye. Something I didn't see before. I stop still, my blood running cold. There's a photograph stuck to the shiny silver fridge with a magnet. I'm too far away to see it properly, but close enough for my instincts to know something isn't right. For my stomach to tighten.

Afraid of what I'll find but needing to be sure, I walk around to the other side of the kitchen island. I lift my hand to the photograph, then drop it again. It's as I feared – it's not a picture of Eloise or even of Pixie. It's the one of me and Joanna outside the art room, our arms looped around each other's shoulders. The one from Mark's apartment. How did it get here? I hadn't even noticed it was missing.

Why is it here? It's not as if I even know Eloise. I only met her once.

There's a sound behind me and I spin round, but it's only the rain battering at the window. Apart from me, the room is empty.

A feeling of unease insinuates itself under my skin. I want to be out of here. Out of the dead woman's apartment. Pulling the photograph from the magnet that holds it, I stuff it in my pocket and hurry back out into the corridor, closing the door behind me. Then, using the rough brick wall to steady myself, I limp along the corridor and shoulder open the door to the stairwell. Once I'm through, I look up, seeing the stairs wind away from me.

My heart sinks.

Reaching for the bannister and putting as little weight as I can on my bad foot, I manage to hop onto the first step. I manage the second too. But however careful I am, the pressure on my ankle as it bears my weight, sends white-hot shooting pains up my leg. It takes just four more steps for me to realise I'm never going to make it back up two flights. Sweat beads my forehead, and I wipe it with my arm. What am I going to do? I curse myself for not having thought this through.

Through the glass panel of the door, I can see the lift. I don't have any choice. Lowering myself onto my bottom, I bump back down the stairs then retrace my steps, every footfall sending a sharp pain through my ankle.

But the discomfort is nothing compared with the fear of what I know I'll have to endure in a minute.

CHAPTER THIRTY-FIVE
Joanna

My hair felt lank and greasy and the sweet, musky smell that followed me everywhere was coming from my own body. As the hours stretched ever onwards in the darkness, my despair and isolation made my body sluggish. My brain slow. With nothing to do but wait, I couldn't stop my mind from wandering to the past.

I wished now that I had never given in to Mark. Gone against my parents' wishes. My heart gave a lurch. Could they have found out about our secret marriage? If they had, my father would have been humiliated. I remembered all the competitors he'd brought down. The cocky salesmen who had been dismissed under a cloud of accusations that had never rung true. If I was right and they knew, is it possible they could have had something to do with this? Planned it all along to teach us a lesson?

I pressed my hands to my face. How could I be even thinking like this? My mum and dad might have been self-centred and uncaring, but they weren't monsters. I'd read too many books. Seen too many movies where the villains were right under your nose.

But why had no one come for me? Why did no one care? There'd been no wail of a siren, no shouts or barking of Alsatians outside the unit, no clang of metal on metal as they jemmied the door open. I forced myself to my feet. No, as in every other part of my life, it was clear the only person I could rely on was myself.

I'd already investigated the crates and boxes. The ones I could reach anyway. There were others, stacked higher, but it would have been suicide to climb up in the dark to search them. Everything I felt or pulled out was either too heavy or too light to be of any use. Books… china ornaments… what felt like curtains with a smooth, silky lining. The contents of a house waiting to be rehomed.

My stomach rumbled. Soon the door would open, and a new tray of food would arrive. But what if it didn't? What if my captor had forgotten me too? I pinched myself to stop the cold lick of fear from growing. I needed to concentrate.

Crouching down, I emptied the tray of its bags and drink carton and ran my hand along its hard, flat surface. Feeling the sharp plastic edge. Was it enough? I didn't know if I was strong enough, brave enough, to make this work, but I had to try. What other option was there? All I needed to do was get them off balance. Give myself a few minutes to run out of the door and disappear into the darkness.

Feeling my way along the wall to the cold metal door, I put my ear to it and listened. There was nothing to be heard but the mournful cry of a seagull. Clutching the tray to my chest, I sank down into a crouch. I would be ready when the door opened. Would draw the tray back as the light entered the building and, with two hands and all my force, drive it into their face as they bent to slide in the tray. It might not work, but what other choice did I have?

At last, after an interminable wait, I heard a car. The slam of a door.

I counted silently as I pictured my captor's feet walking the few steps to the door, every nerve of my body stretched. Waiting.

Alone in the darkness, I braced myself for whatever was going to happen.

CHAPTER THIRTY-SIX

Alice

Without letting myself think, I force my hand to rise to the call button and press it, watching as the numbers above the door rise. My heart beating furiously against my chest. There's a *ding* and the doors slide open.

I look at the concertina inner door, then force myself to open it. It slides back with a metal clang. Swallowing back my anxiety, I step in, then slide the door shut, hearing it click into place. At the moment, I can still see the bare, brick walls of the corridor, but I know that when I press the number six, the silver doors will slide closed.

A wave of panic washes over me as I imagine the gap between the doors getting smaller and smaller until, at last, the world outside disappears. I can't do it. I have to get out.

But I've taken too long and, before I can do anything, the metal doors slide shut of their own accord, trapping me inside. There's a jolt, and the lift begins to move. I press myself against the cold side and am shocked at the terrified face that stares back at me from the mirrored panel at the back. It's supposed to make the lift feel more spacious, but it's an illusion that does nothing to comfort me. Being confronted with evidence of my distress is only compounding it.

What if the lights go out? What if I'm trapped in the dark in this small airless space?

As the lift rises, I try not to think about the space I'm in, the metal sides, the silver doors that are tightly shut behind the metal-latticed inner door. Instead, I watch the number change from four to five, willing it to move faster.

There's a judder and the lift stops, but something's wrong... it's not my floor. It's floor five not six. Someone must have summoned it and I know, even before the doors open, who it is. Recognise the black nylon sleeves of his bomber jacket, the word *security* stitched on the front.

When he sees me, Derek's eyebrows raise in surprise and his lips twist into a smile. He doesn't get into the lift but leans with his shoulder against the concertina door, looking at me through the metal diamonds. Making me feel like an animal in a cage. 'I was just on my way up to give Mr Belmont a message.'

I rub my sweaty palms down the outside of my jeans. 'He's not there.'

Derek nods as though I haven't told him anything he didn't know already. 'When are you expecting him?'

My panic is taking hold again. For some reason being stuck inside the lift this way, Derek looking in at me, is worse than if the metal doors were to slide closed again.

'Later.' The word comes out too shaky. I hate that he's witnessing my distress. 'Please, Derek. Can you either let me get out or stand away from the doors so that I can get to my apartment.'

'*Your* apartment?' It's said with amusement. 'I wonder what Joanna would make of that.'

'I didn't mean anything by it.' My voice is rising. 'Please. Just get away from the door.'

Derek gives a smile that doesn't quite reach his eyes. 'Oh, and I thought you'd like to know that the problem with the car park doors has been fixed. Everything's working fine now. So there's nothing to stop you from leaving.'

I hate the way he's looking at me, his freckled cheek pressed against the grill. I want to cry, but I don't. Instead, I force the words out. 'I'll leave when I'm ready.'

There's a sudden rhythmic tune that echoes in the brick-walled corridor. Swearing under his breath, Derek takes his mobile from his trouser pocket. He stares at it, then frowns before answering, turning his back fractionally away from me.

'Yes? Speaking.'

It's my chance. While he's distracted, I jab at the button that will take me to the next floor and the doors glide shut. I will the lift to move, scared Derek will press the call button to make them open again, but he doesn't. Almost immediately I feel the lift start to rise, and I press my back against the mirror, my eyes glued to the numbers as they change. Praying that soon we'll reach my floor, and I can get out.

After what seems an age, the doors slide open, and I lurch out, hobbling along the corridor as quickly as my bad leg will allow. When I reach the apartment door, I fumble with the key, my eyes darting between the lift and the lock, before finally it turns. Sighing with relief, I fall into the room, shutting and locking the door behind me.

I check the time. It's seven. Three hours until the deadline. I wonder what Mark's doing. Whether he'll manage to get the rest of the money. In my building society, I've savings. There's some in my bank too, if Mark needs it. Once he's back, I can go with him to a cash machine and withdraw as much as I'm able. It won't be much, but surely anything is better than nothing.

Despite its size, the apartment feels oppressive tonight. I'm sick of the brick. Sick of the wooden floorboards. Sick of the shiny chrome and steel accessories. For the first time since I got here, I'm not looking at Joanna's living space with envy. There's nothing homely or comforting about it. No stamp of personality. When this is all over, I'll leave. Go back to my own small house and try to appreciate what I have. Going to the wooden doors between the windows, I draw back the bolts and pull them open, taking in lungfuls of night air. Trying to steady my nerves.

Time creeps by. I sit on the edge of the velvet settee, my arms wrapped tightly around me, staring at the lights across the river. I'm on edge, wondering what's taking Mark so long. Where is he? Walking around the vast room, I turn on all the lights, but it does nothing to calm the fear that's gripping me. What if Mark doesn't get back in time? What will happen to Joanna?

I think I hear a car driving past the front of the building and jump up, but when I get to the iron railing and look down there's nothing to be seen. Is it Mark? I wait, but there are no footsteps in the corridor. No key in the door.

In the silent room, the large station clock's tick is loud as it counts down the minutes. Each one taking me closer to an end I can't possibly predict. I feel overwhelmed with all the lies Mark and I have told and all the things we've not said. If anything happens to Joanna, the fault will be both of ours equally.

There's now only an hour before the drop-off. Why isn't he here?

I sit with my hands clasped, my nails digging into the flesh. My gaze darts around the room, not settling for long on anything. The wait is interminable. Eventually, not able to stand it any longer, I walk to Mark's bedroom and open the door. I switch on the light and look at the bed the two of them shared. There's a faint smell of Joanna that I hadn't noticed before, bringing back memories of the perfume we used to spray on each other's arms in her bedroom when we were teenagers.

A moan breaks from my lips as I remember the words written in the note Mark showed me. Those terrible, terrible words describing what they'll do to her if the money's not paid.

Dropping to my knees, I peer under the bed. The holdall is there, as Mark said it would be. I know in my heart that he isn't going to get here in time. That the only person who can do something is me. I drag the bag from the dark space and, with shaking hands, unzip it, staring at the bundles of notes. I've never seen so much money in one place. But it isn't enough. Mark said it wasn't. Surely, though, delivering something would be better than nothing. Or, if I go now, I could add my own meagre offerings to it.

Can I do it, though? Do I have the strength of mind to brave the lift again? Go back to the car park and drive out into the night? I tentatively feel my ankle, wondering if I'd even be able to drive. As I stand undecided, the old station clock on the wall chimes the hour. It's too late. The deadline has passed. The ransom has not been paid.

Icy fingers work their way up my spine. Somewhere, maybe not so very far from New Tobacco Wharf, someone is waiting. Angry that their scheme has come to nothing. Deciding on Joanna's fate. I picture the swinging chain I'd seen hanging from the crane outside Eloise's window and shiver. Joanna is out there somewhere. Terrified. Wondering why no one has come to help her. Will they have told her what's happening, or will she be sitting alone not knowing why she's there? I feel my panic rising. Will they have tied her hands? Will they have gagged her?

I think I hear a bark below the window. High and sharp. It sounds like Pixie, but I know it can't be. Picking up the holdall, I go back out to the living area and, leaning over the iron railings, look down at the quayside. There's nothing to be seen, but I knew there wouldn't be. My imagination is playing tricks on me.

Tick. Tick. The station clock looks down at me accusingly, its sound a form of torture. What if something's happened to Mark? In that split second, I make my decision. Hefting the holdall onto my arm, I go to the door. I'll drive to the chapel and make the delivery myself. I can't let Joanna down a second time.

As I look down the corridor, I'm aware of the camera. Will Derek be back in his room by now? Will he be watching? Joanna's life is at stake, and I can't afford to make any mistakes. This time,

I don't care if he sees me. With any luck, he'll think I'm leaving Black Water Dock for good.

I'm just closing the door when I hear footsteps in the corridor. The key falls from my hand, but I'm too scared to pick it up. I don't want to see who it is, but I have to. I force myself to turn and the breath escapes my lungs in relief.

'Mark, thank God.'

He's striding down the corridor towards me, and the question I'm desperate to ask him dies on my lips. It's clear from the hunch of his shoulders that he hasn't been able to get the rest of the money. A shadow clouds his face. It's not me he's looking at but the holdall by my feet.

'What the hell do you think you're doing?'

Without a word, he gets his own key out of his pocket and unlocks the apartment. He picks up the holdall and throws it inside, then places a hand on my back and pushes me roughly through the door.

I look at him, forcing myself not to cry. 'It was after the deadline. I was scared and thought it better to deliver some of the money than none at all. I just wanted to help.'

Mark runs his hand through his hair and when he speaks again, he's unable to disguise the anger in his voice. 'Christ. Are you insane? You have no idea what you might have been getting yourself into. You could have been hurt.'

'I'm sorry.'

He looks at me and then his face softens. 'Look, Alice. This is my problem, not yours. It's up to me to sort it out.' As he says this, he reaches out a hand to my hair before dropping it again quickly. The gesture is tender, at odds with the rude way he'd pushed me only a moment ago.

With a shock, and despite my worry about Joanna, I realise my body is responding to his touch.

CHAPTER THIRTY-SEVEN

Joanna

I ran until there was no more breath inside me. Not taking the road but cutting between buildings, their insides choked with weeds. Their broken windows staring blindly out onto flattened plots overseen by cement mixers that hadn't turned in months.

I was terrified I'd hear their footsteps behind me, stumbling over the assault course of bricks. Hear them swear as a foot caught in the brambles that lay like tripwires across the paving.

Or worse still, my name being called. *Joanna.*

I ran from what I'd done. Didn't want to think about what I saw. What it meant. All I knew is I had to find help. Needed to get to a main road and flag down a car.

Thank God the night was moonlit, as the street lights here hadn't been lit in a very long time – not after it became clear no one wanted to live in Black Water Dock. All that wasted money poured into the site. All those expectations dashed.

At the next brick building, I stopped and leant against its side, hands on knees, trying to catch my breath. I couldn't stop long as they'd have recovered and would be after me by now, and I was terrified of what would happen if they caught me.

Breaking away from the building, I ran as fast as my legs, weakened by lack of exercise, would let me. Ahead, in the distance across an area of wasteland, I could see the lights from a block of flats. A trail of white street lights behind, signalling the road.

Crying with relief, I forced my legs to move faster, aware that I was now in full view of anyone following.

I'd got to reach the road. I had to.

How long it took me, I don't know, but finally there it was ahead of me. The road. Running to it, I waved my arms, not caring that I must look like a madwoman. The first car didn't stop. Nor the second. I screamed at their disappearing tail lights in frustration, too terrified to look behind me in case of what I might see.

The next car slowed, signalled and moved over. The driver wound down the window, leant across.

'You okay?'

It was a middle-aged man who peered at me from behind thick-rimmed glasses. He took in my filthy clothes, my lank hair, his face registering first shock then uncertainty. He straightened and, with horror, I saw the window start to glide back up. He must have thought I was a drug addict looking for a fix. Or maybe a prostitute. He was going to drive away. Leave me here.

Grabbing the handle of the passenger door, I yanked it open and threw myself into the seat beside him.

'Please. I don't have time to explain. You've got to take me to the police station.'

The man looked startled but didn't argue. As the car pulled away from the kerb, I dared to turn and look through the back window, terrified someone would be standing there watching me.

But the street was empty.

CHAPTER THIRTY-EIGHT

Alice

Mark's at the door of the stairwell. He's going to try to deliver the money even though it may be too late. Although I'm relieved it's now not me who's doing it, I'm as much worried for his safety as he was for mine.

'Please, Mark. Be careful. Don't take any stupid risks.'

'I won't.' His face is tense, his eyes focussed on the bag he's holding. Although he's hiding it well, I know he's scared. 'I'll see you later. It would be best if you stay inside the apartment until I'm back.'

'I will. You don't need to worry about me.' Without thinking, I reach up on tiptoe and kiss him on the lips. Instantly, I regret it, feel my face flush angry red and my skin prickle with embarrassment. 'I'm sorry.' I bite the inside of my lip. 'I shouldn't have done that.'

To my huge relief, Mark smiles. 'Don't apologise. If anything, it's made me feel a tiny bit better. It shows you care.'

With a small smile, he pushes open the glass-panelled door and disappears down the staircase, leaving me alone in the corridor, my finger touching my lips.

After a few moments, I go back inside, closing the door and locking it behind me. But I need to see Mark one last time. Crossing to the wooden doors, I unlatch them and pull them open, then lean out over the iron railing. Waiting for the sound of the car. I don't have to wait long. I see it now, coming round the side of the building, Mark in the driving seat. He's driving fast, the headlights lighting up the quay as he passes by the front of the building. Then he spins the wheel and turns off the quayside onto the road that leads out of the dock, in a shower of loose chippings.

I haven't yet moved from my position when I hear a nightmarish noise that roots me to the spot. A sound that sickens me to the core. Even from this distance, there's no mistaking the nauseating sound of wheels skidding. The slam of metal as it hits stone.

I stand in the middle of the living area, a police officer next to me, while the other closes the door behind us. I'm trying to process what they've just told me.

'How bad is it?'

The officers exchange looks. 'It's quite serious, I'm afraid. Mr Belmont has sustained injuries to the head and chest area.'

I can't stop shaking. Noticing, the policewoman puts an arm around me and leads me to the settee. 'I'll make a cup of tea, shall I?'

She's different to the one who came here before, but the younger officer is the same.

They're not telling me much, and I wonder why. 'Where is he?'

'He's been taken to intensive care at The Royal London. Mr Price heard the crash and rang us.'

'Mr Price?'

'Derek Price. The security manager. He's the one who let us in. He saw Mr Belmont leave the building earlier and was worried it might be him.'

I sit in silence while the policewoman makes the tea and brings it over. She sits next to me.

'Could you tell me why Mr Belmont was driving your car, Ms Solomon? Why he wasn't driving his own?'

I nod. 'He took my car because he said his own had been playing up.'

It's the truth. A warning light had come on, and he didn't want to risk it breaking down before he could make the drop-off.

The policewoman hands me my mug of tea. 'It appears that Mr Belmont was driving too fast. The chippings on the road are a skid risk and there really should be signs.' She looks at me with sympathy. 'I'm sorry, this must be a terrible shock for you.'

'It is.' Every word she says is too loud. Too harsh. 'I can't take it in.'

The young officer is seated on the other settee. He leans forward. 'And you say you don't know where he was going in such a hurry?'

'No, he didn't say.' I hope they can't tell by my face that I'm lying.

'Yet you were happy to give him your car keys?'

I look down at my tea as though somehow it will give me a sign as to what I should say. 'Yes.'

'There was no argument? No reason you can think of for your friend to take the car and drive off at this time of night?'

'I told you. No.'

They've told me what happened. That my car was found embedded in the side of the old pumping station that I'd passed on my way into Black Water Dock last Saturday. Only Saturday? How could that be? It seems a lifetime ago.

My heart clenches as I remember her words. A write off, she'd said. They'd had to cut the roof to get Mark out.

Will they have found the holdall of money? Did he leave it on the seat or hide it somewhere? It will only be a matter of time before they find it.

I cover my face with my hands. I don't know what to do. What to say. I thought things couldn't get worse, but it's like a nightmare that won't end. This is the time to tell them about Joanna. About Eloise too. It can't be long before they find out the body Mark identified is hers. But something is stopping me.

What about Joanna?

My chest tightens. I'm so tightly bound in the web of lies and omissions I've told, it's almost impossible to break free. Bile rises to my throat, and I wonder if I'm going to be sick.

'Are you all right, Alice?'

I swallow. 'Yes, I'm sorry. It's just such a shock.'

'And Mr Belmont's wife.' The policewoman consults her notes. 'Joanna. You say she's not here? I've got down here that Mr Belmont reported her missing earlier this week but later contacted us to say he'd heard from her. We really do need to speak to her to let her know what's happened. If you've a contact number or any idea of how we can get hold of her…'

'I have a number for her, but she's not answering. Mark said she'd phoned to let him know she was fine, but that she needed some space.'

Why am I doing this? Mark is injured in hospital, and there's no reason to be sticking to his story but I am. How will I ever now be able to tell the truth about the ransom note?

'Can I see him?'

The policewoman nods. 'We can take you there now, if you like.'

'Thank you. I hardly knew him, but until Joanna comes home, I'm the only person he has.'

'And will you be staying here when you get back?' She looks around her at the show-home style interior, all brick, wood and chrome. I wonder what she's thinking.

'No. It doesn't seem right to stay now Mark's in hospital. I'll leave as soon as I've got back from seeing him. It's time I went home, but I'll leave my number with you in case you want to get hold of me. Well, I would if I had any charge left on my phone. The cable of my charger's faulty and the battery's been dead for days.'

'There's nothing you can do about it tonight, but you'll probably be able to get one in a garage or service station on your way home. Give us your number anyway.'

I do as she asks, then pick up my bag and follow them to the door. As I reach it, I realise something. This will be the first time I've left the building in days and it feels strange.

Like I've been let out on parole.

CHAPTER THIRTY-NINE

Joanna

Detective Constable Armstrong leans across the table, his fingers linked. He looks a nice man. The kind who would have a wife and two lovely children, a boy and a girl named Thomas and Olivia. The kind who wants justice to be done. I like him. I trust him.

'You've done well telling us all of this, Joanna,' he says. 'Especially after what you've been through.'

'Thank you.'

It seems an inadequate thing to say under the circumstances, but he smiles at me and looks at the notes he's made. I've been talking for so long, going over every detail I remember, and finally it's his time to speak. 'Just a couple of things. You say you don't remember how you came to be locked up?'

I shake my head. 'I remember being on the riverbank. I thought I heard my name being called, my foot slipping. I don't remember anything else until I came round.'

Lifting up the first sheet, DC Armstrong runs his pen down the page beneath. 'And you don't remember hearing any other voices while you were in there?'

'No.'

'That's fine. Maybe you'd like to read through what you've told me so far and make sure you're happy I've got it all down right.' He turns the sheet of paper he's been writing on towards me. 'It's late now and I can see you're exhausted, but tomorrow I'm going to have to ask you to come back in for a video interview. Are you all right with that?'

'Of course.'

'That's good. I can get this typed up as a formal statement, and then you can sign it.'

I look up at him, trying to hold back the tears that have been forming while I've been talking. 'I'm sorry I've made it so difficult, that what I've told you has been so rambling. I've been alone for days and it's hard to think straight.'

'Please don't apologise. You've given a very detailed account of what you remember. It will help us enormously once we start the investigation.'

With shaking fingers, I draw my lank hair from my face and stare at the words, but they're moving around the page and I can't capture them. Pressing my index fingers to the inner corners of my eyes, I wait until the letters finally still, and I'm able to make sense of them. Somehow, despite my stops and starts – the breaks I've needed in order to pull myself together – DC Armstrong has turned my long-winded account into something coherent.

I read the statement through to the end, my heart beating so loudly I'm sure he'll be able to hear it, but when I reach the end, I turn my head away. There's something I've held back. Not told him. The most important thing.

The thing that will change everything the moment I say it.

Why haven't I told him? Is it because I'm scared of what might happen if I do? Of course it is. Because the thing I've left out is so terrible, so far-fetched, that I don't know if I can bring myself to say the words. If I'd ever be believed.

DC Armstrong's forehead creases slightly. He can tell I'm struggling with something. 'Are you sure you're all right, Joanna? Would you like some water?'

My throat feels dry, my tongue sticking to the roof of my mouth. 'Yes, if it's not too much trouble.'

Since I've been here, everyone has been so thoughtful. Anxious to address my immediate needs: the civilian office assistant who took one look at me as I burst through the doors of the waiting room and ushered me through to an interview room, the police officer who placed a blanket over my shoulders when she saw I was shivering.

That was nearly an hour ago and a lot has happened since then. After I'd been given a seat in the interview room, I hadn't had to wait long before the door opened and DS Barnes walked in, introducing herself along with DC Armstrong. Since then, DS Barnes hasn't said much and now she's standing at the window staring out into the dark car park. Every now and again, just when I think she hasn't been listening, she looks over and smiles encouragingly at me.

I tip my head back, exhaustion washing over me. The room is brightly lit, two strips of lighting running the length of the ceiling. DS Barnes sees me looking at them. 'Is it too bright? Your eyes might not be accustomed yet to the light.'

'Thank you, but I'm fine.' I don't want to make a fuss.

Their concern for me brings a lump to my throat. Reaching my hand into my sleeve, I take out the tissue I was offered earlier from the box on the table and blow my nose. I know I must look a sight. Eyes red-rimmed, hair greasy and uncombed. Unrecognisable from the girl who only a week ago was drinking cocktails in an upmarket bar in Canary Wharf.

'Would you like a few more minutes?'

'No. That won't be necessary.'

I thought I was brave, but I'm not. I'm scared. A voice in my head screams *tell them,* but I can't do it. If I do, I'll forever live in fear of the consequences. Despite what he's done to me, the thought of having him punished for it makes me sick to the stomach.

DC Armstrong waits. 'Joanna?'

'Yes. Sorry.'

Pushing the tissue back up my sleeve, I turn my statement back towards him. DC Armstrong starts to pull it, but I keep my hand on it, my palm covering his slanting handwriting.

What if he does it again? With someone else?

'There's something else I need to tell you.' The words come out in a rush. 'Something important.'

'I see.'

Out of the corner of my eye, I see DS Barnes nod her encouragement. It gives me the confidence to carry on.

I knit my fingers together, my fingertips pressing into the skin on the backs of my hands.

'It's about the person who abducted me.' A band of pain tightens around my chest, as though a hand has wrapped itself around my heart and is squeezing hard. 'I know who it was.'

My eyes meet DC Armstrong's warm brown ones and I wonder, even now, if what I saw was real or something my imagination had conjured up. But the awful, savage pain in my heart tells me everything I need to know. What I saw was the truth. I know now what he's capable of.

DC Armstrong lets go of his notes. He folds his arms on the table and leans forward. 'You're safe, Joanna. If you tell us who it was, we can make sure they never do anything like this again.'

I push the page with my words on towards him, my eyes locked on his, hoping they will give me the strength to say what has to be said.

'It was my husband.' Emotion chokes me. Roughens my voice. 'It was Mark.'

CHAPTER FORTY

Joanna

DC Armstrong's head shoots up. He looks across to DS Barnes who is staring at me, whatever she'd found so interesting in that dark car park forgotten.

'Just to be clear. It was your husband, Mark Belmont, who abducted you?'

'Yes.'

My voice is barely a whisper, and DC Armstrong has to lean forward to catch what I'm saying. I wait as his pen scratches across the page, wondering what he's thinking. Eventually, he finishes what he's writing and looks up.

'So, you're saying that it was Mark who knocked you unconscious and kept you locked in the storage unit?'

I stare miserably at my hands, the knuckles still raw and bloodied. 'Yes.'

DS Barnes leans against the radiator. 'Is there a reason you didn't tell us this before, Joanna?'

I look at her, wishing I had. Wishing my feelings for Mark hadn't made me so weak.

'I think it was because I was frightened of what he might do.' I pick at the frayed skin around my knuckles until beads of blood form. Putting them to my lips, I suck them away. 'I don't think he ever meant for me to see him.'

'I'm sure he didn't.' DS Barnes frowns. 'Is that the only reason you didn't tell us?'

'No.' I look away. 'It's not. I was afraid you wouldn't believe me.'

DC Armstrong reaches out and pats my arm. 'We're here to help you. You shouldn't be scared to tell us anything. It really is important that if there's anything else we should know, you tell us now.'

'No, there's nothing more and I'm sorry.' My voice doesn't sound like my own. 'It's just that I can't think straight. Everything that's happened. I can't…'

'It's all right. I know this is difficult, Joanna, but you're doing really well. This has been a traumatic time for you.'

DC Armstrong's fatherly tone makes the tears that have been pooling in my eyes, spill down my cheeks, dampening the neck of my blouse.

'He said he loved me.' I'm talking to myself as much as to them. 'How can he have done it?'

The detective's gaze is steady. He's sympathetic, but I know he's wanting to get on. Needs to get to the bottom of things.

DS Barnes remains at the window, her face impassive now. 'It was your husband who reported you missing.' She waits while this sinks in. 'But three days later he said you'd made contact and that you were no longer a missing person. Can you think why he would do that?'

'No longer missing?' Her words make me catch my breath. Why report me missing and then tell them that? What's been Mark's game?

My head is starting to ache with all the thoughts that are racing through it, searching for a reason. 'I'm sorry. I have no idea. Mark.. my husband… he's a complex person.'

'Complex? Can you explain that, Joanna?'

'I've never felt as though I've really known the real Mark.' My fingers stray to my wedding ring. 'But that might just be because we haven't been together very long. Did he say we've only been married for a week?'

DC Armstrong says nothing but watches as I twist the gold band round and round my finger. He leans forward in his chair and my heart thumps as I wonder what he might say next. What new bombshell he might drop.

'You mentioned in your statement that you're Mr Belmont's second wife.'

I stop twisting my ring. 'Yes. His first wife, Tanya, died. In a car accident.'

'I see. And you say he never hurt you during the time you were in captivity?'

'No. There's a bump on my head, but I don't know how I got it and I know I must have been tied up at some point.' My thumb seeks out the tender skin of my wrist. 'But after I woke up, he didn't come near me. The only time I saw him was when he pushed the tray of food through the door. It was pitch black in there, and he didn't say anything to me, or I would have recognised his voice. Like I said, I didn't know it was Mark until I escaped.'

I take a gulp of my water, scared I might spill it as my hand is shaking so much.

Suddenly, the weight of what has happened, the seriousness, the danger, is starting to sink in, but I can't let it overwhelm me.

I stare at DC Armstrong, wide-eyed. 'Oh God! Do you think he was planning to kill me?'

A groan escapes me, and I bury my head in my hands, my fingers grasping at my hair, tightening the skin at my scalp.

'Please, Joanna. Don't upset yourself. At this stage, it's impossible to say what your husband's motive was until we've apprehended and questioned him.'

I shudder. 'His first wife, Tanya, left all her money to him. Oh Jesus. What if her death wasn't an accident?'

DC Armstrong clears his throat. 'There's nothing to be gained from jumping to conclusions.'

I can't leave it, though. 'Mark is in financial trouble. I have a trust fund. What if that's what he's after? What if it's why he wanted to marry me quickly?'

'Please, Joanna.'

I grip the edges of the table, my fingers whitening, and push myself up. 'Will he be able to find me?'

'Please sit down. You don't need to worry. You're safe now.' DC Armstrong pushes his chair back. 'Is there anything else you want to tell us at this time? As I said earlier, we'll want you to do a more detailed interview tomorrow, but what you need now is rest. We'll be arranging for you to spend tonight in a hotel.'

I collapse back onto the chair. 'Please, can't you just let me go home?'

'I'm afraid that's not possible. We can't be sure that your husband won't return there. Until we know where he is, it would be better for you to be elsewhere. Besides, forensics will be wanting to take a look around the apartment to see if there's any evidence that will back up your account.'

'You don't believe me.' It's a statement not a question. Folding my arms around my body, I hug myself, my fingernails digging into the soft flesh of my arms. 'I knew you wouldn't. I expect it's what Mark's banking on too.'

DC Armstrong frowns. 'I didn't say we didn't believe you, Joanna. It's normal procedure, nothing more.'

I feel like screaming, but I force myself to stay in control. 'When will I be able to go back home?'

'I can't say for certain. Maybe in a day or so. We'll know more tomorrow. I'll make a call, then, once everything's arranged, I can get a car to take you to the hotel. Before you go though, I'd like you to see the police surgeon so he can make sure you're okay.'

'I don't need to see them.' The tears are starting again, stinging the back of my eyes. I can't face anyone poking and prodding me. Asking more questions. 'I said Mark didn't hurt me. I just need to sleep.'

DC Armstrong looks doubtful. 'That's not quite true, is it. There's the injury to your head... your wrists.'

I look down at the ring of red skin above my palm that's starting to fade. 'It's fine. I don't have to, do I?'

It's DS Barnes who answers. 'We can't make you, but if you don't want to see the police surgeon, I'd advise that you make an appointment with your own GP tomorrow, Joanna. Just to be sure.'

I let out a breath, relieved. 'I will.'

'We'll leave it there for now then.' DS Barnes comes over to the table and picks up the sheet of paper her colleague has been writing on. 'We won't be long. As soon as we've made the hotel arrangements, we'll let you know.'

'Thank you.'

They both leave the room, and I want to shout after them not to, but I don't. Instead, I sit on my red plastic chair and think of everything that's happened. Realising I'm trembling uncontrollably, I clamp my hands between my legs, willing them to be still.

The minutes tick by, and I wonder what they're doing. I picture DS Barnes on the phone, giving orders in her calm, reasonable voice. DC Armstrong waiting for her to finish before the two of them can discuss me. The missing bride.

Lowering my head, I stare at my linked fingers, the shiny gold band on my ring finger still waiting for the inscription Mark had wanted us to add once things settled down. Once everyone knew about our marriage.

Love at first sight.

Bile rises to my throat as I rock forward in my chair then back again. Forward. Back. On and on... not caring that if they come back and see me, I'll look as though I've lost it. For that's how I feel. Mad. How could you do this to me, Mark? Is this how you treat someone you're supposed to love?

Eventually, I come to my senses. Make myself get up and go to the window. The blinds are open and outside the night sky is black. Starless. To pass the time until they come back, I try and think of as many words as I can to describe it: inky, jet, coal, raven. There must be more, I'm sure, but I'm not very good at this game. To me, darkness is simply the absence of light. Nothing more. It's always made me feel safe. Like a comfort blanket.

Where is Mark now? Is he out there looking for me or has he moved on?

I'm starting to feel sick again, the enormity of everything that's happened pressing down on me. When they find him, Mark will pay for what he's done, most likely go to prison for it, yet still the doubts won't leave me. I could tell them I made a mistake, that now I'm not sure I can be certain it was him, let Mark carry on with his life as though nothing has happened. But what about me? What will happen if I weaken? After all, I'm the victim, not him.

I think of all the other things I could have told the detectives, words that DC Armstrong would write down in his slanting hand, but what I've told them is enough.

There's no time to think any more as the door opens again and the detectives come back in. DS Barnes' face is serious. She indicates for me to sit again, then pulls out a chair opposite me, the one DC Armstrong had occupied earlier.

'Since you spoke to us and told us what happened, there have been some further developments.' She clears her throat. 'Though whether you will consider them good or bad I'm not sure.'

I look from one to the other, not understanding. 'What sort of developments?'

DS Barnes picks up a biro from the table and clicks it. Once. Twice. I watch as the nib pops out then retracts, wondering what she's going to say.

'It's your husband, Joanna.' She lays the pen flat on the table. 'He's been in an accident.'

'An accident?' I try and get my head around what she's just said. 'What sort of accident?'

DS Barnes picks up the pen again. 'He was cut out of a car on the road leading out of Black Water Dock. He'd lost control and it hit the wall of the old pumping station not far from where you live.'

My stomach falls away from me. 'I don't believe you. It can't be Mark.'

'I'm sorry, but there's no doubt. He had his driving license with him.'

It can't be true. It can't.

'Are you sure there hasn't been some mistake?'

'I'm afraid not. Are you all right, Joanna?'

I clutch my stomach, wondering if I might be sick. It can't be my husband, they're lying. But why would they?

Slowly the power of speech returns to me. 'Tell me how? When...?'

'Around ten this evening. He was taken to A & E. I've organised for a police watch to be put on your husband's room and as soon as he's in a fit enough condition to be interviewed, we'll be able to find out more.'

'You mean he's not dead?'

'No, but he's in intensive care. It will be a while before he can tell us anything.'

'Will I be able to see him?' Despite all that's happened, I have a desperate need to.

DS Barnes steeples her fingers under her chin. 'Under the circumstances, it wouldn't be a good idea.'

The room is starting to spin, and I close my eyes. It feels like a long time since I slept. 'I just can't believe it.'

'I'm sorry... I know it's a shock.' DS Barnes tucks a strand of thick blonde hair behind her ear. 'Is there someone you'd like us to ring for you? Your parents, perhaps?'

I shake my head vehemently. 'No. I don't want you to call them.'

'A friend then. The one who's been staying at your apartment maybe? Apparently, she left a while ago, but you could ask her to come back if she doesn't live far.'

I look up at her. 'A friend?'

'Yes, Alice Solomon. She told our uniformed colleagues that you invited her to stay. She was with your husband when they reported you missing. In fact, we'll be needing to speak to her as well.'

'Alice.' I smile as a memory comes floating back. A girl with auburn hair stands in the doorway of the classroom, looking nervous. Out of place. When the head teacher asks if anyone would like to look after her on her first day, my hand shoots up unbidden. *I'd like to look after her, Mrs Talbot.*

'It's a shame she left, but your message to Mark made it clear that you weren't planning on coming back. She obviously felt there was nothing to stay for.'

'But I didn't send any message. Mark made it up.'

DS Barnes looks at me. 'We know that now.'

'But how do you know Alice has left? She could still be there.'

'According to the local officers who took her to see Mark in the hospital, she was planning on packing her things and leaving directly. Probably just wants to get back home. The whole thing must have been very upsetting for her.'

'She went to see him?' I stare at her in disbelief. 'Yet you won't let *me*.'

'There was no reason for her not to. It was before we knew the true story.'

I look away. Nobody knows the true story.

'I'll phone Alice later... ask her to come back. I know she will.'

When DS Barnes had said she'd gone back home I'd been glad, but now curiosity has got the better of me. After ten years, I'll see her again. Alice who sucked up to my parents. Alice who copied all my clothes. Alice who's been living in an apartment that she wishes was hers.

Alice who I saw kissing my husband.

CHAPTER FORTY-ONE

Joanna

The police car pulls up outside the hotel. It's just a Travelodge, but I don't care. I press my forehead against the cold window and force my eyes to focus on the vertical blue sign with its white writing. I'm tired of hotels. The windows of this one are small and plain, and I wonder about the people sleeping behind the heavy curtains that shut out the night. Businessmen and tourists, I expect – not women who have come straight from a police station.

It's not home, but I don't care any more. I want a shower and a drink from the minibar. Time to myself to think about what I'm going to do next.

The uniformed officer who's been driving turns around in his seat. 'Here we are then.'

All the way here from the police station, I've watched his eyes in the rear-view mirror. Concerned eyes that every so often would leave the road to check I was all right, even though there's a female officer sitting beside me.

'Let's get you inside.' The policewoman gets out, comes around to my side of the car and opens the door.

'I'll see you in. I should warn you I've had word that because it's so late, forensics won't be able to get a team out to your apartment until the morning. You might have to stay here a couple of days.' She leads the way to the hotel entrance, turning to me when we reach it. 'You know it's important you don't go back to the apartment until we give you the all-clear, don't you?'

'Yes, they told me.'

We go inside, and I wait as the policewoman collects a key card from the bored looking girl who's sitting behind the reception desk. She hands it to me.

'Do you want me to come up with you?'

'No. I'm fine.'

'And you're sure you'll be all right here on your own?'

'You don't need to worry. When I get to my room, I'll call my friend, Alice. She'll come straight away. I won't be on my own for long.'

She seems happy with my answer. 'That's good. As you were told at the station, DS Barnes and DC Armstrong will pick you up tomorrow morning and take you back to see if you can identify the unit where you were kept. Do you think you'll be up to it?'

In the locked unit are the furniture and fixtures from the house Mark once shared with his wife. His dead wife. I wouldn't let him bring any of it with him when we moved in together, into the apartment my father bought for me when I was twenty-five. After all, why would I want to share my space with a dead woman's things? It was bad enough having to look after her crackhead son. Not that I minded at first, when he genuinely needed me. No, it was once he'd got clean that he started to get on my nerves. Followed me around like a lost puppy. Him and Derek.

'Of course. I'll be all right once I've had some sleep.'

The policewoman smiles at me. 'You've been very brave. From the information you've given us, the unit shouldn't be difficult to locate.'

The words are so genuine, so kind, that I feel a stab of guilt. I'll show them where it is and they'll find the mattress, the tray, the dried blood on the metal door. They won't know I only stayed one night, long enough for it to be clear I was there. For the others I was in a cheap hotel... well, not all the others.

But now isn't the time to start wrestling with my conscience. I smile back at her.

'Thank you,' I say.

I take the lift to the third floor and let myself into the room. It's clean and functional, and I can't help comparing it to the places I've stayed with my parents or with Mark. The hotel bedrooms in New York with floor to ceiling windows that looked out over the New York skyline. Mosaic-tiled rooms in Marrakesh facing on to courtyards whose fountains played as I fell asleep. The apartment in Cannes where the bed was twice the size of this small double with its striped bed runner.

Going over to the window, I part the curtains and watch as the police car drives away, then I take my shoes off and lay on my bed, thinking about Alice. Remembering when we were young, and she'd spend more time in the holidays at my house than her own. Mum had loved it, as it meant she didn't have to spend time with me. Entertain me. I was just an inconvenience to her, filling her ordered life with first nappies and bottles, then later, arguments and school fees. It wouldn't surprise me if she wished she'd had her tubes tied... or given birth to a quiet, well-behaved child like Alice.

Ever since the day I last saw her, all those years ago, I've wondered what Alice looks like now, whether she's morphed into a self-assured, red-headed beauty or whether she's as she was then, her auburn hair pulled into a ponytail and her face bare of make-up. Unable to think for herself. Unable to make decisions unless someone made them for her. Unless *I* made them for her.

Of course, I know now.

What I don't know is how life's been treating her. How she's managed without me. She thought she'd be able to, but I've always known better. Known that it would only be a matter of time before she realised her mistake. That she still needed me. A sudden white-hot surge of anger and disillusion washes over me. I wasn't to know she'd let me down again.

On the bedside table is the basic phone the police gave me. It's so they can keep in contact. I pick it up and, knowing Alice's number off by heart, punch it in and wait. It goes straight to voicemail. She'll have switched her phone off, but that's not surprising as it's almost three in the morning. It looks like my best friend won't be running to my side tonight after all.

For the moment, at least, my anger abates. I leave a message. *Alice, it's me, Joanna. Call me*, then end the call and drop the phone onto the white duvet.

I wait for the disappointment to set in, but it doesn't, and I realise it's because I don't really care if she gets the message or not. After all, her job is done. She's played her part.

CHAPTER FORTY-TWO

Alice

In my dream Mark is standing over me, his face swollen and bruised, the skin crazed with blooded glass from the windscreen. He's trying to tell me something, but I don't know what it is and even now I'm awake, he's there still in the cold and lonely bedroom, his colourless lips pleading with me to understand.

Forcing the image away, I sit up. Even though my nightdress is damp with sweat, I'm shivering; the heating hasn't come on and the room is freezing. Reaching across to the bedside light, I switch it on and check to see if my phone has charged, offering up thanks to the police who, on the way back from the hospital, stopped at a garage to let me buy a new cable. I'm surprised that it's only forty per cent charged, but I haven't been back that long and when I see the notifications of emails and messages on the screen, my concern turns to relief. I'm back in contact with the world again.

The dream has rattled me, and I know there's no way I'm going to get back to sleep. Hardly any wonder when only a few hours ago I was standing by Mark's bed, watching his vital signs trace across the monitor. Trying not to give in to my distress when I saw the tube in his mouth, the cannula in his hand, the breathing machine that made his chest rise and fall.

Of course, it should have been Joanna at his bedside, not me, but Joanna is somewhere else. Scared. Wondering, maybe, if she'll die. A tide of panic rises up my body, but I refuse to let it get a grip on me. Instead, I push back the covers and get out of bed, the floorboards frigid under my feet.

Putting my sweatshirt over my nightdress, I unplug the charging cable from the socket and take it with me to the kitchen. As I pass the fridge and switch on the lights under the eye-level units, I look at the empty place where the photograph of me and Joanna had once been, realising as I touch my finger to the champagne-shaped magnet, that it's exactly the same as the one Eloise had. The one that's now in the pocket of my jeans.

I still haven't said anything to the police about Eloise. Neither have I told them about the ransom note. Mark had insisted that by telling them, it might have put Joanna in more danger, but now I'm scared he was wrong. Besides, Mark is unconscious in a hospital bed. My thoughts are in free fall. Spinning out of control. Even as I try to persuade myself I'm doing the right thing, I know I'm acting irrationally. Yet I'm unable to do anything about it.

As I plug my phone into the socket in the wall above the steel worktop, the screen lights up and I take a closer look at the notifications. I'm just thinking there's nothing of much interest when I see that at 2.50 this morning I had a missed call from a number I don't recognise. There's a voicemail too.

Taking a mug from the cupboard and spooning in some coffee, I put the phone onto loudspeaker and click play on the message. It's as I'm filling the kettle that the recording starts, and a woman's voice fills the kitchen.

I freeze, my hand on the tap, wondering if it's just my imagination that's conjured up her voice. But by the time the message has ended, I'm certain.

'Joanna.' The word echoes in the high-ceilinged warehouse.

Turning around, I stare at my phone as if expecting to see her standing there holding it. It's only when a spray of water bounces off the side of the kettle, soaking my sleeve, that I come to my senses.

I turn the tap off, and wait to hear if there's anything more, but there's nothing.

The voicemail was short, giving nothing away. No mention of where she is, where she's been. Just a request for me to call her back.

Christ. I don't even know if she's safe. Where did she send this message from? Where is she?

Clanging the kettle down onto the metal worktop, I run to my phone and go to my missed calls. Pressing the most recent number, I wait for Joanna to answer. Eventually, when it becomes clear that she's not going to, I start to leave a message, but I'm still in shock from hearing her voice and I can't think what I want to say.

When I play her message again, I listen more carefully, searching for clues – background noises, the nuance of her words – anything that might tell me where she is and how she's feeling. There's nothing obvious, though.

Have they still got her? Could this be a trick?

Not knowing what to think, I refill the kettle and make the coffee, my hand shaking as I pour the boiling water into the cup. Then, unplugging the phone again, I take it with me to the settee and type a message, clicking send as soon as I've finished.

CHAPTER FORTY-THREE

Joanna

I reach across to the minibar, take out a bottle of wine and unscrew the lid. Pouring some of the amber liquid into the water tumbler, I take a sip of it, then lean my head back against the headboard and let my eyes wander around the room. Opposite the bed is a veneered desk, a red leather-look tub chair pushed under the space beneath. On it, next to the phone and the tea tray with its assortment of beverages in their coloured sachets, is a tablet of plain paper and a pen. Clearly, the space is designed so visitors to the hotel have somewhere to write. But what would they be writing on that plain white pad? Letters to loved ones? Shopping lists? Ransom notes?

I don't use the phone the police gave me, instead, I run to the main road, which, despite the hour, is still busy. I think about hitching a lift, but then a taxi drives by and I hail it. With luck, I'll be back here at the Travelodge before dawn.

I'm glad the taxi driver isn't one for making idle talk, and I lean my head back against the headrest, barely noticing the empty shops we drive past, grills covering their entrances, or the rows of terraced housing either side of the road, their blank windows staring blindly at each other across the road.

It's only when we turn off the main road and head south in the direction of the river that I pay more attention. The taxi takes us past the Tesco Metro, now closed for the night, past the disused bus shelter covered in graffiti, past the electricity substation inside its spiked metal prison. Then it swings around a corner, and we're heading towards the disused pumping station.

Suddenly, the taxi slows to a stop, jolting my head against the headrest. The driver unfastens his belt, leans forward in his seat, cupping his hand to the windscreen to see better.

'What the fuck's happened here?'

I lower my window, knowing, even before I see it, what's picked out in the headlights. It's Alice's Mini embedded in the brick wall. The white and blue police tape rippling in the wind. I'd thought they would have removed it by now.

I try to keep my voice steady. 'That's some accident.'

The driver rubs his nose with the back of his hand. 'Can't believe anyone survived that. Only if God was looking down on them.'

He pulls a crucifix from his T-shirt and kisses it before tucking it back inside.

I look back at the car. Mark is in hospital, but he's alive. Maybe the taxi driver's right. Maybe God *was* looking down on him.

My heart aches with all that I nearly lost. Oh Mark. If only you had proven your love for me on your own. Not just the ransom note. It all went wrong before that – maybe I should never have persuaded you to marry me so quickly. You hadn't wanted to, I know… didn't want to upset my parents. But I was scared that if we waited any longer, you'd get cold feet and pull out of the big wedding they were planning. Can't you see, I needed that ring on my finger? I needed to know you wouldn't leave me.

The taxi driver crosses himself, then pulls away. What he's seen has clearly rattled him, and we travel a few hundred yards in silence until I tell him to stop. I've already taken some notes from the money belt hidden under my blouse and I hand them to him, telling him to keep the change. He doesn't seem to think it's odd that I've asked him to drop me in the middle of nowhere; he's probably keen to get home to his warm bed.

He reverses into a layby, then drives back the way we came, past the accident site, leaving me in the place I stood only a few hours ago. I watch his tail lights disappear around the corner and wait for grief to wrap me in its arms, but it doesn't. I feel empty. It's a moonlit night and the words WELCOME TO BLACK WATER DOCK stand out clearly against their white background. I stare at the sign, the blue paint obscuring some of the words. Is it any wonder it's been defaced? There's nothing welcoming about this barren place. Never has been – despite what my father and Mark thought in the early days of the scheme.

Mark wasn't happy. I could see it. It was only a matter of time before he bailed out. But what if it wasn't just the failing business that he wanted to move on from? What if he had wanted to move on from me too? No one can blame me for wanting to know.

My phone vibrates against my leg. Taking it from my pocket, I see I have a message and a missed call. From Alice.

Joanna! Is that really you? Where are you? Please answer. I'm at New Tobacco Wharf and I need you.

I look out across the black wasteland. In the distance, too far away for me to see, Alice is sitting in my apartment. In my bed, maybe. The police were wrong. She's still there.

Quickly I type my reply. *Sorry. The police say I'm not allowed to go back there. They need to search the place.* When I've pressed send, I turn my phone off and put it back in my pocket.

I hold the breath tight inside my lungs. What the hell is Alice still doing in my apartment? I think of her eating my food, kissing my husband, visiting him in hospital when I've not been able to. My fingernails dig into my palms.

I hate her.

It should never have ended like this. When I stepped out in front of the Mini, consumed by the red-hot flames of my jealousy, and watched it lose control. When I heard the skid of tyres, the crunch of metal on brick and the shatter of glass, I wasn't to know that it would be my husband driving the car.

It was never meant to be him.

It was meant to be Alice.

CHAPTER FORTY-FOUR

Alice

Through the square-paned windows, the sky is lightening. The tal
buildings across the river, that when I'd got home had been lit up
as if with fairy lights, now just blank grey faces.

I'm in limbo, not knowing what to do for the best. The impor
tant thing is that Joanna's alive, and it's making me look at the
apartment with new eyes. Eyes from which the scales have fallen
Her phone message has brought me back to reality. What have
been doing this last week? Sleeping in a bed that Joanna once slep
in. Sharing meals and a table with her husband. Acting as though
the place is mine. In what stupid fairy tale have I cast myself i
the leading role? There must be one where the poor village gir
covets the rich one in her palace?

Suddenly, my phone pings, and I grab at it. It might be Joann
telling me what's going on. I look at the message and see that
it is indeed from her, but there's nothing about where she is o
where she's been, just that the police are coming here to search
the apartment. That she can't be here.

I shouldn't be here either. And I don't want to be.

It's over. Joanna is no longer missing, and Mark isn't m
responsibility; he never was. I don't know what's going on, but
wish I'd never come. That she'd never sent me that message.

I've got myself embroiled in something I don't understand, an
I'm sickened by the lies I've told. The things I should have sai

but didn't. Mark's accident has put things into perspective, and it's time to stop playing foolish games. I'll stop at the police station and tell them everything. Explain why we never said anything. How scared we were. I'll answer their questions truthfully, then I'll go home and wait for whatever happens next.

Maybe once this is all over, I can look for another job and start my life again.

Going into the bedroom, I push my clothes into my bag. It's only been a week and yet the time I've been here has seemed so much longer. Being here has made me weak. Made me do what Mark wanted even though I knew it wasn't right. Just like I used to with Joanna.

It's like New Tobacco Wharf has infected me. That Joanna's absence, even more than her presence, has turned me back into the person I once was. But I'm not that person any more. I haven't been for ten years.

At the bedroom door, I stop and look behind me. The photograph I found in Eloise's apartment is in my mind, and I can't resist having one last look before I leave. Crossing to the wardrobe, I open the door and stare at the drawer where I found all the photographs of me and Joanna. Even though I know it should be locked, I reach out a hand and give a tentative pull.

To my surprise, the drawer slides easily. It's still full of photographs, which I never looked closely at. Too shocked to find them there at all. The top one is face down. Putting my hand in, I pull it out and turn it over, my blood freezing when I see what's happened. It's another photo of the two of us, and from the shiny paper, Joanna's smile is wide... but my own face has been blacked out. The next one is the same, only this time the black marker has been scrawled so thickly that it's worn a hole right through my face. The ruined picture created by a hand made heavy with hatred.

More and more. All the same.

CHAPTER FORTY-FIVE

Joanna

I tip my head to look at the iron-railed balconies, the tall mullioned windows with their arched tops and the heavy wooden doors. Despite the development being such a failure, the building's still impressive as it stands in front of me.

I touch the fingers of my right hand to the money belt beneath my blouse, feeling the shape of my key. In there too is one for Eloise's apartment, copied from the one she gave me so that Mark wouldn't notice it was missing from the hook. I also have one for the apartment where Nathan is squatting.

As I walk to the large double sliding doors, I see that Derek is in his office. He's at his monitors, his back to me. What is he still doing up? My father thinks the sun shines out of his arse just because he's ex-army. *Diligent* is the word he uses. Too bloody diligent. That's why he's the only creep I haven't managed to persuade my father or Mark to dispense with.

I think of Derek's thin ginger hair, his freckled fingers that I know would like to touch my skin and shiver. In his dreams.

Stepping up to the glass entrance door, the area around me is immediately lit up by the security lights. There's no way I'm going to get in without Derek seeing me, so I need to do this right. Reaching out a hand, I press the buzzer and wait. Slowly, he swivels his chair around, his pale freckled face drawn into a frown. Clearly, he's not expecting anyone so late at night. After all, it's not as though the area is bursting at the seams with residents.

Slowly, he stands. Beside his desk is a white plastic pot containing a large green yucca plant. Bending to it, he stubs out the cigarette he shouldn't be smoking, then straightens and zips up his black bomber jacket. He's in no hurry to get to the door, but as he passes the reception desk and sees me through the glass, his pace quickens.

'Joanna!' Although I can't hear him, I recognise the shape of my name on his lips.

I wait as Derek presses the large button at the side of the glass doors. There are blotches of red on each of his cheeks, a tide of pink creeping up his neck. The doors slide open, and he steps forward. For one dreadful moment I think he's going to embrace me, but then he checks himself, chewing at his bottom lip to keep it under control.

'Jesus, Joanna. Where have you been?' His small eyes sweep my face, taking in the dark circles under my eyes, the skin he's never seen without make-up.

I bite my tongue hard until tears form in my eyes. 'It's been horrible, Derek. Just horrible. I can't believe what he did.'

'What *who* did? Tell me.'

He puts a hand on my upper arm, and I resist the urge to pull away. I need to keep Derek on my side.

'Mark. He's evil. I think he wanted to kill me.'

Derek's eyes widen. 'The bastard. He'll be the one who's dead if I get my hands on him. What did he do?'

I let my face crumple. 'I don't want to talk about it now, Derek. I just need to collect some clothes from the apartment. The police will be here tomorrow. They'll be asking questions, but I'd rather you didn't tell them I was here.' I raise my hand to his face, tracing a finger down his cheek. 'I can trust you, can't I?'

'Of course, you can. I'd never do anything to hurt you... not like that girl who's been staying here.'

'Who, Alice?'

'Yes, her.' Derek's lips twist into a sneer. 'She wormed her way in here good and proper.'

I try not to react. 'She's my friend, Derek. Please don't talk about her that way. Anyway, she's gone now.'

It's like Derek hasn't heard, though.

'From what I can see, she treated the place as her own personal boutique hotel. Getting your lapdog husband to wait on her hand and foot. Jesus, you should have seen the food delivery. You'd think it was the Ivy. Who eats asparagus anyway?'

I don't answer. What would I say? That asparagus has always been my favourite food? That the thought of Alice dipping it into the hollandaise sauce and putting it to her lips while my husband watches makes me feel sick. Why was he buying it for her?

'What's going on, Joanna?'

'I'll explain everything tomorrow. They won't let me stay here. I'll just get my stuff and go.' I point to the camera on the wall, then put my finger to his lips. 'Just our little secret.'

Derek looks unconvinced, but he doesn't argue. 'Yes, of course. I'll switch off the CCTV.' He jerks his thumb at the dark night outside, his face unreadable. 'Is Mr Belmont okay?'

His question unsettles me. I think of the white Mini embedded in the side of the pumping station, the blue and white police cordon. And, as I do, different emotions flow through me: disappointment at Mark's weakness, despair that I might never see him again, anger that Alice was the one to ruin it all. 'I don't know. They won't let me see him.'

I walk over to the lift, feeling Derek's eyes on my back, and press the button. The doors slide open straight away, and pulling the concertina inner door aside, I step in, thankful when the doors slide closed again against Derek's prying eyes. A worry is nagging at me. What if Mark recognised me when I stepped into the road? What if he picked me out in his headlights? If he regains consciousness and tells the police, everything will be ruined.

The lift stops. It's only travelled one floor, but that's the one whose shiny silver button I pressed. There's something I need to do before I go home.

Before I see Alice.

CHAPTER FORTY-SIX

Alice

I drop the photographs onto the floor, standing immobile as shock courses through me. Someone has been in here since I last looked at them and done this.

I count off on my fingers the few people who might have had access to them. Mark's stepson was here this week. Derek too when he came to fix the air conditioning unit. Eloise also had a key... Mark told me so. Can it be that one of these people disliked me so much they'd do such a thing?

More worryingly, why?

Cold fingers of fear work their way up my spine as I remember that one of these people is no longer alive. What if someone is preying on the women who live here? First Joanna, then Eloise. How long before the police find my friend's body washed up on some muddy river beach, her black hair full of silt.

How long before they find mine?

Adrenaline kicks in. I must leave this place. Immediately. Leaving the photographs on the floor, I throw my bag over my shoulder and hobble from the room. I pull open the front door and step into the corridor, checking for my car keys in my bag before realising my stupidity. My car is no longer in the garage. It's either still embedded in the wall of the pumping station or the police will have towed it away.

It might take all night, but I need to get out of this place. I haven't got very far down the corridor though before I see something that makes my breathing become shorter.

The numbers above the lift are moving. Steadily rising. 3... 4... 5...

It can't be Mark; he's in hospital attached to a machine that's helping him breathe. Who else would be riding the lift to floor six? Might Mark's stepson be paying me another visit?

No. There's only one person who knows everything. Would have seen on his monitors the police arrive, watched them escort me to the apartment, bided his time until they left again. What does he want with me? I picture Derek in the small, confined space of the lift. His feet astride, his eyes fixed on the door, waiting for it to open. The word *security* on his jacket giving him all the permission he needs to do what he wants.

The doors to the stairs are at the end of the corridor. Can I make it before the lift arrives or should I go back and shut myself into the apartment? Put the chain on the door and pray that he'll leave me alone?

I've taken too much time thinking. The number has already reached 6, and I have no choice. Turning around, I limp back the way I came and force the key into the lock, nearly crying with relief when it turns, and the door opens. Behind me, I hear the lift ping, then the grate of the concertina door as it's pulled open. Throwing myself into the room, I slam the door closed behind me and pull the chain across.

I wait, my ear to the door. There are footsteps on the wooden floor, then silence. He's outside. I know it. With my back against the door, I sink to the ground, not wanting to hear the shrill buzz that lets me know he's here. Knowing it's going to come. But it doesn't. There's nothing except the sound of my laboured breathing.

CHAPTER FORTY-SEVEN
Joanna

I stand in front of my own front door. It's been just over a week since I was last here. Since I ate at my table, sat on my purple settee or slept in my bed with my husband. I lean my shoulder against the door. Has Alice been sleeping in that bed too?

I think of Eloise's bed two floors below, its expensive memory foam mattress covered in a bright patchwork quilt. She'd told me once that she'd made it herself. She had nothing better to do than stitch bed linen.

That huge reproduction four-poster bed under its floating canopy of red muslin, had been more comfortable than my own though and certainly more comfortable than the bed in the cheap hotel or the mattress in the unit. One night between those four metal walls had been enough. I don't think I could have stood another, for even with the duvet I'd dragged out of one of the boxes, the place had been freezing.

That's why I'd been so relieved when I let myself into Eloise's apartment and realised she'd gone. I'd only popped in to have a snoop around, waiting until the time I knew she always took her dog for a walk. Imagine my surprise when I saw her suicide note stuck to the fridge with a magnet along with a photograph of me and Alice. I'd recognised it straight away as the one I had on my own fridge door, but how it had come to be there I had no idea. As I'd read her words, I'd felt sad – of course I had – but there was a little part of me that had felt glad too. What Eloise had done was evidence of how much I'd meant to her. Evidence too of how Alice's visit had affected more people than I thought.

What I wanted to do was have a hot shower, wash my hair and dress myself in some of Eloise's clean clothes, but of course I couldn't. Instead, I'd gone into her bedroom and locked the door, falling asleep as soon as my head hit her pillow. What would Alice have thought if she'd known I was only a heartbeat away from her when she'd stopped by? Or that only a few hours later, I'd be on my way to the police station?

Putting my ear to my own apartment door, I think I hear something. A muffled sob. It comes again, but this time it's the sound of a scared and wounded animal. I smile, placing the flat of my hand against the wood. I know it's Alice who's in distress. I know she needs me. The realisation floods my body with warmth, every instinct making me want to go to her. But I fight it. A few more minutes won't hurt.

The sweet smell of tobacco in the corridor is more pungent than I remember, but I like it. It reminds me of the stories Mark liked to tell me of the docks when they were still full of life. A time when the black water of the wharf was full of tall ships and a hangman's gibbet stood proudly on the quayside waiting to welcome the traitors.

Outside the window, at the end of the corridor, the sky is the pale milky blue of dawn, the black bulk of the warehouse next to ours, silhouetted against it. Smiling to myself, I take Eloise's letter from my back pocket and unfold the page. It's just light enough to make out the words.

Leaning my back against the door, knowing that Alice is on the other side of it, I read Eloise's letter for the second time.

Dear Joanna,

I don't know where you are and, to be honest, I don't really care now I know our friendship meant so little. Once, you made me feel special, helped me pull myself out of the dark place I was in, but I see myself now for what I really was – nothing more than another of your little projects.

It was never about helping me, was it? It was about how good it made you feel to be needed. Being there when I was at my lowest ebb was your way of controlling me, wasn't it? And when I started to get better, less dependent, you dropped me for someone weaker. Another fool who would look up to you as I did. Poor Nathan.

I expect you'll be surprised to hear that we met. He knocked on my door and told me who he was. How you'd helped him when his life was spiralling out of control. He looked bad, Joanna. Really rough. He said he knew all about our special friendship. That you'd told him… only it wasn't that special, was it? There was someone else who meant more to you than either of us, and that person wasn't Mark. Nathan gave me the photograph of you and Alice – said there were more in your apartment. Hundreds of them. That you were obsessed. He wanted to hurt me – it's what jealousy does to you.

Only I knew already. I'd met Alice briefly and had seen it in the way her eyes lit up when she talked about you. It's a shame, as she seemed nice, and, in some ways, not unlike me. We were both blinkered. Both naïve. It was clever of you to know the right time to click your fingers and have her running back. It's like you have a sixth sense that tells you when someone is at a low point in their lives. Just like me. Just like that poor kid who thinks you've replaced his dead mother. Now he's clean and getting his act together, have you thought what will happen to him when you dump him too? Yes, of course you have. I just hope he doesn't blame himself for what I'm going to do. It wasn't the photograph that did it. I'm just tired of life. Everything's turned dark again.

I don't know where you've gone, but when you get back, I'll be gone too. I've taken Pixie with me. Someone will find her, and if not, she'll make her way home in time. Hopefully, she'll find someone who loves her as much as I do.

If you're reading this, it means that in the end I was the strong one. I broke away from you... not the other way round.

Eloise

CHAPTER FORTY-EIGHT
Alice

I hear a knock. Once, twice. A third time. So quiet, I can barely hear it. I hold my breath, but there's nothing more. The minutes tick by, and I wait, my forehead resting on my bent knees, listening to the silence.

Please. Please. Just go.

Is he still out there? And, if so, what is he doing? I imagine him leaning against the brick wall, a cigarette in his hand, waiting for me to get bored. Waiting for me to open the door and look out. Or maybe he's gone. In some strange way, the not knowing is worse. Panic is taking hold of me. He knows I can't stay in the apartment forever.

Slowly, I stand and move aside the brass cover of the spyhole. I'm just pressing my eye to it when the knock comes again, making me jump. But it's not this that sends my pulse racing, it's who I see standing in the corridor.

Grabbing at the chain, I slide it back so quickly my skin catches on the sharp metal edge. Using my other hand to unlock the door, I pull it open, sucking at the cut on my finger.

'Joanna!'

I can't believe what I'm seeing. She's here. She's back. Standing like a lost soul on the doorstep, her dark hair freshly washed and shiny, her face deathly pale. She's wearing clothes that look too large for her as though they're not her own. Stepping forward, pull her into a hug, tears of relief running down my face, feeling her heart beat against mine. It's only now she's here in the flesh, not just in my memory, that I realise how much I've missed her.

Standing back, I take in her pale, heart-shaped face. The shadows under her green eyes. 'Oh my God! What happened to you? Where have you been?'

Joanna looks over her shoulder. 'Not here.'

'I'm sorry. Come in. You look tired… I'll make some tea.'

She stares at me, and I realise how stupid my words must sound. Joanna has escaped from God knows where, and I'm inviting her in as though it's my apartment and she the visitor.

Saying nothing, Joanna steps inside. She has nothing with her. No bag. No coat.

I start to walk to the kitchen, then stop. Why am I acting as though everything is normal when it's not? Coming back, I take her hand in mine, my fingers tightening around hers. 'I can't stand not knowing. You must tell me where you've been.'

Joanna doesn't move. Just stands and looks beyond me, her eyes roving over the dining table, the settees, the kitchen island with its stainless steel counter. Her free hand moves to her hair, her fingers drawing back a strand that she tucks behind her ear. It's then I see the thin gold band on her wedding finger. In my relief at seeing Joanna, I've forgotten about Mark.

'There's something I need to tell you, Joanna. It's not good. Maybe you should sit down.'

Putting an arm around her, I lead her to the purple settee and gently make her sit, just like the policewoman did with me earlier. I sit beside her, our knees touching, like we're children again pressing close to one another, still trying to come to terms with the fact that she's really here.

Joanna lowers her eyes. Clasps one hand with the other, her knuckles whitening. 'I know about Mark, if that's what you were going to tell me, Alice.'

'You know?'

She nods. 'The police told me about the accident. They thought, being his wife, it was something I ought to know.'

I put my own hand on top of hers, wondering if I imagined the emphasis she put on the word wife. 'It will take a while, but he'll be all right. I'm sure he will.' I give her fingers a reassuring squeeze. 'I went to see him in the hospital.'

Her eyes lock with mine. 'They told me that too.'

'Yes. I was worried. I…'

'Of course, you were. Why wouldn't you be?' Joanna rubs at her wrist. There's a faint welt around it like a bracelet. The other one has it too.

'Your wrists? What happened?'

Joanna doesn't answer. Pulling the sleeves of her cardigan over her hands, she gets up and walks to the window. There's a pale tangerine glow to the sky, but it only serves to accentuate the velvet darkness of the river. On a morning like this, it's easy to see how Black Water Dock got its name.

'You need to know the truth,' Joanna says eventually.

Her back is to me, and I notice how her dark hair is longer than it used to be, falling to just below her shoulders. It suits her. It brings back a memory. We're sitting on her bed, in our halls of residence, and I'm drawing a brush through the fine, straight strands. Following it with my hand, mesmerised by its shine.

I hold my breath. 'Yes.'

'It was Mark who did it. He knocked me unconscious, then locked me in an industrial unit by the river.'

I stare at her. Not comprehending what she's saying. I think of Mark – the man who welcomed me into his apartment and cooked me a meal even though he hadn't a clue who I was. The man who did everything he could to scrape together the money to pay off Joanna's captives. Who loved her enough to marry her without a second thought after only a few weeks, just because it was what she wanted.

'I don't understand. He can't have. You're lying.'

Her voice catches. 'I wish I was.'

I study Joanna's face. In all the years we've known each other, she might have had her faults, but she's never lied to me. In some ways, she's been too honest.

'Oh, Jesus.' Can it really be true? I try to picture it but can't. 'Where was this unit?'

Joanna turns her profile to the window, points her finger at the glass, her face a picture of misery. 'It was further along the dock. Near the Devil's Staircase. He rented the unit to store the contents of his ex-wife's house after he sold it.'

That first day, when Mark had shown me the ancient mildewed steps with their iron rings embedded into the stone, we'd passed by several units to let amongst the derelict buildings. How had Joanna been in one of them without me knowing it? Feeling it? I feel sick to my stomach.

'But it can't have been Mark. He received a ransom note. Someone was asking him for money for your safe return.'

I watch Joanna run her finger down the glass, hoping that her face will give away that this has all been a big joke.

It doesn't. Instead, she's looking at me as though I'm the biggest fool alive.

CHAPTER FORTY-NINE

Joanna

I shake my head. 'Oh, Alice. You're so naïve. Don't you see? Mark sent that note to himself.'

Alice stares at me stupidly. 'He can't have. It's not possible.'

'And why do you think that?' I wait, genuinely interested to hear her answer.

Her hands are loose at her sides. She looks helpless. 'Because I know him.'

I want to laugh, but something tells me it's better that I don't. 'You've only just met him and, besides, you've never been a very good judge of character, have you?'

A phone rings, breaking into my thoughts. It's an upbeat tune, something that's in the charts, and it takes a moment to realise it's my mobile that's ringing. The one the police gave me. Taking it from my pocket, I answer it.

'Hello? No, don't worry, you didn't wake me up. I wasn't asleep.' I look across at Alice, my face impassive. 'Yes, I see. Thank you for letting me know. I'll see you in the morning.'

Shoving the phone back into my pocket, I turn and hold my hands out to her. Palms upturned. The pink tender skin on my wrists exposed. 'He tied me up, Alice. Left me alone in the dark.'

Alice's hand rises to her throat, her fingers hovering at the soft dip between her collarbones. 'The dark?'

'It was awful,' I carry on. 'I was so scared.'

I cover my face with my hands, guessing that Alice wants to come over and comfort me, wondering if she will. When she doesn't, I wonder whether it's because she's not used to this role reversal. She's used to me being the strong one.

'But why?' Alice remains where she is, her head bent, forehead creased. 'Wouldn't it have been better if he'd sent the note to your parents?'

'My parents?' I know my voice is incredulous. Why would she think that? 'Fuck all they care about me. It would be like getting blood out of a stone. No, his plan was different. This way, when it was all over, he would look like the victim.'

Alice's head shoots up. 'What do you mean *when it was all over*? Christ, Joanna. What did you think Mark was going to do? Surely you can't think…' The words stick in her mouth.

'You don't know him, Alice. You don't know what he's capable of. If it wasn't for the fact he was in hospital, I would have been too scared to come back here. The police know. They've sent officers to the ward.' Walking back to the settee, I sit beside her again.

Alice stares ahead, her arms wrapped around her body. 'Do you really mean to say that for a week I've been sharing the apartment with a monster?' She shudders at the thought.

'I was so scared for you, knowing that I'd invited you here and as a result you'd be here… with him. Part of me hoped that you'd just turn around and go back home when you found I wasn't here, but the other part of me knew you were my only hope.' I take her hands in mine, remembering the feel of them. 'Knowing you wouldn't let me down was what kept me strong. I knew that if you stayed, you'd realise something was wrong and eventually see through Mark's lies.'

Yet we both know she hadn't. Even now, I'm not sure she completely believes he could do what he did. And that's the thing I'm uncertain about. The thing that's been puzzling me. At no point during my interview with the police did they mention the demand for money. No one showed me a ransom note.

I picture the sheet of paper, the words written in red ink. Each one formed from the little wooden blocks with their rubber letters, which I'd pressed into the moistened ink pad. I'd found the printing set in a box in the unit, along with other toys belonging to Nathan, though why he hadn't got rid of them I don't know. It was what had given me the idea – the perfect way to prove how much Mark loved me.

Could it be that the police don't know about the note? That no one told them? I need to make sure it stays that way. Things have escalated since the day I left. Going to the police had never been part of the plan, but when Mark didn't deliver the money to the chapel, my disappointment had been crushing. I'd wanted to punish him for not loving me enough.

Punish him for Alice too.

To expect the police to believe Mark sent the ransom note to himself is a step too far without her help; I need her to believe too. I never thought anyone other than my husband would read it, but if it's found, it could be easy to link it to me.

Alice looks uncertain, as though she's still trying to decide what to believe. She's perched on the very edge of the settee, her back ramrod straight, watching me with nervous eyes. I have to up my game.

'It was so cold,' I continue. 'So dark in there. No windows to let in any light. The only sound was the scratching of the rats. I was terrified they'd run over my face as I slept.'

Alice turns away from me… from my words. Not wanting to hear. Not wanting a picture to form. What I'm telling her is taking her back to a place she doesn't want to remember. I know I should stop, that to carry on is dangerous, but I can't. I've missed that look on her face. The fear in her eyes. Her lip caught between her teeth.

At first, my voice is flat, but as I carry on, it becomes more animated. I'm picturing the place of my captivity, describing it as though it's a scene from a film.

'Each morning, I'd wake, and it would be as dark as it was when I fell asleep. It made my skin crawl, but at least then I knew I was still alive. I'd press the palms of my hands against the wall. Move them along until I felt the place where the door was. Pounding with my fists in the hope that someone might hear me.'

I can see from Alice's face that she's there again, in that garage at the end of my parents' gravel drive. Her fist raw from trying to make someone hear. From wanting *me* to hear.

'Stop it. Please.' Her voice is a plea.

Taking her gently by the shoulders, I turn her so she's facing me again. Her pupils are dilated with horror. I can't stop. My power over her intoxicating. 'And with every minute, every hour, the suffocating darkness would press in on me until at last I knew, with absolute certainty, that I'd gone blind. That my fear was slowly shutting down each part of my body and I was going to die.'

Our eyes are locked, and I feel the shiver that runs through her body, making her shoulders shudder.

I think she's going to break down, fall into my waiting arms as she always used to in times of distress, but she doesn't. Instead, she stands, and it's only when I see the look of disgust in her eyes that I realise I've made a terrible mistake.

CHAPTER FIFTY

Alice

I stare at her.

These are *my* words. The ones I used all those years ago, sitting in her parents' living room, a cup of sweet tea in my hand to help me get over the shock.

I think of Mark in his hospital bed. How desperate he'd been to find the money. The effort it took to control his trembling lip as he'd told me Joanna was missing. If I was going to fake my distress, I'd have put on more of a show – sobbed and pulled at my hair. And what about the silent tears that soaked the collar of his shirt? The tiny red blood vessels that reddened the whites of his eyes? The desperation in his voice? No… they were real.

I look at Joanna and I know, with certainty, that something's not right.

'You used my words.'

Joanna stops speaking. 'What do you mean?'

'Those things you said, the way you said what it was like.. all of it. They were *my* words – the ones I used to describe how it was when I was locked in your parents' garage that time when we were children. You've never been afraid of the dark, Joanna. Not in all the years I've known you. You might have been scared of what Mark might do – that he wouldn't come back, leave you there with no food or water, or worse still, what he'd do if he did come back – but the dark is something you would never be scared of. That has always been *my* fear, not yours. You've stolen my memory.'

Joanna's face grows stony. 'And you've never taken what wasn't yours? Don't pretend you didn't ever wonder what it would be like to live here. In an apartment bought with money you'd never make in a lifetime.'

How can she know? How can she read my mind? But of course, she would remember how I never invited her home, how I'd always made excuses: my mum was too tired and then, when we were older, too ill to have people to stay. It was always me who'd invite myself to Joanna's. Every holiday. Pretending I lived there. Pretending it was my home. Wanting her life.

And when I'd got her message, it hadn't taken much to send me running back – just a lost job and a broken heart – the invisible cords of our friendship pulling me in. I'd basked in the idea that she wanted to help me again, that our friendship was as strong as it ever was, but my obsession with her had stopped me recognising that nothing would be different. Joanna would use me in the same way she'd always done.

Nothing is real. It's all a lie.

Joanna is scratching at the welt on her arm, pinpricks of blood needling the surface. I grab her hand to stop her. 'Don't! Tell me the truth. You made this whole thing up, didn't you?'

Narrowing her eyes, Joanna pulls her hand away. 'What if I did?'

I stare at her. Gobsmacked.

And then slowly it all comes to me – the rumours Joanna encouraged me to help spread about any girl at school she didn't like. How when we fell out, it would be Joanna who would decide when the fight was over, but I'd never hear an apology. And when I was brave enough to question why she wanted to hurt people, she'd call me attention-seeking and needy.

But that wasn't all. Joanna had always played the victim. Nothing was ever her fault.

'You're sick, Joanna, do you know that? What made you do it?'

Joanna brings her face close to mine, and I see now how the features, once so pretty, have hardened.

'Isn't it obvious?' she says. 'I wanted to see how much Mark cared. How much I was worth.'

'How much you were *worth*?'

Her lips stretch into a smile. 'Everyone has a price. I needed to know what mine was.'

Getting up, she paces in front of the settee like a restless animal. 'Mark let me down. Just like *you* did. He couldn't even be bothered to raise the money.'

I don't like the look in her eyes. The way she's wringing her hands. A gut feeling makes me know I must appease her. 'But he tried to get the money, Joanna. He did everything he could.'

'Did he?' She sneers. 'Did he really?'

'He borrowed some, I know that. Made up some story and got a loan from your father.'

Joanna snorts in disgust. 'So the money came from that tight arse after all. Ironic.'

'Mark did his best. He was only a little short. He was on his way to deliver it when he had the accident. That was why he didn't make the deadline.'

'Maybe he did, but if he passed *that* test, he failed the other. Why *are* you still here, Alice? Why *are* you in my home?'

'You invited me. You asked me to come… to meet Mark.'

'And you didn't think it strange I contacted you after ten years?' She stops pacing and stands in front of me. 'Oh, no. You were too busy thinking about yourself. Wondering how you could insinuate yourself into my world again when I'd made it clear I didn't want anything more to do with you.'

Her words sting, and I remember again how she'd dropped me. Told me we were no longer friends. We'd been standing outside the crematorium, the wind shivering the petals on the wreaths. The ervice and saying that final goodbye to my mum had brought back another loss. All I'd wanted to do was make Joanna understand what it had done to me. Understand her part in it. It was the first time I'd stood up to her. Raised my voice. Become stronger.

She hadn't liked it. It made me a different person.

'It wasn't like that,' I whisper.

Joanna gives a mirthless laugh. 'No? Then why was it *me* the stewardess called when you had your pathetic little panic attack on the plane? Why not someone else?' She sneers. 'Because you can't leave me alone. You want to be *me*.'

I freeze. 'The stewardess said she hadn't rung you.'

'Oh, she rang all right. Told me about your little turn... that it was *me* you wanted. When she phoned me back almost straight away and said you'd changed your mind, I didn't believe her. You needed me, just like you did all those years ago. Only this time I needed you too.'

So that's why Joanna messaged me. It hadn't been out of the blue after all.

'And when you arrived and found out I wasn't here,' Joanna continues, 'you thought it would be normal to stay a week. It's what anyone would do, right?'

'Yes... no.' My eyes flick to the door wondering how quickly I can reach it. 'I wanted to help find you. I didn't want Mark to be on his own.'

Reaching out a hand, Joanna takes my chin, turning my face from left to right, her nails digging into the flesh. 'I thought it might work with Eloise, but she wasn't interested in him. You though... you were another matter. You've always wanted what's mine. I knew you would be the one to tempt him. The perfect honeytrap.'

I push her hand away. 'Mark and I... nothing happened.'

She gives a hollow laugh. 'Just like you and Jez never happened.'

'That was different, Joanna. He wasn't your fiancé... your husband. You weren't even really going out.'

'And that made it all right. Even though you knew I loved him.

'I loved him too.'

'Of course you did.' She jabs a finger into my stomach. 'Enough to get knocked up.'

CHAPTER FIFTY-ONE

Alice

Ten long years and not a day goes by when I don't think of my baby. So many things that make me remember: an infant's cry in the street. A programme on the television about midwifery. The sight of a child's toy dropped on the pavement.

Worse, though, is when I see someone who is following that same precious path I should have taken all those years ago. Like the colleague who announced her pregnancy in the staffroom, holding out the scan photograph, not knowing how the sketchy white image on its black background tore at my heart. Not realising how deep I'd had to dig in order to paste that smile on my face and congratulate her. The woman who lives opposite me hadn't known either what it took to ask if she'd thought of a name yet and how I'd had to force myself not to watch as her hand strayed to the swell of her belly as she answered that they were going to call him Alex.

I never got the chance to give that baby a name. Couldn't let myself think that way as it would only have made it harder. That's what I was told anyway. And so I'd tried not to think of my baby at all, even when it broke my heart not to. I'd tried to think, instead, of how much easier my life would be without it. I could finish my studies. Get a job. Carry on as though it had never come into my life.

Only it didn't happen that way. Nobody had told me of the grief that would rise unexpectedly and threaten to swallow me.

That what I'd done was something I'd have to live with every day of my life.

If only I'd had the courage to tell Drew what had happened all those years ago. If I had, things might have turned out differently. Instead, I'd kept my grief and guilt locked inside and pushed him away. Would I have done that if I'd known that he'd end up having the one thing I've ever truly wanted. A child.

How I wish I could have been stronger.

I think of that tiny, innocent baby inside me. My anxiety. My indecision. It was Joanna who'd said it would be all right. She'd go to the hospital with me, look after me when I came out. She said it would be for the best as it was clear Jez didn't love me. I had a year left of my degree and I had to think of my future. Make my parents proud after all the sacrifices they'd made.

I'd never told Jez about the baby or what I'd done. What was the point after what Joanna told me? I couldn't face him so, instead I'd left a message on his phone telling him I needed space and that it was best we didn't see each other any more. When he'd rung me straight back and tried to change my mind, told me he loved me I hadn't believed him. Besides, it wasn't about Jez, it never was.

Knocked up. Such a blunt expression. So cruel.

In the years after we last saw each other, I'd presumed that Joanna had done it out of jealousy, but now I wonder if I was right. I'd never have started seeing him if it hadn't been for the fact that I knew Joanna hadn't even liked Jez that much. It was something she'd told me over a vodka and Coke in the student union bar one evening. As she'd downed her drink and listed his faults, she'd already been planning how to get the attention of the guy behind the bar.

No, it wasn't jealousy; it was something else. Something more unsettling than that.

'I know why you did it. Why you persuaded me to terminate the pregnancy. It wasn't about Jez, it was because you wanted to keep me to yourself. Couldn't bear the thought of me sharing my love with someone else. Not even a baby.'

Her lips twitch. 'You don't know what you're talking about, Alice. You're living in cloud cuckoo land. You always did have a vivid imagination.'

Just as they always used to, her words seep into my pores, filling my being until I wonder if she's right. But I won't let her win. Can't let her see how her throwaway description of what happened has crushed me. Not now the truth is crystal clear.

Outside the window, the sky has lightened further, and I'm glad. It makes me stronger.

Without realising it, my hand has strayed to my belly. 'That little life would have been completely dependent on me. I'd have become the giver instead of the taker and that would have been more than you could stand. I should never have listened to you. I should never have let you persuade me to ring the clinic.'

Joanna puts her head on one side, amused. 'You didn't have to do everything I said.'

I know that now, but it's how I was then, and there's nothing I can do to change the past. I shouldn't have let her persuade me, but I did. The irony was, two months later, I left anyway. Left the flat. Left university. My mother was dying, and I came home to be with her. Locked in grief at the prospect of losing her and the baby I'd never had, it had been my chance to break away from Joanna. Yet, still I'd thought about her. Obsessed over what she was doing and what her life was like without me. She was like a drug and even when I finally settled down with Drew, there was a Joanna-shaped hole he couldn't fill.

Joanna places her hands on her hips. 'You know something, Alice?'

'What?' I'm scared of what else she's going to tell me.

'Mark is the first man I've been with who's strong. I don't mean physically, I mean mentally. He's no lame duck – doesn't rely on me the way the other men have. Waiting for me to praise them for selling a shit painting of Tower Bridge or making enough from their busking to buy dinner. Wanting me to massage their egos. He's not interested in my money or who my parents are. He doesn't need me. And do you know what, Alice? I liked it.'

Disbelief is written across her face as though she can't believe what she's just said. I can't either.

'Mark's a good man.' I know it now. Think, deep down, I knew it all along. 'How could you do that to him?'

Joanna frowns at me as though I'm stupid. 'I needed to know that Mark was different. That he wouldn't be like the other men I've been with, but I had to be sure. Would it be money that would be his weakness or sex?' She jabs a finger into my chest. 'Now I know.'

'We didn't do anything.' Anxiety is making my voice rise. 'It's you he loves.'

'That's not what it looked like from where I was standing. Did you know that the only camera that's turned on in the corridors is the one on our floor? That creep Derek's got an obsession with me, likes to watch me come and go.' She shakes her head sadly. 'But what can you do?'

So that's why he never knew about Nathan. How he had managed to stay hidden from prying eyes. There were no working cameras on his floor. The one time he'd visited this one, he must have been lucky. Picked a time when the security guard was doing something else.

'I know Derek's routine... when he patrols the corridors, when he does his maintenance. And, of course, even he needs the toilet sometimes.' Joanna looks amused. 'It's surprising what those monitors of his will pick up – especially the one in the car park. Sorry if I gave you a fright with the doors. I couldn't help myself – it was just too tempting.'

'It was *you* who stopped them from working? Even though you knew how much I hate the dark... being trapped.'

'Like I said, I'm sorry, Alice. You'll get over it.' She cups her chin in her hand, tapping her cheek with her fingertips. 'Yes, those monitors… quite the soap opera. Take that kiss. It would have been rather moving if it hadn't been with my husband.'

I feel the colour drain from my face. With certainty, I now know it was Joanna who came into the apartment. She who scribbled over my face with the black marker until I was obliterated.

'It wasn't anything. I was scared for him, that's all. Please, Joanna. You have to believe me.'

I stand and, without any concrete plan, begin to move away from her. It's an effort to keep my voice steady, but I know I have to if I have any chance of getting away from Joanna. I'd come here imagining the friend I'd had when I was younger needed me, and, in a way, I was right. But it wasn't my friendship she'd craved, it was my weakness. I'd known it that day at Mum's funeral. Why had I let myself forget?

'I'll make us a drink, and then we can talk properly. Soon, we'll be laughing about it, just like we used to.'

The shove she gives me sends me reeling back onto the settee. Joanna stands above me, her dark hair swinging as she lowers her face to mine. 'Do you know where my husband put the ransom note… what he did with it?'

'No. He didn't tell me.'

'Stay where you are. Don't even think about leaving that chair.'

As I look on, Joanna moves through the apartment, pulling out drawers, rifling through cupboards, lifting cushions. I know I have to get out of here. If Joanna's mad enough to do what she did, who knows what else she's capable of. In the kitchen, on the shiny steel counter, I can see my mobile, but it's too far away.

All I can do is wait.

'Where the hell did he put it?'

Finishing in the living area, Joanna goes into the bedroom she shares with Mark, and I hear the bang of the wardrobe doors being flung open. The sound of drawers sliding and furniture being moved. When she finally comes out, her face is triumphant. She waves the ransom note above her head like a prize.

'There we go.'

Going into the kitchen, she rummages in one of the drawer and pulls out a box of matches. Then, taking the note to the sink she strikes one and touches the end to the paper. I watch as th flame creeps up, blackening it. When it licks at her fingers, she drops it into the sink and smiles.

'That's the end of that. We wouldn't want the police to trac the ink and think I had anything to do with this, would we?'

I stand up, willing myself to stay strong. 'I'll tell them anyway and, if I don't, Mark will when he wakes up. We'll tell ther everything.'

Turning on the tap, Joanna washes away the burnt remnants of the note, then carefully wipes her hands on the towel. She come back to me and places her hands on my shoulders.

'Oh, did I forget to say?' When I don't reply, she carries on 'That phone call… it was from the police.'

I stare at her, the hairs raised on the back of my arms. I know what she's going to say even before she's said it.

'I'm sorry, Alice.' She shakes her head sadly. 'But Mark die two hours ago.'

CHAPTER FIFTY-TWO

Alice

Joanna holds out her arms. Her tone has changed. It's no longer vindictive but motherly. 'You poor thing, this has all been a huge shock for you. Come here.'

I stare at her in horror. This is exactly how she used to behave when we were younger, saying things to shock, then consoling me. Can she really expect me to forget everything she's told me? Batting away her hands, I step back.

'Leave me alone, Joanna. I'm not thirteen any more. I don't need you to be my saviour.'

Joanna is taller than me, and there's a pent-up energy about her that makes her strong. Fearless. I watch her walk over to the sleek wooden sideboard under the wall-mounted TV. She picks up a controller and, for one idiotic moment, I think she's going to suggest we watch a film like we used to when we shared a flat at uni.

Then, with horror, I see that it's not the TV controller she's picked up.

I feel the first cold lick of fear. My voice comes out as a whisper. 'No, please don't.'

She looks at me and smiles. Points the controller at the window. 'Don't be such a baby, Alice.'

With a soft whirring sound, the hideous blinds at the windows begin to lower. The room that was flooded in daylight is growing darker, the sky and the tops of the buildings on the other side of the river disappearing behind the metal slats.

I try to grab the controller, but she jerks her hand away. 'There's nothing to be scared of. Face your fears, Alice. I dare you.'

The blinds are almost down, just a thin strip of light showing under them. Every instinct tells me to get out, but I can't as Joanna is in front of me now. In the gloom, I see the controller in her hand, but in the other is something that catches the last of the light. The glint of sharp metal before the light is extinguished.

'Please, Joanna.' Every nerve in my body is taut. Ready to respond to the fight or flight instinct.

Joanna's voice comes out of the deepening darkness. 'I chose *you* that day in the classroom. It could have been one of the others, but the moment you looked at me with those nervous eyes, I knew you were special. That you'd make the perfect friend. And do you know why?' I can no longer see her face, just hear her voice as the metal shutter clicks into place. Fighting my rising panic, I will my eyes to adjust to the lack of light. But there's nothing but the pitch-blackness. 'I asked if you know why?'

I'm crying now. Fighting for breath between the sobs. 'No, don't know.'

'Because I knew that you needed me as much as I needed you. I could see it in your eyes. You want me to open the blinds, don' you? You want me to save you.'

My arms are hugged tight around me. 'Yes. Yes, I do.'

'Just like you wanted me to save you from the scary dark garage. Like you wanted me to save you from life as a single mother.' Her voice is mocking. Hateful. 'I knew you'd be grateful. It's why did it.'

My fear is turning to anger. '*You* shut me in there, even though you knew I was terrified of the dark? How could you?'

I can't see her, but I take my chance. Raising my arm, I swing it out in front of me with as much force as I can muster. There' a sharp pain as it makes contact, and I hear the clink of metal on wood. Joanna swears. I hear her drop to the floor, feel her hand as she sweeps the floor for the knife.

I feel it by my foot and kick it away, hearing it skid across the floor. Then I'm on my feet, lurching across the room in the pitch-darkness. Praying I'm going in the right direction for the door.

When my side makes contact with the corner of the kitchen island, I know I haven't gone far enough. There's a blue light from the kettle, digital numbers on the oven. These small beacons of light give me hope. Turning from them, I cross the empty space until I reach the wall, then feel my way along it until my fingers meet with the doorframe.

There's a noise behind me, the metallic rock of a standard lamp on the floor. Reaching up, I desperately feel for the handle, forgetting in my panic whether it's set high or low. I look behind me. I can't see anything. Just the solid darkness. But then there's a sound. A small click and a whirr. The shutters are rising again, and my sight is returning.

Joanna is staring at me from across the room. I don't know if she found the knife, but I've no time to find out as she's running towards me, a dreadful expression on her face.

I turn back to the apartment door, fumbling with terrified fingers for the handle. 'You'll never get away with this.'

I feel her hand slam into mine, prising my fingers away, but I jab my elbow back. Hear her groan as the wind's forced out of her. Thanking God I didn't lock the door, I push on the handle and yank it open. The corridor is empty as it always is, but I know Derek will be in his room. He'll be watching the monitor, waiting for his crush to come out. Wanting to get his fix. I shout and scream. Wave my arms. He'll see. He'll phone the police.

But Joanna has made it to the door and, with one hand holding her stomach, she runs towards me. Fighting against the pain in my ankle, I stumble down the corridor, past the open doors of the lift, past the doors of the empty apartments, in the direction of the stairs. When I get to the camera, I wave frantically again, my heart sinking when I see the woollen hat that's been hooked over it. The window pole that's been used to put it there, leaning against the wall.

It's Nathan's hat; the one he was wearing when I last saw him. Did she go to his room to get it? Did she see him?

I'm at the glass door now, pulling it open, but a force on my back sends me reeling, my weak ankle buckling under me, pain tearing through my knees as they hit the ground.

She's on me, her fingers gripping my hair, pulling my head backwards. Reaching behind me, I find her ankle and yank at it, bringing her down on top of me. The breath knocked out of me. I look to my right. We are at the edge of the stairs, the stone steps falling away to the landing below. Joanna is rolling over, pulling me with her. My hand reaches out, trying to grab hold of something that will anchor me... anything. But all I feel is the cold rough stone.

The edge of the top step cuts into my cheek, and then I'm falling, falling.

And the world goes black again.

EPILOGUE

don't know how long I've been asleep, but when I wake up, the oom has grown darker. I lift my head and see that it's a different urse who sits at the desk behind the panel of windows.

I want her to come in so I can speak to her, find out what's oing on, but my arm is too heavy to reach the call button. So, nstead, I lay my head back down on the starched white pillow nd think. Searching through my subconscious to find something, nything, that will help me remember what I did yesterday... the lay before even. There's nothing. Just a black void that makes my eart rate quicken.

The nurse gets up. She walks around her desk, and I will her to ome in, but she doesn't. Instead, she disappears from my eyesight or a few minutes before returning with an armful of folders.

My mouth is dry. My throat parched. On the table beside me s a plastic beaker with a straw, but I can't reach it. Soon someone ill come. At regular intervals since I've been here, I've been aware f people coming in to take my vital signs. Check my drip. Surely, won't have to wait much longer.

But then, through the gloom, I see a movement. It's from the hair by the window. Someone is sitting there, a blanket draped ver them. Through heavy eyelids, I watch them yawn and stretch. ee the blanket drop to the floor.

They're coming towards me, and my fingers tighten around e sheet at my neck.

'Who is it?'

The figure hovers over me. 'How are you feeling?'

A hand slides under my head, and I feel the poke of a straw as it's guided to my lips. Then the blessed relief as the cool water slips down my dry throat.

'Joanna? Have you been here all night?'

In the dimly lit room, I see her nod. 'Yes.' Her brow furrows as she pauses. 'You asked me to stay.'

I smile, though the simple movement hurts my head. 'Thank you.'

Joanna lowers my head gently back onto the pillow and smooths my sheets. Behind her, there's a gentle click as the door of my room opens. A nurse comes in – one I haven't seen before. She clips the heart rate monitor to my finger and tightens a cuff around my arm. As the cuff compresses, I feel a corresponding tightening across my chest.

'Please tell me what happened.'

She smiles. 'You were very lucky, Alice. If you hadn't been found, who knows how long you would have been lying there in that empty building.'

'Found?'

'Yes, you fell down the stairs at your friend's apartment. It was the security guard who found you and called the ambulance.'

'Derek?' I have a vague memory of him. A man in a black bomber jacket. White freckled hands.

'Yes. He was very worried about you. Has been up to the hospital twice already, but we couldn't let him see you until you were feeling a bit better.'

'But I don't remember anything.' My head hurts from trying. 'Why can't I?'

The nurse writes something on my chart. 'After a traumatic brain injury, short-term memory loss is common, and some patients have no memory of the injury or the events leading up to it.'

'Will it come back? My memory?'

'Let's hope so. But, in a few cases the memories never return.'

I press my fingertips to my forehead as though it will help me remember, then turn to Joanna, my cheeks wet with tears. 'All I know is you were missing, and I thought you were dead. What happened?'

A vast room with bare brick walls comes to my mind, the sluggish brown Thames moving beneath a window, a tall man with a neatly trimmed beard.

I clutch at Joanna's arm, knowing who he is. His face comes to me. Swollen. Bloodied. He's lying in a hospital bed like this one. 'Your husband had an accident, Joanna. He's in hospital. Maybe even this one. Does he know you're safe? Has anyone told him?'

The nurse and Joanna glance at each other, and I see the look that passes between them.

'What is it? What's wrong?'

The nurse straightens up. 'Now's not the time to be worrying about anything except getting better. When you're feeling stronger, the consultant will come and talk to you about your treatment and you can ask all the questions you want. But for now, what you need is rest.'

Joanna smiles at her. 'Can I stay with Alice? Just for a while.'

Loosening the cuff, the nurse takes it off my arm. 'Just for a short while but don't tire her.'

She goes out and closes the door. It's just the two of us now, and I'm glad.

I try to pull myself up the bed, the sheet twisting around me. 'How is your husband? I don't care what they've said – you must tell me.'

'You don't remember, do you?'

'Not much. I know he was nice to me. Made me feel welcome. He was worried sick about you. We both were.'

Joanna looks away. 'There's a lot you don't know.'

'What do you mean?'

It's then she tells me. Everything. What Mark did.

'After the accident, the police found a holdall of money in Mark's car.' Joanna's fingers hover over the faint pink circles on her wrist. 'I'd managed to get away, and when he knew his plan had failed, he emptied our savings account and was leaving.'

I can hardly believe it. 'How did he think he'd ever get away with it?'

'He was desperate, Alice. You'd be surprised what people will do when they feel there's no way out.'

I feel dizzy. Unable to comprehend. 'But I remember Mark seemed so upset when he thought you were missing.' I sink my head into my hands.

Joanna reaches out a hand. Places it over mine. 'You might be remembering that correctly, but you were simply taken in by him… just like the rest of us.'

How could Mark do such a terrible thing? I shiver, thinking of the nights I spent in the warehouse apartment alone with him. The danger I'd inadvertently put myself in.

'There's something else, Alice.'

'Yes?'

'Mark regained consciousness briefly. He told the police that someone had stepped out in front of him on the road. It was what made him lose control of the car. They've searched the area and arrested his stepson, Nathan, this morning. His woollen hat was found near the scene of the crash. I can't believe it. He used to be such a sweet boy, but it's impossible to know what someone will do when they're off their head.'

Nathan. I remember him now. His sunken eyes. The track marks on the pallid skin of his arm. His obvious dislike of his stepfather.

Joanna gives my hand a short squeeze. 'They've charged him with manslaughter.'

I struggle to sit up. 'Manslaughter? What do you mean? Mark's going to be all right. He's…'

Joanna looks at me sadly. 'I'm afraid not. I know they didn't want to tell you until you were well enough, but it's only fair you know.' Her eyes fill with tears. 'He died, Alice. My husband died last night.'

The room spins, and my head pounds. I have the sensation that I might float away. But Joanna is there, holding my hand. Pulling me gently back to earth.

'I know it's a shock after what happened to you. Would you like me to sit on the bed with you?'

I nod, dumbly, and she climbs next to me. I feel the weight of her arm around my shoulders, and a memory stirs. Joanna and I are teenagers. We're sitting outside the art room, and her arm is around me like it is now. We're laughing at something to do with Charlotte, a girl in our class. I think it was when we prank called her one day when Joanna's mother was out with the horses. We'd pretended to be from a local radio station and said she'd won tickets. She'd been so excited, told all her friends at school. I'd seen her crying in the toilets when she found out it wasn't true, and I'd felt bad. It had been Joanna's idea, but I could have said no.

We were only kids then, barely fourteen. I'm glad we've left our younger selves behind, but what we have instead is pain and uncertainty.

I rest my head on Joanna's shoulder, my tears wetting the material of her blouse. 'I'm so sorry you've lost your husband, Joanna. I don't know what to say. I don't know what to do.'

'It's all right, Alice.' Joanna smooths my hair back from my face, just like Mum used to, just like *she* used to, and smiles down at me. 'It won't be long before you can go home.'

Home. There's nothing waiting for me there except a broken heart.

It's like Joanna's read my mind. 'Or if you prefer, you don't have to go straight back. You can stay with me. I can look after you. We'll get through this together, and things will be just like they used to be. We're all each other needs. You'd like that, wouldn't you?'

I watch the sun flicker through the metal blinds at the windows. Something's hovering at the edge of my memory, but I can't grasp hold of it. I know it's important. Know it could ruin this moment.

I nudge it to the back of my mind; it can't be important.

'Yes,' I say, feeling my anxiety lift. 'I'd like that.'

A LETTER FROM WENDY

want to say a huge thank you for choosing to read *The Bride*. If ou did enjoy it, and want to keep up-to-date with all my latest eleases, just sign up at the following link. Your email address will ever be shared, and you can unsubscribe at any time.

www.bookouture.com/wendy-clarke

The setting of a novel is very important to me and the idea or the setting of *The Bride* came to me after seeing a black and white photograph of an old dockland warehouse in a coffee shop. loved the small-paned windows with their arched brickwork, the eavy wooden doors that opened onto iron railings, the rope and ully system used to haul goods to the upper floors, still bolted o its wall. I know a lot of these buildings have been converted nto up-market apartments, and it was this marriage of old and ew that attracted me.

I'd already decided that I wanted *The Bride* to be set in one lace… in one building. I wanted it to be a place of contrast. On he one hand, an open, modern living space that would showcase oanna's lifestyle but, on the other, a place with an industrial eritage: bare-bricked corridors with functional lifts that could ighlight Alice's claustrophobia.

An old tobacco warehouse would be perfect. I'd been on a alking tour of the old East End docks and had seen such a uilding, but I didn't want my warehouse to be in a place bustling

with life. I wanted it to be alone in a sea of derelict buildings an
half-finished apartments – a London that no longer exists. But th
is the beauty of fiction – the author can create their own worlds t
suit the needs of the plot. In this way, my fictitious Black Wat
Dock was designed and came to fruition.

I hope you loved *The Bride* and if you did, I would be ve
grateful if you could write a review. I'd love to hear what you thin
and it makes such a difference helping new readers to discover or
of my books for the first time.

I love hearing from my readers – you can get in touch on m
Facebook page, through Twitter, Goodreads, Instagram or m
website.

Thanks,
Wendy x

🖥 www.wendyclarke.uk

🐦 @WendyClarke99

f WendyClarkeAuthor

📷 wendyclarke99

ACKNOWLEDGEMENTS

Receiving the phone call from Jennifer Hunt, my editor at Book-outure, telling me she loved my debut and would like to publish it was one of those special moments in life I'll never forget. Three psychological thrillers later, Jennifer and I are still working together, and I couldn't wish for a better editor. After brainstorming ideas for *The Bride*, a seed was planted, nurtured and eventually grew into the novel you are reading today. Jennifer's intuition is second to none, and her input helps to make my books the best they can be. Thanks also to the rest of the Bookouture team, especially Kim Nash and Noelle Holten, who work tirelessly to get my novels in front of readers.

Although our heads are crowded with fictitious characters, we writers would go mad if we didn't engage with people in real life from time to time. So, once again, I owe a huge thank you to my best writing buddy, Tracy Fells, who is always there for me, whether it be in times of jubilation or crisis. Our monthly teacake and coffee sessions help to keep me sane. Also, thanks are due to my lovely RNA writing pals, with whom I meet regularly to put the writing world to rights!

Sometimes, though, it's good to get away from the writing world and whenever I feel the need to emerge from my writing cave and talk about something other than the written word, it's to my 'Friday Girls' I turn. Thank you, Carol, Linda, Helen, Barbara and Jill for your twenty plus years of friendship.

The Bride has some police procedure in it and once again it's the fabulous Graham Bartlett I turned to with questions that I'm sure he thinks are amusing. Any mistakes are entirely my own.

Thanks also to all my family – especially my children, stepchildren and their partners, and my mum, who are always there cheering me on from the sidelines. But my final mention must, a always, go to my long-suffering husband, who is there by my side supporting me, putting up with a house filled with my writing detritus and taking care of the technical side of things which I hate. Thank you, Ian. I couldn't do it without you!

Made in the USA
Coppell, TX
29 September 2020

38918945R00166